Behind in the Count

A Second Chance Baseball Romance

Nashville Songbirds
Book 1

Kat Summers

Behind in Count (Nashville Songbirds, Book 1)

Edited by Emma Jane of EJL Editing

Cover Illustration by Booked Forever

ISBN-13: 979-8-218-25097-3

To all the people, dreams, and interactions that inspire the stories we tell ourselves. This one made it on paper. Yours can, too!

Seriously, Mom, don't read this.

Playlist

1. Love Me Harder – Ariana Grande, The Weeknd
2. Comeback – Jonas Brothers
3. Stay Stay Stay – Taylor Swift
4. Austin – Blake Shelton
5. IF YOU GO DOWN (I'M GOING DOWN, TOO) – Kelesea Ballerini
6. Girlfriend – *NSYNC
7. Work Song – Hozier
8. SO DONE – The Kid LAROI
9. Until The End of Time – Justin Timberlake, Beyonce
10. Bejeweled – Taylor Swift
11. Dark Paradise – Lana Del Ray
12. The One That Got Away – Katie Perry
13. I Choose You – Mario
14. Wanted – Hunter Hayes
15. Everything Has Changed - Taylor Swift
16. Kiss and Make Up – Due Lipa, BLACKPINK
17. I GUESS I'M IN LOVE - Clinton Kane

18. When I Was Your Man – Bruno Mars
19. 23 – Sam Hunt
20. Stay Fly - Three Six Mafia
21. The Last Time – Taylor Swift (ft. Gary Lightbody)

Listen to it on Spotify.

Dick-tionary

For those of you who want to find or avoid the spice in this book, take note of the following chapters:

- Chapter 25
- Chapter 26
- Chapter 29
- Chapter 32
- Chapter 33
- Chapter 37

Prologue

Robby

The energy at Amazon Field is electric as I step up to the plate. There is a bite in the air that is more from tension than the damp, early May Seattle weather. The energy of the crowd is vibrating through my muscles. It's hard to make out much in the roar, but it sounds like an even mix of cheers and boos, making me smile beneath my eye black. Since my major league career started in Seattle, the home fans love me as much as they hate that I am wearing a Songbirds jersey. I get it. I'd miss me, too.

I know that may seem cocky, but at a certain point, facts are facts. Not only do I average 11.2 strikeouts per game and have a 99 mph fastball, but my batting average of above .275 makes me as much of a threat in the batter's box as on the mound. Plus, I'm having a killer game.

No one on the Eagles has been able to hit against me, which is pissing them off. As their pitcher winds up, I can picture what he is going to throw in my head. I know this guy. I played with him for years. He is as predictable as they come. I tighten my grip on the bat and prepare for the changeup coming my way.

Bam! That ball is flying high into left field. I kick my ass into gear and don't wait to see it land in that nice alley between center and left field. That's another double added to my stat sheet. When my teammate Miller heads into the box, I peer over to the third base coach and prepare to steal.

As the ball heads into the catcher's glove, he drops it, and I have my chance. I race to third base. When I am about to make it, something catches my foot. I suddenly lose my balance and hit the dirt hard. Unfortunately, I used my hand to break my fall, and now my elbow hurts like a bitch. I get on my feet and try to shake it off when I hear the umpire call me out.

When I search for what tripped me up, I see Derrick fucking Jones smirking back at me. I don't know what this dude's problem is, but he has always been a major jerkwad. While I've never personally had any issues with him, that changed today. Because the reason I fell to the ground? Derrick fucking Jones tripped me. Worse than that, thanks to his schoolyard antics, I didn't even make it to the base, and now I have to walk of shame back to my dugout. At least I will, after Derrick and I have a quick chat.

See, what the asshole third baseman doesn't know is that today, May 7, is not the day to fuck with Robby Becker. May 7 and I have a history, and it is not a good one. Ever since that drizzly, shitty day in Houston four years ago, I have had chronically bad May 7ths. I may be overly superstitious due to my profession, but there is something about this day that spells bad luck for me.

Last year, my team ended a twenty-five-game win streak. We were so close to tying the record. The year before that, some chick slashed my tires because I canceled a date—if you can even call what we were doing dating. The year before that, my childhood dog,

Vader, died and before that I had food poising. Clearly, May 7 has it out for me. But that ends today with Derrick fucking Jones.

Derrick can see I don't have the best of intentions as I turn his way. He doesn't have much time to react before my punch lands right on his smarmy face. Unfortunately, it hurts me more than it does him. If my elbow wasn't messed up before, it is now.

My base coach pulls me away from Derrick and pushes me toward the dugout. I can hear the ump yelling at me, but the blood rushing between my ears doesn't allow me to hear him. I don't need to, though. I know what he's saying. I'm ejected. Glancing over my shoulder as I head toward my trainer, I smile at what I see. Hopefully, the satisfaction of seeing blood on Derrick's jersey is worth it.

"What do you mean grade two ligament sprain? Did it fucking fail first?" I practically yell at the team doctor. I know he's trying to help me, but this news blows. I knew my elbow wasn't good. It hurts more now that the adrenaline has worn off. I've had it wrapped and iced for the last thirty-six hours. I didn't realize it would be this serious, though. I thought it would be a strain at worst, a tweak at best.

"How the hell does punching someone lead to an elbow sprain?" I ask.

"This most likely happened when you tried to catch yourself on the ground," Doc says with a pointed stare. "You couldn't sprain your UCL decking anyone—unless you were doing it really, really wrong. The punch was a stupid move that led to your bruised knuckles and a two-game suspension."

Unfortunately, that momentarily satisfying punch I landed earned me a suspension for the rest of the series. Not that it matters with my elbow being messed up.

"What's the prognosis, Doc?" I ask the team's head medical personnel. Doc has been with the organization for over fifteen years. I trust his opinion on this.

"Do you want the good news or the bad news?" he inquires.

"Hit me with the good first, I guess? I've always been a glass-half-full kind of guy."

"The good news is you'll be back to pitching again in six to eight weeks."

"Okay, that isn't as bad as I expected," I reply. "If that is the good news, what is the bad news?" Doc looks me in the eye with his no-nonsense expression before he drops his bomb.

"Your next pitch won't take place in Nashville."

"Okay, so Phoenix? That series is six weeks away," I say.

"Phoenix *is* the series that is six weeks away, but you won't be there. Your next pitch is going to be in Memphis. You may be mostly healed by the Phoenix series, but I'd estimate you won't be up to MLB standards for another four to six weeks after that."

I stare back at him in shock. "Whoa, whoa. Are you saying I'm being sent down? Do you think that is necessary?" I only spent two years in the minors, but I am not exactly keen to relive them. Plus, Memphis holds nothing but complicated memories.

"Not only do I think it is necessary," he declares, "but the boys upstairs agree that some time to cool off might be what your attitude needs. You didn't hurt yourself fighting this time, but you're not some twenty-one-year-old punk anymore, Robby."

Even after four years, it still makes something tighten in my chest to be called that name. For twenty years, I was Rob or Robert Matthew when my mom was mad about something. It wasn't until a sassy little brunette that I got called Robby. Somehow the name followed me to the league, and now I'm stuck with the ever-present reminder of who I used to be.

"You can't be going off like that. Next time you could seriously injure yourself." I wince. Doc is someone I respect. For him to be calling me out on my shit, I know I messed up.

"Pack your bags, bud. The Bluff City is calling your name. We'll see you back here later this summer," he remarks as his mouth tips slightly. Cheeky bastard.

See, I told you. May 7 has it out for me. Injured, tires slashed, dog died, food poisoning, made the biggest mistake of my life. And now I'm being sent to a city I haven't been to in years that represents everything I could have been. It's as if the universe is taunting me. But why?

Chapter One

As I walk in the door of my mom's house, I'm hit with the sense of home. I only lived here for five years—plus the occasional college break—but this is the place where Mom and I were finally able to let our guard down. Mom made the dingy apartments we lived in before homey, but they were always temporary, never a place to return to. But here, in the house we moved into with Steve after they married, she made us a home.

As I round the corner into the kitchen, I take a moment to watch Mom knock Steve's hand away from her homemade croutons. Their love is inspiring to me. While he might appear to be a typical, stuffy lawyer, Steve is one of the most kindhearted men you'll ever meet—outside the courtroom, anyway.

He took one look at the gangly thirteen-year-old his new girlfriend came with and still decided he was all in. I mean, I don't blame the guy. Even at forty-four, my mom is still a total smoke show. She says it's the Italian blood. I say it's karma for all the hard work she did to support us after she was left a single mom thanks to an IED in Afghanistan.

I thank grown-up and baby Jesus every day that I take after her in appearance. We're both petite with olive skin and small features. With long, chestnut hair and matching brown eyes, people often mistake us for sisters instead of mother and daughter. While I know I got her beauty, I hope people think I got her kind temperament, too, even if I may be a tad sassier than her gracious nature.

Not once growing up can I remember my mom complaining about our circumstances. She took the crap lemons that life handed us and made limoncello. And then she shared that limoncello with anyone she could. "There is always someone who has it worse than you, *bambolina*," she used to tell me. And that is why karma made Teresa Ballerini Shaw an ageless goddess well into middle age.

I don't mind. For years, we were all the other had. Mom moved to Memphis when Dad was stationed at the military base here. All her family is back in St. Louis, including my cousin, Lola. Being only two years apart, we were thick as thieves growing up. We spent time together when Mom and I could afford to visit Missouri for the holidays and Lola would spend her summers here.

Speaking of Mom, she finally noticed me watching her from the doorway.

"*Mia bambolina!* You are right on time. The lasagna will be ready in five minutes, and I am about to plate the salads. You can help."

"Hi, Mama. Hi, Steve," I say as I enter the room.

"Hey, kiddo, how ya doing?" Steve asks.

"Hanging in there as always, Steveo. How is the world of business litigation treating you?"

"Can't complain," he says. "It pays for all the fancy spices your mom insists she needs to make her lasagna."

That earns Steve another swat from my mom.

"That type of talk is how you end up with Stouffer's, honey. You know I only serve the best to my loves."

"I would never insult the Francelli family lasagna, Teresa," he says with a twinkle in his eye as he carries plates into the dining room. I swear he has as much love for her, if not more, as he did the day he married her.

"Usually, on Mother's Day, the daughters make the meal, not the other way around, Mom," I admonish.

"Hush," she chides. "Mother's Day is supposed to be about me doing what I want to do, and what I want to do is cook."

"And we wouldn't have it any other way," Steve yells from the dining room, where I see him stealing croutons off the top of the salad. He winks at me, and I shake my head at his antics.

As we sit down for dinner, my mom and Steve catch me up on their lives. Steve is working on a big case about two local dry cleaners who are feuding. My mom swears her tennis coach is out to get her and always hits serves to her too hard.

"What about you, *bambolina*, solved world hunger yet?" she asks cheekily.

"Not yet," I sigh. "Honestly, I believe we're barely scratching the surface. Yeah, we're getting food to people through our outreach programs, but there is more we could do if Camila would open herself up to new ideas. Our school lunch program means that kids are getting a meal while at school, but it is ignoring their table at home. And the other people at it! One balanced meal isn't enough, especially when they have no idea *why* it's nutritious."

Mom senses I am getting heated and places her hand on mine. "*Roma* wasn't built in a day, Carina. It will take some time, but I know you can make it happen with your passion."

Seemingly tuning into the conversation after inhaling his lasagna, Steve asks, "What's missing? What aren't you doing, and what is stopping you?"

"Well," I ponder out loud, "what we're missing is dinner. Kids may be getting lunch at school, but if they're going to bed hungry, they don't sleep as well, which affects their energy level, attitude, and academic performance. The bigger issue is that even if they have dinner, it might not be nutritious because their parents either don't know how or think they don't have time to make something healthy. Or, the even bigger issue, getting fresh ingredients is too much of a hassle." Glancing at my mother, I see understanding in her eyes.

She remembers the days of stretching our budget as far as it could go—the nights she created masterful Italian dinners with jarred tomato sauce, spinach, and Vienna sausages. It's why she imports those 'fancy spices,' as Steve calls them now. Because she can. She struggled for years. Now that she can, she wants to treat herself—and Steve and I—to the best ingredients she can get her hands on.

"So, what's your plan?" my stepfather prompts.

"Huh?"

"You've identified the problem. What is your solution? I know you've got one. All that long hair of yours is covering a big ole brain," he teases.

"Oh, I've got one. But I know my boss isn't going to go for it. She'll say we don't have the funds. We don't have research to support the efficiency. It will be too hard to implement. Blah, blah, blah."

"Then raise your own money," Steve says, eyeing the cheesecake that appeared out of nowhere.

"I can't just raise my own money," I chide.

"Why not? She says your budget can't support it, fine. Find a way to support it yourself." With that comment, Steve is lost in the delightful strawberry-covered concoction Mom made for dessert.

As I ponder his statement, my mom catches my eye. "All your life, *bambolina*, you've defied expectations. I have no doubt that if you set your mind to this project, you can prove your boss wrong and help more people."

Thanks to my conversation with my mom and Steve, I walk into work the next morning ready to seize the day. As I sit at my desk, Kim, one of my work besties, comes over.

"How was your weekend Care Bear?" I both love and hate the nickname Kim gave me on my first day of work. My cousin Lola calls me that, too, and I miss her terribly.

"It was good," I say. "I vegged out on Saturday and had dinner with the parentals for Mother's Day. What about you?"

"My parents went to Oklahoma to spend Mother's Day with the only people they actually like," Kim remarks.

"So, their grandchildren," I deadpan.

"Bingo."

Kim is a beautiful curvy redhead with a heart of gold and a penchant for trouble. She is too much of a wild child for her strait-laced Southern Baptist parents with her tattoos and septum piercing. I have no doubt they love her as best they know how, but they aren't peas in a pod like my parents and me.

"It is hard to compete with the missing teeth and dimples your niece and nephew are sporting," I reply.

"You're not wrong there. How kids that cute came from my brother is a mystery to me."

"Good morning, ladies," Haley sings as she strolls in.

"On time as usual," Kim smirks, holding up her watch and showing the time as 9:03.

"Hush, the traffic in the Starbucks line was bad," Haley murmurs while sipping her iced latte, eyeing it as if it is the only thing keeping her alive.

With beautiful mocha skin and shiny relaxed hair, Haley is one of the most beautiful women I have ever seen in real life. She may come across as standoffish and reserved, but Haley is the hardest worker here. I swear this place wouldn't run without her. Plus, despite her work persona, no one is more fun at karaoke.

Camila may be the director of Feeding Memphis, but everyone knows Haley is the one who gets things done. Her technical title is assistant director, but she does it all. Kim serves as Feeding Memphis' volunteer coordinator, while my title is programs director. Our merry band of millennial office mates is rounded out by Alex, who handles marketing and communications.

"Why are you tense, my little Venus?" Haley questioned.

"I'm pitching my new program idea to Camila at today's staff meeting," I respond.

"The one with the food truck?" Kim interjects. I nod. "Wow. I can't wait to see what the Wicked Witch of Central Gardens has to say to that."

"Come on." I laugh. "Camila is not that bad. It's a good idea!"

"It is a great idea," Haley says coolly, "but it is new, and we all know how Camila feels about that."

That we do. It took almost a year after I was hired for Camila to decide *I* was a good idea. As if summoned by our conversation, our boss enters the room with a flourish.

Camila is what would happen if Cruella De Ville and Miranda from *The Devil Wears Prada* had a baby. But instead of high fashion, puppies, and magazine publishing, that spawn cared about expensive eyewear, essential oils, and schmoozing with the who's who of Memphis. With half her grey hair shaved and the other half in a bob, Camila has a severe appearance to match her cold personality.

"Ladies," she chirps, "I don't see how standing around and chatting is getting food in anyone's bellies. We have our weekly staff meeting promptly at ten. Let's see what we can get done before then, hmm? Kimberly, I am expecting to have the latest volunteer retention numbers."

With that, she flounces into her office, and we all return to our desks to kick off the day.

Chapter Two

"Before we dive into the weekly metrics report, does anyone have any items not on the agenda they wish to discuss?" Camila asks as she eyes us dubiously.

"I do," I squeak out, raising my hand.

"Well, on with it then," she huffs.

I pass out the proposal I have made to the team. "Thank you for the floor. We have done a fantastic job feeding two of the most vulnerable demographics: school-aged children and senior citizens. We've created a lunch program for the kids and a meal delivery service for the seniors that has helped these demographics immensely. However, there is a big piece of the hunger puzzle that we are neglecting."

Peeking over to Kim and Haley, I see them sending me reassuring glances.

"We're getting kids fed during the day, but many are still going to bed hungry. Doing this reduces the quality of sleep kids are able to achieve. This can lead to mood swings, reduced academic performance, a weakened immune system, and stunt their growth.

"The kids in our program who *are* getting dinner at home may not receive the most nutritious meals. We all know the vast food deserts that exist in our city, which result in limited availability of fresh and healthy food options. Even if families are able to get more nutritious options, parents often don't have the time or knowledge on how to prepare balanced meals.

"That feeds—no pun intended—into the demographic I believe is underrepresented by our services: single moms. Forty-three percent of female-headed households in Memphis live under the poverty line. These women are busy trying to keep the lights on and a roof over their kids' heads. They don't always have the time or additional funds to purchase healthy options for their kids and themselves. This is part of the reason Memphis is the second most obese city in the country."

As I finally stop rambling, Camila is processing what I've said. "What exactly is it you are proposing, Carina? A lunch program for moms?" she inquires.

"I want to create a program that not only supplies single mothers with fresh produce, meat, and other healthy food but also teaches them how to turn them into simple, nutritious meals. I'm calling it FM Mobile Market.

"FM Mobile Market is a take on the food truck. Instead of a serving window, it has retractable storage bins that will allow participants to pick out their own fresh produce. It is equipped with refrigerated lockers inside to store perishables. We'll record videos of the recipes they can make each week with the ingredients and even host cooking classes when we're able."

Before Camila can respond, Kim jumps in, "We've had interest from local farmers hoping to get involved with our mission. They are more than willing to donate a small percentage of their crops to the cause." I smile at her appreciatively. Our boss loves anything locally sourced.

"A Cincinnati nonprofit similar to ours recently made national news for a program that helped teens learn to cook before heading off to college," Haley supplies helpfully.

"Okay, I get it. You ladies are all into this program," Camila responds. "You make some... interesting points, Carina. However, I don't see it being a priority this year. Maybe we can revisit the topic in Q2 of next year. We simply don't have the funds or the manpower to support a program of this magnitude. It would take too much work to get it off the ground, and with our limited resources, we need to focus on programs we know will succeed. Frankly, I am not convinced education is the reason these mothers can't make their children healthy meals. Everyone has the internet these days, no?"

Kim is about to disagree with Camila, but I send her a discreet head shake. While I appreciate her willingness to go to bat for me, I know when to pick my battles.

Camila continues, "We don't have the budget to pick up any new programs right now. We are barely hanging on as it is."

I'm not sure exactly what she means by this. We are pacing well above where we were this time last year and exceeded our quarterly fundraising goal by twenty-eight percent.

"I understand your concerns," I say to my boss. "For my clarification, should we come across a grant or additional budget, would this be a program you'd be interested in pursuing?"

"I supposed if, what does this proposal say, $18,000 were to somehow fall in our lap, then yes, this is a program we could consider. But it would be a massive undertaking. Now, if there is nothing else?" Camila eyes the room, clearly done with this conversation. "Great. Alex, explain to me how these silly videos you made for that talk app are going to bring in more donations."

After a brutal forty-five minute meeting—most of it Camila forcing Alex to explain how he can't just 'make something go viral'—I return to my desk.

Kim and Haley give me tight smiles as they return to theirs, and Alex seems dazed as he exits the conference room. "You did great in there," I say.

"Thanks," he mumbles. "Trying to explain digital marketing to Camila is like trying to teach my husband to play Catan. At a certain point you have to give up and play Candy Land."

His analogy makes me giggle. Mostly because I know his husband, John, and I can't see him having the patience to sit through either game. He's more of a basketball and poker guy. I sometimes wonder how jock-y John ended up with long-haired, nerdy Alex, but as they say, opposites attract.

Before heading out to lunch, Alex turns to me. "You did awesome in there, too. It's not as simple as Camila thinks. John came from a household similar to the one you described, and his mom could have used a program like that. She may have had access to benefits, but that didn't mean she knew how to create healthy and filling meals for a growing boy. They ate a lot of fast food and TV dinners growing up, and it has taken a toll on her body. Last month she had to start taking a new medicine for her diabetes. She was also referred to a specialist for her heart, but damn if that woman can't bake a casserole."

I smile at him warmly.

"What I'm trying to say is that you should find funding yourself, I know I speak for the rest of the team when I say we'll do whatever it takes to make the program a success."

"Thank you, that means a lot."

As I heat up some of the leftover lasagna my mom sent me home with, I consider what Alex said and how John's mom and mine weren't that different. Mine, luckily, had my Nonna, who taught her the value of fresh ingredients and how to make a balanced meal on a budget. Single-income, immigrant families know how to stretch a dollar. If only John's mom had benefited from similar training. It could have helped then and now as she struggles with the effects of a lifetime of poor eating choices.

With renewed enthusiasm, I spend my lunch searching for a way to fund my program. I don't think Camila would appreciate me hitting up existing donors. Instead, I look for grants, contests, and anything I can find that might give us a fraction of the funds we need. After I've applied for what must be a million government grants and billionaire philanthropy *cough tax write-off* initiatives, I find an opportunity giving a hefty grant to one Memphis nonprofit. I cringe at the competition, a softball tournament, but shake off the bad memories and hit apply. Hopefully, one of the things I applied to will stick.

Four days later, I get a call that leads me down a path I never saw coming.

"Hi, is this Carina with Feeding Memphis?"

"Yes, this is she."

"Wonderful," a smooth voice replies. "My name is Stacy Howard. I'm the public relations manager for the Memphis Blues Birds, the local minor league baseball team."

"Hi, Stacy! Yes, I am familiar with the team. How can I help you?"

"Wonderful! I came across your organization's application for our nonprofit softball tournament and wanted to see if you were still interested. We have one more spot to fill, and your organization would be a great fit. The Mid-South Food Bank had to drop out last minute, and we don't have any other hunger-focused nonprofits involved."

"Oh my gosh, that is incredible!" I reply. "Not that they had to drop out, but that we can fill in."

She laughs. "Yes, yes, I understood what you meant. I know it is last minute, but applications were technically closed when you applied. However, since we've had this opening, we were hoping you all would be able to make it work on short notice?"

"Absolutely, we can do whatever you need."

"Perfect," she chirps. Stacy goes on to explain the details of the tournament and that we will meet our coaches, two Blues Birds players, Saturday and have our first practice Tuesday. After two weeks of practice, we will have eight games. Since there is an odd number, the team with the best record will automatically go to the championship game on National Nonprofits Day, August 17. The rest play a single-elimination playoff to decide who they will face off against. The winner will get the $25,000 grant. Everyone else will get a $2,500 donation.

I thank Stacy for all the information and practically race over to the office Kim and Haley share.

"Guess what?!" I yell.

"You decided to try that acupuncturist I recommended?" Kim responds excitedly.

"What? No. That's never going to happen. I got a call from the Blues Birds. We are officially taking part in their nonprofit softball tournament!"

"What do you mean 'we'?"

Haley eyes me wearily as Kim murmurs, "Softball?"

"You are on the team, Miss All-Star track athlete. They're giving the winning team a $25,000 grant! It's more than enough to fund my program, and we could all use more exercise in our lives. We meet our coaches tomorrow." I give them my best puppy dog eyes and an exaggerated pout.

"Ugh, fine," Haley admonishes as Kim groans. "But if you're making me get all hot and sweaty playing softball, then you are getting all hot and sweaty going dancing with us tonight."

I grimace but quickly agree. I am in the mood to celebrate, and it's been a while since we had a girls' night out. Seems like a fair trade to me.

Thinking about dancing makes me miss my bestie and all the fun we had partying in college. I make a mental note to call her later while Kim and Haley iron out the details of where they want to spend our evening.

Chapter Three

Robby

As I sit in the physical therapy room at Express Delivery Park, I am struck by how unimpressive it is. I'm either spoiled by MLB-level facilities, or I'm in a mood because I thought I'd never see myself sent back to the minors after my initial two years. Regardless, this treatment room leaves a lot to be desired.

After I was drafted, I spent two years playing for the Baytown Bucs, Seattle's AA team. It was a step above where most rookies start out in the baseball hierarchy but still two degrees below the big boys. Most draftees get sent to a single A or farm team and then work up to AA, AAA, then the major leagues.

A combination of injuries, trades, and working my ass off got me called up to the big show sooner than expected, and I am grateful for it every day. For the last four years—really my entire life—I have lived and breathed baseball.

Some people might say I take the sport too seriously, but what else do I have? A supportive family? Not me. My sister may be my number one fan, but she's been all about hockey ever since she married the Wayne Gretzky of the Soviet Bloc. My parents were too busy working to pay the bills to come to my games as a kid, let alone now. Not to mention they are way too practical to encourage me to pursue such an 'unstable and unpredictable' career. That's a narrative I'd prefer to be excluded from.

A girl waiting for me back at home? Hell no. I haven't had more than a fling since my rookie year. Don't get me wrong; I get my fair share of ladies. However, I haven't had the time or desire to get to know someone well enough to decide whether they're worth being a priority in my life. Hence, slash-y tire girl from May 7 a few years ago. The last time I had a girl worth prioritizing, I wasn't mature enough to balance a career and my love life, so I lost her.

She supported my dream to play unconditionally, and I've yet to meet a woman as beautiful, kind, and intriguing since. All the cleat chasers that hang around are two-dimensional; they make me want to fall asleep, which I do after I rock both our worlds. Again, it's not cocky if it's a fact. Although my world has been somewhat less rocked recently after my late-night encounters. I wonder why that is...

Before I can get too sucked into thinking about my lackluster sex life, pain shoots up my arm.

"Oops, sorry," the bouncy, blonde trainer says sheepishly.

I find it funny she's going all shy on me now, considering she spent most of this appointment not-so-subtly hitting on and touching me unnecessarily. I mean, I get it. I'm an attractive dude. I don't have the surfer image I used to since I cut my signature long brown locks when I joined the big leagues. What I lost in inches of hair, I've gained in inches of muscle on my 6-foot-4 frame.

I'd want to touch me, too, if I was a woman. My focus, though, is on my recovery, and she is supposed to be helping me get better; no funny business allowed.

"It's cool," I send her a dazzling smile. "How is the injury looking?"

Blushing from my attention, she has to clear her throat before she replies. "I'm impressed with the strength you've been able to keep despite resting your arm, but I am not loving where your dexterity is right now. I'm going to give you some exercises to add to your routine to hopefully get you back on track to play in the next few weeks."

Not exactly what I wanted to hear, but it is what it is. I majored in kinesiology in college, so I have a basic understanding of how all this stuff works. I'll give Doc a call to make sure he agrees with her assessment. It's not that I don't trust her, but she looks fresh out of the dorm. My career is too important to put in the hands of someone that green.

When my session is over, the physical therapist, Anastasia, seems disappointed that I'm leaving and not sticking around to flirt. I don't have time to get involved with anyone, let alone someone tasked with helping me heal. It's much safer to lay low in my apartment and focus on the game.

On the way home, I stop at a food truck and pull up to the family group chat while I wait for my order. My sister Morgan is talking about her husband Ralphie's schedule for the next week. Ralphie, more widely known as Ralph Nokavik, is a Right Winger for the Tampa Thunder. His team is in the middle of the NHL playoffs.

I can't help but be annoyed at how supportive my parents are about *his* career. They've hardly ever shown interest in mine, but they are all over Ralphie's as if he's God's gift to earth. I'd honestly hate the guy if he didn't treat my sister like a queen.

Morgan dated a string of douche canoes before she met him at a party. She was working as a bottle girl during her off night as a flight attendant. Now she gets to spend her time being a hockey WAG—the term for wives and girlfriends of professional athletes—and influencer. I can't blame the dickheaded guys for flocking to her; she is objectively beautiful. I had to knock a few heads together both on and off the field for comments about her during my early years as a player. I'm glad that is Ralphie's job now; that dude is way scarier than I could ever be.

She may be older than me, but the little shit doesn't always behave that way. She loves getting under my skin; case in point, her latest text in the group chat.

12:15 PM

DEAREST SISTER

> Bobert, I know you're injured and all, but do you think you'll be able to crawl your broken body to Ralphie's game this weekend? If they win the next two series, they're in the cup!

> Sorry, Sis. The team still expects me to be with them for all the games, and I have physical therapy appointments I have to keep up with. Also, short notice much?

DEAREST SISTER

> Boo, you suck!

> Ralphie says that is a reasonable explanation. He wouldn't be allowed to leave midseason, either. We're going to come visit after the hockey season is over. I miss you.

DAD

> Don't waste your time on Rob, Mo. He was never able to appreciate quality sports.

I frown at my dad's response. Shoving my phone into my pocket, I can grab my order and make the walk home.

When I get to the courtyard of my apartment complex, I see one of my new teammates, Leo Davis, lumbering toward me. If you didn't know him, Leo would be an intimidating dude. He is an inch or so shorter than me, and the blond has a solid extra fifteen pounds of muscle on him. That bulk comes in handy as a catcher but makes him seem tougher than the teddy bear he is.

Several members of the team live here since it is right next door to the ballpark, and we get a discount on rent. Well, they do. My apartment is supplied through the team since I am only here temporarily. The accommodations couldn't be more basic if they tried. It's essentially a glorified hotel room. It makes me miss my condo in Nashville. Don't get me wrong, the apartment is nice enough, but there is nothing like home. Plus, with what I spent on that condo, it has all the bells and whistles. This place is all neutral decor and staged furniture.

"Hey man, how is the arm doing?" Leo asks. And I know he means it. Leo is a stand-up guy. Being from a small town in Iowa, he is as genuine as they come.

"It's coming along," I say. "The trainer gave me some workouts to add, but it's back to normal for day-to-day stuff. Got work to do before I'm back to playing form."

He nods. "I hear that. I don't know if you have plans tonight, but a few of us are going out and would love for you to tag along. I'm sure the nightlife isn't what you're used to, but there are still some cool spots on Beale and other places downtown. You in?"

My first instinct is to say no, but after the dig from my dad, I could use a night letting loose. "That could be just what the doctor ordered," I comment. "Text me the details."

Leo takes my number, and I return to my temporary home to relax until we meet up later. I have enough time for some quick cardio, a shower, and a nap before I have to be ready to go. I have this nagging sensation that something is on the horizon, but I brush it off and go to my place to get on with my afternoon.

Chapter Four

Carina

When I get home after work, I quickly wash the work stink off and put on my cozy robe as I pull out all my nail supplies. Giving myself a manicure has always been my biggest act of self-care. I'm sure it has something to do with money being tight growing up and Mom and I enjoying special moments treating ourselves to manicure parties. Going to the salon isn't the same. After picking out a color and some cute decals, I click the video call button, and a familiar blonde face pops in.

"Hi, Babs," I greet. Tiffany has been my best friend since my freshman year of college. Even though she was a sophomore, fate decided we were destined to be together, and thank the Lord for that. I was struggling when she got on campus fashionably late. Resembling a quintessential Malibu Barbie, people often underestimate Tiff, but she is one of the smartest people I've ever met, especially emotionally. Just because she's a makeup artist doesn't mean she couldn't have been the next Elizabeth Holmes—without the scandal.

"Hello, my little Italian meatball," she responds. I roll my eyes.

"You know I hate when you call me that."

"I know," she smirks. "What's the nail design of choice this evening?"

Lifting my hand into view, I say, "Going for something glam. The girls and I are going out tonight." I'm going with a light pink polish with silver metallic stars overtop. I'll cover both in a sheer shimmer to give my nails a cohesive and glittery vibe.

"Ohhhh, we're getting lit, are we? Are we talking freshman year spring break or junior year homecoming?"

"Um, neither, I hope. We're celebrating a work win, but I am planning to make it to a 10 a.m. Pilates class, so I need to be alive in the morning."

Intrigued, she asks, "A work win? Did your shrew of a boss finally quit, and they decided you should be running the show?"

"No, not quite," I retort. I go on to explain about the grant and my plan to Tiffany. She knows how important this cause is to me. I've only been talking about feeding food-insecure people for as long as she's known me.

"I can't remember the last time you seemed this excited about something," Tiffany states, smiling at me. "Don't get me wrong, it's not as if you've been a sad sack—recently anyway—but 'excited' isn't an emotion I would say you show that often. I'm usually the effervescent one."

She isn't wrong there. That isn't to say that I am grumpy. The word people most often use to describe me is 'sweet.' I appreciate the sentiment, but it is slightly demoralizing, depending on who it is coming from. The second way people would define my personality is "sassy." I'm not too proud to admit I can be a bit bratty, which is why I respond to Tiffany by sticking my tongue out.

"Hey, it was a compliment!" she snickers. "All I am saying is that it is good to get a glimpse of the bright-eyed and bushy-tailed girl I met in Harkings Hall."

"Ah, that girl. Well, you know what happened to her. You were at her funeral. Anyway, we're celebrating with a night of Mexican food and dancing because we 'aren't nineteen anymore and need something to soak up the liquor,' according to Haley," I admit trying to change the subject from the heavy comment that slipped out. It doesn't work.

"Hmm," she hums. "Well, I think it is good you're getting out there and not staying at home watching Ross and Rachel break up for the fifty-seventh time." That earns her a middle finger that I present as I blow on the nail.

She laughs at my antics. "Speaking of getting out there, have any gentlemen suitors requested to promenade in your lady garden recently?"

"Finished Bridgerton, did you?" I laugh. "Um, no. No interested parties at the moment."

"No interested parties or no parties aware you're open for business?"

"Oh my God, don't say it like that!"

"What?!" she exclaims. Appraising me, she sighs, "Care, you deserve to be happy. You deserve to have someone to celebrate this 'work win' with that isn't paid to hang out with you."

"Hey, Kim and Haley are real friends!" I defend.

"I know they are, and you have your mom, Lola, and me. But come on, you can't tell me you don't want someone tall, dark, and handsome to share your successes with."

"I already tried tall, dark, and handsome, and you saw how that turned out," I mutter.

"Fine. Try short, pale, and mid-looking for all I care. But I'm serious, Carina; I don't want you to end up alone. Don't follow my example. I mean, I am killing it by myself, obviously..."

"Obviously," I interrupt with an eye roll.

Glaring at me, she continues, "But you didn't grow up with an ice queen for a mom and a rotating door of detached and weird stepfathers. You are a squishy, rom-com-loving smoke show who deserves a hot dude to celebrate your wins and make your eyes roll in the back of your head before taking you out for pancakes."

"My battery-powered boyfriend is taking care of me fine, thank you," I say flippantly.

"Yes, and I bet that Kindle Unlimited subscription is getting the job done, but neither will keep you warm at night." She shoots me an expression full of concern that I'm not sure I'm comfortable with. "Promise me that you'll be open to meeting someone. I have a good feeling, and Venus is totally in your favor tonight."

"Okay, Babs," I yield. "For you, I will keep my eyes open for my dream man tonight. If I find him, I promise to let him scramble my eggs and then make me some for breakfast."

"That's all I ask," she giggles.

After a few more minutes of catching up and getting fashion advice, I say goodbye to Tiffany and finish getting ready to meet the girls. Luckily, our first stop is dinner at my favorite Mexican restaurant, which is conveniently near my house. I stick my ID and credit card in the back of my phone case and lock my door.

"I can't believe you sent that guacamole back!" Kim marvels as we show the bouncer our IDs.

"What can I say?" I shrug. "After four years in Cali, my guac standards are high."

She shakes her head. "At least the margaritas were up to Her Majesty's satisfaction. Now, let's go to the bar, do a round of shots, and hit the dance floor. I am ready to get my groove on."

Downing a shot of Jose and grabbing my tequila sunrise, the girls and I make our way out to the back of the dance floor. I love this place. The vibe at Paula's is unlike anything else. The disco balls make the light play off my silk dress. Was silk the best choice for a club where I will surely get a drink spilled on me and/or sweat on? Doubtful. But Tiffany insisted this was the outfit the universe wanted for me, and who am I to argue when the universe speaks?

The little lilac dress is gorgeous. It's form-fitting at the top but then flares out from my waist until it hits mid-thigh. I am average in the chest area, but the straight cut and tiny straps highlight what I do have well. Combined with the beachy waves in my long brown hair and my signature red lip, I am not ashamed to admit I look damn good tonight.

The DJ is on fire, and we are having a great time. Resident mom friend, Haley, goes to grab us some water since we've all had a few drinks at this point. While she's gone, a pair of guys move closer to us. One is taller with flaming red hair and a baby face. The second one resembles a shorter Tom Selleck since he's rocking the eighties mustache that has become popular as of late. I'm undecided on my take on staches in general, but this guy is not pulling it off.

"Dibs on the ginger," Kim whisper-shouts. I nod at her. Her desire for redheaded babies is well-documented, and I am not about to get in her way. As Kim and her guy dance, his friend puts out his hand, which after a moment of hesitation, I take.

He spins me around until my back is to his front, and we move along with the music. He is a decent dancer, though he seems more preoccupied with smelling my hair than dancing to the beat. Since the club is packed, we don't have much room to move anyway. I peek over at Kim, who gives me a thumbs up.

Midsize PI, as I've dubbed him, breathes directly into my ear and tightens his grip on my hips. "You are fucking hot in this dress, sweet cheeks," he says. Sweet cheeks? Gag.

"Thanks," I murmur, barely loud enough for him to hear.

"It will look better on my bedroom floor later."

I laugh but don't say anything. I told Tiffany I would be more open to finding a guy tonight, but I'm not a hookup kind of girl. There is no chance any of my clothing will be seeing his bedroom floor anytime soon or ever. Plus, he is so not the one.

Not getting that memo apparently, he continues, "Are there going to be panties joining this dress on my floor tonight?" Okay, we've officially crossed over from gross to creepy. I squirm, trying to put some space between us, but he takes it as encouragement, trailing his hand down my dress and inches it up my thigh. When I put my hands on top of his to stop him, he grips my thigh hard enough that it might bruise.

"Come on, honey. The way you were grinding all over this dick tells me how much you want it."

"Um, no," I assert as I try to separate from him again. I manage to get a step away, but he turns me and grabs my forearms.

"Listen, thanks for the dance, but this," I say, pointing between us, "is not happening."

Moving closer into my space, his eyes get a predatory gleam. Searching for Kim and his friend, I realize they joined Haley on the side of the dance floor, and we're isolated in the corner, backed up against the mirrors. "Don't be a cocktease. How about we get you another drink and see what you think then?" he suggests. As if another drink will make me go home with someone who smells like he drank the entire bar and insulted me.

I shake my head, but before I can get out a verbal response, he's gone. He was ripped away so violently that my body spun to face the mirror as I hear yelling behind me. The relief that hits me from his absence is short-lived when I gaze into the mirror and make eye contact with the person who pulled him away. A person I never thought I'd see again: the man who broke my heart four years ago, Robby Becker.

Instead of saying 'thank you' like a normal person, I turn around to make sure what I am seeing is, in fact, real and not my imagination. Once I confirm I am face-to-face with Robby, my fight-or-flight instinct kicks in. Usually, I freeze, but this time my body chooses flight and gets the hell out of dodge. One second, I am locked into Robby's ocean-blue eyes, and the next, I am standing with Haley and Kim. The guy's ginger friend is nowhere in sight.

"Are you okay?" They both yell at the same time. Shaking my head no, then yes, then no, the lump in my throat finally lessens.

"Can we go?" I ask shakily. They both agree. "Thank you! I'm going to run to the bathroom and wash that slime ball off me. Y'all call an Uber, and I'll meet you out front."

I'm introspective as I wash up in the bathroom. You'd think it's because of the altercation with that creep, but it isn't. It's due to a whole different interaction altogether. I'm blaming the fluttering of my heart—and dampness in my panties—on the drinks. It has nothing to do with the 6 '4" ghost from my past who just went all knight and shining armor on that shady perv. It *absolutely* has nothing to do with the way his muscles bunched as he flung around that jerkwad in defense of me. Nope. These tingles are a result of tequila. That's my story, and I'm sticking to it.

Chapter Five

Robby

Riding in the car with Leo, he explains that we're going to a dance club downtown called Paula's. When I ask about the club, he tells me I have to "experience its majesty" myself, whatever that means.

We pull up to a brightly neon-lit building in what seems to be a business area of the city, and my skepticism grows. "Are you sure you didn't want to go to Beale Street?" I ask. I've been to Memphis before—not that I told him that—and it seemed to be a better place for a night out than this hole-in-the-wall.

Patting me on the back, Justin, the team's shortstop, responds, "Nah man, you want to get a real taste of the 9-0-1, this is the place." Still on the fence, I follow them inside.

This place is a mix between Barbie's Dreamhouse and Studio 54. Not only is the air smokey, but it also has a pinkish hue. Disco balls and pink balloons litter the ceiling, and multicolored string lights seem to cover everywhere else.

After paying our cover, we venture inside and take a seat in a white leather booth; Leo goes to grab us beers. Dude comes back with forties which honestly shouldn't surprise me based on the vibe of this place. Trevor and Ryan, some of my new teammates, quickly make their way out onto the dance floor, chasing after some blondes they saw on the way in. I haven't had enough time to get to know any of the guys yet, but Trevor is my least favorite. He totally has a 'my shit doesn't stink' attitude which I am not here for.

"What do you think?" Leo asks excitedly.

"It is something," I muse.

"I figured you might want to try something different since you're probably used to being out on Broadway," he states.

He's not wrong that I've spent a lot of time frequenting the bars of the infamous Nashville street. My condo is literally on it. But I am not as much of a party boy as people assume. Don't get me wrong, I have fun, but after partying too much as a new player in the league, I kicked my ass into gear. I wanted to move up to the majors quickly, and partying was a distraction.

"I know you're not thrilled to be down here," Leo comments, "but we're glad to have you for a while. We can learn a lot from you."

"Thanks, man. I'm happy to help you guys however I can, especially while still on the injury list."

He nods while taking in his surroundings. "So, what's your deal?" he inquires. "You got a girl? Chronically single? Hiding a bunch of baby mamas?"

His last question has me choking on my beer. "Uh, none of the above. I've spent the last few years focusing on the game. I guess you could say baseball is my girl."

"I'm sure you've got plenty of offers to change that," Justin chimes in.

"True," I laugh. "But I'm not after some cleat chaser. I'd have to meet someone special to divert any time away from the game, and that hasn't happened in a long time."

"But it has before?" Leo asks.

Shifting uncomfortably, I nod. I don't want to think about her tonight. Not when the anniversary of our break up is top of mind. Not when I am surrounded by countless reminders of her. But the universe has other plans, it seems. This conversation has manifested her right into this fucking club. Where there was once an empty space on the dance floor is now my college girlfriend.

"What the hell is she doing here?" I mutter to myself. It's been four years since I've seen her and she is more beautiful than I remember. Wearing a sexy purple dress that shows off her delicious curves and brown hair cascading down her back, she is a vision. I know I'm not the only one who notices. I swear I saw Trevor's head turn despite the blonde dancing on him.

I can't get over the fact that I'm seeing Carina. I know she grew up here, but I assumed she stayed in Cali after graduation. She loved it there. We never talked about it, but I figured she'd end up wherever I was playing. When that didn't happen, she must have come back home. It's where her mom lives, after all.

I should have looked her up when I got sent down here. Hell, I should have looked her up when I was traded to her home state, but I didn't. A year after the breakup, I stopped stalking her on social media. Seeing her smiling face was too painful, knowing I'd never be the reason for that smile again.

Watching her float around the dance floor like an apparition of my wildest dreams, I notice a guy with what can only be called a pornstache grinding behind her. I want to throttle him for the way he sniffs her hair. I wonder if it is as silky as I remember, if her skin is as soft, if her pouty lips still taste faintly of cotton candy from her favorite lip gloss. Following my gaze, Justin whistles through his teeth, shaking me out of my fantasy.

"Damn, that's a fine woman right there. You should shoot your shot, bro. That overgrown frat boy has nothing on you."

Eyeing me curiously, Leo—the fucking psychic, I guess—says, "I think he's been on that ride before, Pinder." He pats me on the shoulder with a smirk on his face as the pair leaves to go dance.

Saying nothing, I continue to watch Carina and the douche canoe dance. After a while, I notice her friend and the guy she was dancing with leave. I spot them off to the side, talking to the other girl they came with. When I glance back at Carina, the soon-to-be dead man has her by the arms and is whispering in her ear while she searches around uncomfortably. With his grip too tight for my liking, I'm down there in a flash, ripping him off her.

Staring at me in disbelief, he yells, "What the fuck, bro? Get your own."

Wrong thing to say. "Get my own? That's a person, not a Four Runner your dad bought you off Craigslist. Fuck off." He makes a move to get around me and back to her, and that's when I deck him. I'm usually a chill guy, but I've punched two people in less than two weeks. Maybe I should consider that meditation app Morgan keeps suggesting.

The guy scuttles off the ground, and I hear him mutter, "Frigid bitch isn't worth it."

I consider going after him, but I need to make sure Carina is okay. When I turn back to where she was, she is making eye contact with me in the mirror. And damn if I don't get lost in her gaze. Something familiar zips through my body as I stare into those little chocolate orbs. Home. Her eyes look like coming home. What? I don't know what to do with that thought. Shutting it down, I focus back on the sexy siren in the mirror.

Her facial expression quickly shifts from relief to confusion to horror as she turns around to face me. I don't know what response I'm expecting after how we ended things four years ago, but it is not her fleeing as if I'm an eighties movie serial killer.

"You good, man?" Leo asks, appearing beside me.

"Yeah." I shrug as the bouncers who saw the altercation go after the creep. "I'm gonna hit the head," I say, trying to make sense of what just happened.

After splashing some water on my face, I leave the bathroom only to have someone walk straight into my chest. I grab their arms to steady them and peer down to realize it's Carina.

She stares at me, blinking, and we're frozen in time. The slam of a door behind us knocks us out of our trance, and she pulls out of my grip. "Are you okay?" I ask, proud as hell that my voice doesn't crack.

"Yes," she says quietly. "Thanks." She turns to walk away.

"Wait," I practically yell. She stops. Gripping the back of my neck, embarrassed that I'm not even sure what to say, I spit out, "So... um... how ya been?" Christ, is that the best I can come up with?

"How have I been?" She whips around. "How have I been?" she repeats, almost to herself, glaring at me like I am the most audacious person she's ever met. "What answer are you honestly expecting to get from that, Robby? Good? Amazing? Living the dream? It's been four years. I've been many things during that time—none of them your business," she sneers.

"Whoa," I say, throwing up my hands. "Is this level of vitriol how you respond to everyone who comes to your rescue? Cause I gotta say, it isn't the appreciation I was expecting, Kitten."

She cringes at my use of her nickname, and I almost feel bad for saying it, but damn, she is not being the sweet-hearted beauty I knew. It's been a few years, and I did fuck things up, but technically she broke up with me. I'm not saying I didn't deserve it, but I thought if we ever saw each other again, it would be similar to running into an old friend.

Getting uncomfortable by her silence, I dig the hole deeper, "Usually when someone saves a damsel in distress, the damsel kisses them or at least swoons a little." I realize the stupidity of my statement as it is leaving my lips, but it seems to jar her out of her stupor.

"Damsel in distress? You want to be a knight in shining armor? Find another girl. Your role in my story was cast a long time ago. You can't be my white knight when the biggest dragon I ever had to face was you," she states. Apparently done with the conversation, she turns on her heel and is gone before my brain can even process what she said.

I stand there, shell-shocked at the bluntness of her statement. As I rejoin Leo and Justin in the booth, my thoughts go to how I ended up here. I contemplate the actions that led to me being in this smokey club, left in the dust by the woman I was once convinced was my future. The woman who no other has ever lived up to. Even more troubling to consider, why was that interaction we had in the hall the most titillating interaction I've had with anyone in a long fucking time?

Chapter Six

Robby

Four years ago...

After a brutal training camp and first month of the season, I am finally settling into my own on the Baytown Bucs. I joined the team midway through last season after being drafted, but this year I'm finally being utilized to my potential.

"Yo, Robby," one of my teammates shouts as I walk to my locker post-shower. "We're heading into H-Town to celebrate tonight's win. You in?"

"Hell yeah," I respond. "Let me call my girl first. I'm going to go home and change. Text me where we're meeting up." He gives me a head lift as a few of us walk toward our respective cars.

Hoping into the Bronco I bought with my signing bonus after being picked in the first round of the draft, I plug in my phone and dial my girlfriend. It may be 10 p.m. here, but it's only 8 p.m. in Cali. I know she's up.

"Hi, baby! How was the game?" she asks. She has always been my biggest supporter. My parents were never encouraging of my baseball career, but having her in the stands for the last two years in college was everything. She even traveled to Omaha to watch us clinch the College World Series.

I'm glad to hear she is in a good mood. Things have been tense with us since the season started back up. Long-distance is hard, but since she's still in school, we don't have any other option. Thankfully, she graduates next May. We only have one more year of this shit before she can move to me. It might be here, but my agent is hopeful that by then, I'll be in Spokane playing at Seattle's Triple-A affiliate or maybe even playing for the Eagles themselves.

"It was good. We pulled out another win. I didn't pitch tonight, but I'm happy the team was able to make it happen."

"That's awesome, babe. I can't wait to see you. Are you all packed?"

I'm heading back to Cali tomorrow to participate in a charity auction she's putting on as part of her internship. Some shit about playing catch with a professional baseball player. I'm fuzzy on the details, but since it's important to her, I agreed even though we only have a three-day break between games. I was told the auction started at 2 p.m. I should arrive at LAX with time to spare.

"Yep. I'm all ready to get to the airport at 8 a.m. tomorrow."

"Ugh, I wish your flight wasn't tomorrow," she grumbles. "What if there is a delay and you don't make it? It's not as if I have professional baseball players laying around I can call on."

I laugh. "You'd figure something out. I'm sure Tiffany's got someone in her Rolodex. Hell, Sean is technically a professional, even if he stayed an extra year to finish out his degree. He was drafted, after all."

"I guess you're right. I'm just excited to get to spend some time with you. I haven't seen you since camp." She came out to visit me for her spring break. Yeah, I had to work every day, but we still had a good time, and she got plenty of beach time.

"Alright, Kitten, I gotta hop off. I'm meeting some of the guys for a post-game drink." More like post-game bottle service based on the spot Luke texted me to meet him; I don't tell her that, though. She's been on my case lately about partying too much. I think she hates it because I always seem to let my phone die. Last time that happened, she didn't hear from me for over eighteen hours, which is not typical for us. But also not a big deal. With that thought, I make a note to plug my phone in while I change.

"Okay, babe, don't stay out too late. I can't wait to see you tomorrow. I love you," she sighs.

"Love you, too. I'll call you on my way to the airport."

"And text me when you get home tonight," she requests. She's never been the clingy type, but her neediness has been next level lately. I'm playing professional baseball now. I don't have all this free time to devote to her anymore. Since she isn't even here, I don't know why she cares if I spend that time out bonding with my teammates. She is busy and goes out, too. You don't hear me complaining.

Not wanting to fight right now, I reply, "Will do, baby. Bye."

This party is fucking lit. One of the guys on the team is dating a waitress at this club and got us a VIP booth and complimentary bottles of liquor. That's not a perk you get when dating a girl who works for nonprofits, I think, as Luke pours another round of shots.

I smile over at my teammate and throw back the shot. I've never been at a party this crazy. I went to some great clubs in college. Since my friend Tiffany is as connected as a hotel heiress—without the sex tape and drug problems—we got into tons of dope places in LA. But there is something about being out with my teammates. These guys get me, and people here give us the celebrity treatment. We deserve this night after all the work we've put in this season. So, what if we play hard? We worked damn hard to get here.

I know I should head home now, but I am having too much fun. I'm used to being surrounded by friends 24/7. Being out here alone in Texas has been eye-opening. When your girl and your crew all live somewhere far away, there isn't much else to do besides party with the boys. I mean, what else would I be doing? Sitting around my apartment waiting for Carina to call me when she gets done studying? No thanks. I've always been a social guy, and being alone has been hard.

Not that I've told anyone that, though. I'm the easygoing one, steady. I'm the one you come to when you want to chill and not talk about your deep dark secrets. Javi is the one you go to when you need sage advice, and Sean is your guy if you need help getting shit done or emotional support. I'm not good at the advice, but I can offer a sarcastic comment.

I try to avoid confrontations when possible, at least the emotional kind. And it seems as if that is all I've been having with Carina lately. She misses me. She worries about me going out and wants to talk about my feelings. Blah, blah, blah. It has taken a lot of mental energy to make her happy lately. That's the only reason I'm going to this dumb charity event.

Don't get me wrong; I miss my girl. Nothing beats having her in my arms, but I hope she isn't going to be all naggy with me about how I'm spending my time here. Everything I'm doing is for our future. I'm killing myself to be a good ball player, and if I want to have some drinks with the boys, why shouldn't I?

No one else understands this experience the way my Bucs teammates do. Not my old teammates, not Carina, and sure as hell, not my dad. None of them understand the pressure you're under, playing at this level. We may play for some podunk team far from the major league diamonds, but we're working our asses off for a chance at the big stage. Tired of all the thoughts running through my head, I join some of my buddies on the dance floor.

It feels like five minutes later when I come back to our booth for water. Based on the number of empties and the number of guys who have bailed by now, I suspect I was out there longer than I thought.

I go to check the time on my phone, but it's dead. Oops. "Hey Luke, what time is it?" I ask.

"Time to stop letting your phone die all the time, dumbass," he responds, making the girl in his lap giggle.

"It's 3:42," the guy beside me says.

"Shit. I'm supposed to catch a flight at eight," I say to no one in particular. "I gotta go."

Downing the rest of my drink, I grab a cab since I can't exactly Uber with a dead phone. Forty-five minutes later, I stumble into my apartment. Stripping out of my clothes, I go straight to bed, planning to get a few hours of sleep before I have to be up for my flight. Having set an alarm earlier while on the phone with Carina, I pass out the second my head hits the pillow.

I wake up with a groan to the sound of thunder and lightning. I throw my hand over my face to block the flash as I take stock of how hungover I am. I reach over to grab my phone to see what time it is, but it doesn't light up.

Shit. Jolting up, I run into my kitchen to see the time on the microwave—2:17 p.m. Running my hands through my hair, panic seizes my chest. There is no way I can make it to Cali in time now. I'll have to figure something else out. Maybe I can schedule playing with the winner another time. I need to call Carina to suggest a new plan. She'll understand. She's been high-strung lately, but she's typically chill.

Plugging in my phone, I take a shower while it charges. Feeling more like a person when I get out, I grab my phone to call Carina, and that's when I see them. Half a dozen missed calls and seemingly a million texts between Carina and our friends. I open my group text with the boys first.

As I'm reading through the messages, I get a call from my best friend, Sean. "Hey man, what's up?"

"What's up? Seriously, bro. What the fuck?"

"Whoa, chill man, what's crawled up your ass?" I defend.

"What's crawled up my ass is that I'm watching your girlfriend run around this event, wondering if you died or something because where the fuck else would you be? But your location says you're at your apartment, and you sound alive to me, so again, I say, what the fuck?"

Shit. I didn't realize she'd be worried something had happened to me. I figured she'd assume my phone died and I'd missed the flight, a.k.a. what happened.

"What's the plan here, bro?" Sean responds to my silence.

"Uh, I am still sorting that out. I figured I could schedule the game of catch next time I'm in town?" I suggest.

"I'm not talking about that dumbass. I'm talking about what you're going to tell Carina. She's going to be devastated."

"That's dramatic, don't you think?" I quip.

"Not really, no. She's been counting down the days until you got here, literally counting them on her calendar. It isn't only about the event today. It was about getting to spend time with you. She hasn't said anything, but we can all tell things are tense between you guys. She seems less sure of herself and less sure of you. And now you do this? Did you even consider how that would make her feel? Today was important to her personally as much as professionally."

"Alright, Dr. Phil, chill the fuck out," I snap. See what I mean Sean being the practical one? "I don't need relationship advice from a guy who can't keep a girl in his bed for longer than a month. Maybe focus on satisfying your own woman and leave mine out of it."

"Fuck you, man. I'm trying to help you," he sneers. "Let me deal with this. Don't text her until after the event. She doesn't need to deal with that stress on top of everything else."

"Whatever," I retort. "Tell her to call me later, and we can iron out the details."

He hangs up without responding. Who the fuck does he think he is talking to me about *my* girlfriend like that? I know what she needs. She may be annoying the hell out of me lately, but she's my endgame. This is one of those rocky phases we'll discuss in future interviews, explaining how it strengthened our relationship. We'll get through it. We always do. She'll understand. She always does. I'll send her some flowers Monday, grovel a little, and we'll be fine.

Chapter Seven

Four years ago...

Robby didn't text me when he got back last night, but that's fine. He didn't want to wake me, I'm sure. That's why I didn't hear from him before his flight, either. It would've been 5 a.m. here when he got to the airport. He knows I love my sleep. That is totally why he didn't call. Or text.

When I called his phone, it went straight to voicemail, but he had it off while on the plane. His plane should have landed at 10 a.m. Cali time which was three hours ago. According to the airline's app, it did. I bet he let his phone die playing Candy Crush on the plane.

He has always been bad at keeping his phone charged. At least, he was before we dated. He'd been better about it since our short break two years ago, but lately, he's been falling into old habits.

That must be the explanation. It can't be anything else. If it's not that, I'll have to consider that something bad might have happened to him last night or this morning on his way to the airport. I won't even put those thoughts into the universe. With Tiffany always preaching about what I manifest, I don't want to risk it.

I've been setting up at the park for the last hour and a half. Today is a big day for me. I'm hosting a silent auction benefiting the children's charity I work for. I interned there last summer, and they loved me so much that they decided to keep me on. This is the first solo fundraiser I've put on, and I've poured myself into it the last couple of months. With Robby playing baseball in Texas, it's been nice to have something else to focus on.

Don't get me wrong, I still have our friends and supporting the Pelicans from the stands, but being long-distance made me realize how much time we spent together. With that thought, I try Robby's cell again. When his phone goes to voicemail, I text him asking him to let me know he's okay.

As my thoughts spiral, our friend Sean walks up. He was Robby's roommate and quickly became an honorary big brother to me when I joined the crew, which as an only child, I've secretly loved.

"Hey, pip-squeak," he greets me. I may be on the shorter side, but Sean is abnormally tall. I'm talking 6'6". Our height difference is comical to anyone who may be staring at us. "How's it coming along?"

"It's good. Everything is mostly set up. Now I have to wait for everyone to get here."

"Awesome," he replies, glancing around. "What are the chances I can get some insider help winning that round of golf at Pebble Beach?"

"I am not helping you cheat the system, Seany. You want to win it, pony up," I sass.

"Please, for how high that thing will sell for, I'm going to have to start dancing *Magic Mike* style to afford it," he jokes.

I laugh but then go quickly back to worrying.

Sean notices. "What's wrong, Carina?"

"Have you heard from Robby today?" I ask.

"Uh, no?" He responds hesitantly. "Have you not?"

I shake my head. "No, the last I heard from him was as he went out last night. His flight landed, but his phone is still going straight to voicemail. You don't think anything happened, do you?"

"No," he says incredulously. "I'm sure he's fine. I'll get in touch with him and see how long it takes until he gets here. You focus on finishing your setup."

Later, I find Sean talking with my roommate, Tiffany.

"Okay," I say, "That's everything. Bar is stocked, games are set up, and auction items are out. People should arrive in thirtyish minutes." Turning to Sean, I ask, "Any word?"

His features pinch, but before he can speak, Tiffany chimes in, "We've got good news, bad news, and great news. Which do you want first?"

"Good."

"Okay, well, the good news is, Robby is fine—alive and well." The knot in my chest that had been forming since we talked last night loosens.

"Thank God. How long until he's here?" I inquire. The pair share a look. Tiffany gives me the soft expression she usually only reserves for when I talk about fictional characters breaking up or dying, which can be super sad for some people, okay!

"He isn't... That's the bad news."

"What?!" I practically scream.

"The dickwad overslept and missed his flight," Sean grouses.

"What am I going to do?" I panic.

"That's the great news," Tiffany supplies cheerfully as if my entire event isn't slowly crumbling with this information. His was one of the biggest items. "Do you remember that party I did makeup for last month?" Clearly not seeing recognition on my face, she continues with a huff.

"Remember, I did that woman's makeup for the ESPYs? We talked about how funny it was when Peyton Manning hosted and how I'd do your makeup for it one day. The lady had the crazy ass fountain in front of her house?"

"Tiff, focus, babe," Sean nudges.

"Right, not the point. Anyway, she loved her makeup enough that I sent her the product I used, and she said to let me know if I ever needed anything." Still not getting the point of this story, I stare blankly. "She's married to Clayton Kershaw, and he agreed to fill in. He's on his way. Now, that game of catch will go for way more money!"

"Oh my God." I hug her. "Thank you! You're a lifesaver."

Pulling out my phone, I frown when I don't see anything from Robby. Why couldn't *he* have told me what was going on?

"I told him not to reach out to you," Sean explains when he notices. "You need to focus on the event and not entertain his platitudes. I said you'd call him later to talk about it."

It is no surprise that Sean is taking control of the situation and is concerned for everyone's well-being. He's such a dad. I've never heard Sean speak about Robby with such annoyance before, though. They are best friends. The peanut butter to his jelly. The Tiffany to his Carina.

As I spot my boss and other guests arriving, I thank both my friends again and put on the brightest smile I can manage. I've got to get through this event. Afterward, I can consider what it means that Robby isn't here. Until then, I'm going to raise a crap ton of money to help these kids.

Six hours later, I return to my apartment. Between set up, hosting, and clean up, I'm freaking wiped. I've been on my feet for over twelve hours, but I know my night isn't over yet. I haven't had the courage to reach out to Robby. I'm not ready to deal with whatever bullshit apology I have coming my way.

I am beyond disappointed in him. He has always been my biggest supporter—my champion. Sure, we had some ups and downs when we first got together, but nothing compared to what we've been through recently. Lately, every time we talk, I feel like an obligation. As if talking to me is something he has to check off his to-do list.

In a way, my worst fears are coming true. I was worried that when he got drafted, we'd drift apart. Except I didn't imagine he'd drift and I'd stay put. If anything, it's a rubber band. The harder he pulls away, the harder I snap forward to hold on. But now I'm wondering if I'm holding on to something that doesn't exist anymore.

Holding on this tightly hurts. This sense of being a burden and unwanted is familiar, and I hate it. My mom may be financially stable now, but I grew up poor. Like wearing the same clothes to school every week poor and on social services. Even once we were comfortable, I still never felt wanted by anyone but my family. I didn't relate to my new classmates and their silver spoons. They never let me forget where I came from. It gave me an inferiority complex. After realizing I didn't deserve to be treated like that—ironically mostly due to Robby—I decided never to let anyone treat me that way again.

Walking in the door of my apartment, I'm greeted by a smiling Tiffany and a glass of wine. "Meatball," she coos. "How did the rest of the event go? It was popping off when I left. Clayton's wife texted me and said he had such a good time that they want to talk about volunteering regularly."

Sighing, I say, "Thank you again for arranging that. You saved me from major embarrassment. The event was good. We raised even more money than I expected. My boss is thrilled. It's going to make a great case study for my nonprofit management class. All in all, I'd call it a success."

"Of course it was! You put it on. It could have never been anything else," she praises. Clearing her throat, she asks the question I know she's been dying to know the answer to, "Did you talk to Robby yet?"

I shake my head. "Aw, babe. Sit down, tell me what's running through that busy mind of yours."

Joining her on the couch, I tell her everything I've been processing since the event ended. She takes a minute to digest everything I said before she responds, "You know I love Robby—even though I want to throttle him right now. Know that I will support whatever decision you decide to make. It sounds to me that you may be at a make-or-break moment in your relationship."

I tense. I know she is right, but it's hard to consider that. Robby and I have been together for over three years. He's my future, at least, I thought he was. We've talked about forever. Sure, there are issues we've had to work out, but our love is worth overcoming all obstacles. It used to be, anyway.

"I knew that baseball would take over his life," I state. "I just thought there would still be room for me. And it seems right now, he only cares about playing ball and having a good time with his buddies. I don't see how I fit into that, especially when I'll be here for another year. I can't be with someone who makes me an obligation when they're my priority. Putting someone first only works when you're in their top five."

Tiffany hums and nods in response. "No matter what happens when you make that call later, know I am here for you. Sean is here for you. Your mom is here for you. You have people in your corner willing to make you top three at least." She says the last part light-heartedly enough to make me smile. "Love you, Meatball."

"Love you, too, Babs," I say as I enter my room to face my fate.

After showering and getting ready for bed, I pull out my phone and hit Robby's number from my favorites list. He answers on the second ring. "Hey! I was wondering when you would finally get around to calling me."

"Where are you?" I ask. "It sounds loud."

"Hang on." I hear some shuffling, and then it's quieter. "Sorry, my buddy Tony had some of the guys from the team over tonight, and since I was in town, I decided to come."

"You're out partying right now?" I gripe.

"What did you want me to do? Sit around and wait for you to call me all night? It's been eight fucking hours since I talked to Sean, Carina. I wasn't going to waste a perfectly good night off when I didn't even know if you were going to reach out. Besides, it isn't a party. It's a few guys on the team hanging out at Tony's apartment. He got the new Call-of-Duty game."

Taken aback by both his angry tone and casualness, I respond, "I got home forty-five minutes ago and took a shower. I was busy hosting an event all day. An event you promised to be at, by the way."

He sighs loudly. "I'm sorry I didn't make it. My phone died last night, and I overslept without my alarm. I offered to schedule the catch-thing for when I am in town next. We're playing a team in Costa Mesa in a month or so. It would've been fine." His lack of accountability pisses me off.

"That's not the point! Do you know how embarrassing it was when people asked me where you were? I'd told people—our friends, my boss—that you were coming. The fact that you no-showed could've made me appear bad if Tiffany hadn't had a connection to take your place."

"See, it all worked out. FSB saved the day," he says with a huff.

"Tiffany isn't supposed to save the day for me. You are! They knew you were supposed to be coming to support me. My mom even texted me to see how you were doing. What did you want me to tell people? That you partied too hard to make it?"

I can hear his jaw clench through the phone.

"It isn't only about you not showing up to this event, Robby. It's about you not showing up at all lately."

"What does that mean?"

"It means that recently it feels like you don't want to be in this anymore, as if I'm an obligation, a box for you to check off during your day. Wash face, brush teeth, give girlfriend attention, like a freaking Tamagotchi. Relationships take work, investment—both emotionally and with time. Lately, it hasn't seemed you are willing to give me either."

"Oh my God, you're being so dramatic. It hasn't been like that at all."

"No? How has it been?" I retort. "How it appears to me is that my boyfriend would rather party than support me, connect with me."

"Sorry for enjoying myself. I'm playing professional baseball. No one thought I'd get here. My parents were convinced I'd end up working with my dad every day. I fucking made it and am living my dream. Fucking sue me for making the most of it."

"You're living your dream? Right now? Everything about your current situation is your dream?" I ask.

"Well, the needy ass girlfriend isn't, but otherwise, mostly, it is." His words are a knife to my heart.

"I'm sorry, I didn't realize it was needy asking you to make good on your commitments to me and a freaking charity."

I hear people calling his name, and he must walk further away because they fade as I listen to him mutter, "Hey, I'm dealing with something. I'll be back in a minute, man." I almost laugh at the irony. Me. I'm the thing he needs to deal with. The supposed love of his life is now a thing he has to deal with for a minute.

"This is not what I expected it to be," I admit.

"Well, it isn't what I expected either."

I try to stop the word vomit fighting to escape, but I can't. "I need more from you, Robby. I need you to make me a priority. Choose me. I don't think it's too much to ask."

"Choose you?" He asks incredulously. "What does that even mean? Grow up, Carina. This isn't The Bachelor. Besides, I already chose you by dating you. I can't give you any more right now. I have to give baseball my everything if I want to make it to the top. It has to be my number one priority." With his confession, he rips my heart out and stomps it on the ground.

"Is that how you truly feel?" I question quietly.

His response is immediate. "Right now, yes, it is."

As tears form in my eye, I offer up an ultimatum of sorts. "If that's how you feel, then maybe you should take me out of the equation and focus solely on baseball."

"Maybe I should," he replies as if it isn't the final nail in the coffin of our relationship.

"Goodbye, Robby." I sniffle.

"Whatever, bye," he retorts.

With his parting words, I hang up. Curling up on my side, I sob. Tiffany comes in a few minutes later and slides in behind me. I fall asleep to her stroking my hair and tears soaking my pillows.

I wake up the next morning to a simple text from Robby that says, "I'm sorry." Its time stamp says he sent it at 7 a.m. his time.

Later that afternoon, he calls me, but I don't answer. In fact, I turn off my phone. I spend the night in bed crying and staring off into space. He may not fully understand it yet, but that conversation last night was the end of us. I can't do this to myself anymore. I deserve more, but damn, am I broken by that realization.

All I can do is nod when Tiffany asks if this is what I really want. While I lay there, my best friend goes into action mode. She takes all the pictures and mementos of Robby and me and hides them in a box in the back of my closet. She texts our friends and my family to break the news to them so I don't have to field all their questions. They're all shocked except Sean, who shows up later that night with pizza. He sits on my bed and forces me to eat while we—he—watch TV.

When I finally turn my phone back on the next morning, I'm greeted by a barrage of texts that make tears I didn't know I was still capable of producing flow once again. I send Robby a final message before blocking him for good.

6:18 PM

53

Are you going to ignore me?

7:23 PM

I said I was sorry. What more do you want?
I can't go back in time and show up. I made
a fucking mistake, and I regret it, but the
past is the past.

8:28 PM

Kitten, come on. You know I didn't mean
any of the shit I said.

8:45 PM

I choose you. Is that what you want to
hear? I love you, dammit. Forever and
always.

10:02 PM

Babe, call me back. You're being ridiculous.
I'm sorry for what I said last night, but
you're taking this too far. Don't let a silly
fight be the end of us.

Carina. Stop. This is crazy.

12:16 AM

I talked to Sean. Are you really serious? You're breaking up with me because I missed this stupid event? Because I can't give you "more," whatever the hell that means? Three years together down the drain because I'm not giving you enough attention? That's fucking dumb.

Baby, I'm not giving up until you tell me this is over. I know I fucked up by missing the event, but I'm under a lot of pressure to make this happen so that we can have the life we talked about.

12:37 AM

Kitten. Baby. Carina. Tell me what you want. I'll do whatever you ask. Forever and always, babe. I won't lose sight of that again.

8:57 AM

ME

You let your priorities be known last night, Robby. I think you're right. You can't be what I need right now when you're trying to become the man you want. So go do that. Go make something of yourself. Prove to your dad and the whole wide world what an amazing player you are. Just don't expect me to be waiting here once you're done.

I can't keep giving myself to someone who isn't able to give back. You're not only the one who has stuff going on. I may not be trying to make it in the MLB, but that doesn't make my commitments any less important. Until you can get that, don't bother pretending. Goodbye, Robby, and good luck.

55

Chapter Eight

Robby

Present day...

The next morning, I am still stupefied as I make my way into the stadium for PT. I might have thought last night was a dream if it wasn't for my slightly bruised knuckles. It may not have been a dream, but Carina certainly was. Seeing her again did something to my body. It recognized her on some primal level. My blood has been hot, and my pants have been tight all morning. I need to chill out before seeing Anastasia. I don't need her imagining this semi is for her.

On my way to the training room, I run into Stacy. She's the Blues Birds PR director. "Mr. Becker, just the man I was searching for."

This can't be good. "What can I do for you, Mrs. Clemmons?"

"Stacy, please," she says. "As you are probably not aware, the front office here at Express Delivery Park has been trying to find a way to connect more with the community, especially our nonprofits."

Since I don't know what she's talking about, I remain silent as she keeps talking. "We decided to give one local nonprofit a $25,000 grant donated by the team owner."

"That is great," I say. "What is it you need from me? Help give the check? Show up for a photo op?"

"Ah, if only it were that easy," she replies with a twinkle in her eye. "What I need from you is to stick around after PT to meet your team captains."

"Team captains? I already met all the guys," I say, bewildered.

"Not the captain of the Blues Birds. The captains of the charity team you're coaching."

"Come again?" I sputter.

Smiling with amusement, "Yes, to decide who gets the money, we're hosting a softball tournament made up of employees and volunteers from local nonprofits. It will take place over the next couple of months on Tuesday nights. The championship will take place on National Nonprofits Day. I don't have to tell you what having a player of your caliber will do for the profile of the tournament."

"Is this a good idea? We don't know how long I'll be here. No offense, but I think Norris would rather I focus on healing my injury and getting back up to the bigs. Gotta put that paycheck they give me to use."

She gives me a face of derision as she answers. "We are confident you can both work on healing your injury and spend a couple of hours a week with your team. You've coached Little League in the past. Think of it as coaching big kids who are all devoted to a cause with less of a desire to pick their noses while standing on the field. You and Mr. Davis will be coaching a team together, and he is aware he may be solo at some point during the tournament. You can meet your captains on the field at noon after you get done with your appointment. Have fun!"

She walks away, not giving me the chance to argue further. I guess I'm coaching a team of goodie two shoes—color me thrilled.

After an hour of flicking my wrist like I'm fucking Harry Potter and getting felt up by Anastasia, I text Leo to meet me in the tunnel before we go greet our team.

"Hey, brother," he calls.

"Sup man? How ya doing after last night?" I respond.

"I'm good. Ryan seemed a little worse for wear when I saw him this morning, though. Poor kid partied too hard. What about you? How is the hand?"

Ah, the hand. "Yeah, the bruised knuckles did not go over well with PT Barbie. I told her I slammed them on a door frame, but I don't think she bought it." The nickname causes a pain in my chest at the memory of a friend I used to tease with a similar moniker. I make a note to do some social media stalking later to see how Tiffany is. I'd ask Carina, but after she ran out with her ass on fire last night, I doubt I'll see her again during my time here.

It's just as well. My body may want to be around her again, but my brain is smart enough not to go down that road considering the animosity I saw in her eyes. Besides, there wouldn't be a point in spending time together. She knows better than anyone that long-distance doesn't work—at least not for us. There is no way she'd ever be willing to give me a chance again. That's a leaf best left unturned.

"Ready to meet our merry band of do-gooders?" Leo jests.

"Let's get this over with. I want to get some cardio in before I watch y'all play today." We walk out to the field to see our team.

When we get there, a group of four people is standing around home plate. Since they aren't facing us, I can only see them from the back. But that view has something stirring in my mind. As we approach, they turn around and, wouldn't you know, I am met with the same pair of panicked brown eyes I was reacquainted with last night.

"Hey, we know you guys!" The curvy redhead says brightly. "You were at Paula's last night. You saved Carina from that creeper."

"Uh, yeah, we were there last night; glad you remember. I hope you guys are doing okay after everything," I say, examining Carina, who is avoiding my gaze and searching for the off-ramp of this conversation.

"Wait, what happened?" The gangly guy who is with them today questions. Haley and Kim fill him in as Carina looks everywhere but at me.

Clearing her throat, she says, "It was nothing. A misunderstanding with a guy at the bar who thought a few cheesy lines were going to get him somewhere with me. I had it handled."

I snort. "You absolutely did not have it handled, Kitten. He was holding you so tight he practically left bruises."

"Don't. Call me. Kitten," she grits out, and damn if the ferocity doesn't go straight to my dick.

Leo chimes in as the air around us grows awkward, "Okay... Well, it's great to see you guys. I was worried we might get stuck with a bunch of PTA moms or middle-aged pencil pushers. I'm Leo, and this is Robby. We're going to be your coaches. And not to brag, but we're pretty freakin' awesome. I know we're going to kill this competition."

Regaining some of her composure, Carina answers for her group. She appears to be the one in charge of this whole thing. I should've guessed. "I'm Carina. This is Kim, Haley, and Alex. We're from Feeding Memphis and are thrilled for this opportunity to fund a program that will feed hungry moms and kids who otherwise wouldn't have access to fresh meals.

I smile at her spiel. She always said she wanted to work for a charity that dealt with food insecurity, and she is. We both made good on our goals.

"That's amazing," I comment softly, making Carina's cheeks

flush. Everyone is giving us curious glances, but I ignore them as I read from the packet Leo handed me.

"Alright, well, we've been given the next two Tuesdays to practice before the first games, and then we'll have eight to play. We automatically make it to the championship if we're the best after those eight games. If we aren't, we'll play a single-elimination playoff and hopefully kick ass there to make it to the championship."

"Oh, we're going to do more than kick-ass. Losing isn't an option. This grant is as good as ours," Haley cheers.

"That's the enthusiasm I want to see," Leo remarks, eyeing the black beauty. "Well, if you guys don't have any questions, we will see you Tuesday at 6 p.m. Bring your A-game and your best volunteers!"

They say their farewells, and Carina gives me a parting glance as she heads out of the gate. After they leave, Leo peeks over at me and bursts out laughing. "I don't know what the deal is with you and that girl, but this is gonna be fun!"

I sneer at him as we go to the locker room to prep for today's game.

Chapter Nine

I was too dumbfounded last night to even consider why Robby was in Memphis. The only reason he'd ever been here was to meet my parents and see my hometown. Clearly, he wasn't here to see me, not that the universe cared about that.

After we broke up four years ago, I made every trace of him disappear. Well, it was regulated to a box, but that box is hidden in the depths of my closet. After I blocked him, Tiffany and I removed him completely from my life. I muted all references to him on social media—including the team he played for, his family, and anything that could potentially be tied to him. Tiff even banned all our friends from mentioning him in passing, and we referred to him as "the dick who must not be named."

Imagine my surprise last night when I Googled him only to see he has been living in the same state as me for the past two years. Seattle traded him to the Nashville Songbirds in some controversial trade to free up some roster space for a new wunderkind they picked up overseas.

Regardless, it means Robby was within hours of me for the last twenty-two months, and I had no freaking clue. It seems like an oversight in our Robby Becker Amnesia Plan when the chance to run into him was on the table. I didn't go to our friend Kelsea's bachelorette party in Scottsdale last year on the off chance his team was spring training in Arizona! I could've spent a weekend spa-hopping and lounging on a pink flamingo floatie instead of sulking in my apartment here, watching my friends have fun on Instagram. Dumb.

Once scoured Google for info about him, I found that he was sent down. Here. To Memphis. To play for the Blues Birds while he recovers from a UCL sprain. Normally, that wouldn't be a problem. Today, however, it is. It's a problem since I am in my trusty Rogue driving to Express Delivery Park to meet the players coaching us in the charity softball tournament. Since he's still injured and a big leaguer, I'm sure he won't be the team's coach, but I could still run into him again, which is not an experience I want to repeat.

The box where I keep my feelings for him is tied closed so tightly it's bowing. And now the box is freaking shaking because those emotions want to spill out. We had to meet again when he was being all chivalrous and saving me from some d-bag. That shouldn't have been as hot as it was, especially since it wasn't the first time. And yet it was.

Speaking of the past, Robby was even sexier than the last time I saw him, holy cow. His arms and shoulders are much more defined. His luscious long hair is cut closer to his head but still looks as soft as I remember. It makes me wonder how it would feel to grab onto the strands in comparison. Don't even get me started on the scruff. He's a freaking wet dream.

And this, this is the problem. I can't be over here lusting for the only guy I've ever loved. The one who broke my heart. The one who told me I wasn't worth his time. No, thank you. Not again. As I park next to Haley's KIA, I take a deep breath and center myself before I head inside. All I have to do is get in and out without running into him. How hard can that be?

Really freaking hard, apparently. Of course, he's the coach of my team. Why wouldn't he be? The next time I talk to Tiffany, I am lodging a formal complaint with her and the universe. Her 'good feeling' was some complete and utter bull, and I want a refund. I'll even take store credit.

I couldn't tell you what happened in our meeting, aside from the fact that Robby and I's prior connection went completely unacknowledged. I don't know if it was he or I that did that, but I'm glad. The last thing I need is for this to become *a thing*.

Walking to my car, I give my cousin Lola a call. I'm stressed about this predicament, and she has always been my voice of reason. She's only eighteen months older than me, but she's wise beyond her years —a product of growing up without a mother and with a workaholic dad.

She picks up after a few rings. "Care Bear, how are you?"

"Honestly, I'm not sure," I reply.

"What's wrong?" she frets. "Are you hurt? Sick? Do you need me to call someone?"

Since Lola is usually reserved, her burst of panic would be heartwarming if I wasn't this stressed. "No, no, calm down, worry wart. I'm not hurt. But... something did happen."

"Well, don't leave me hanging, you little *cagacazzo!*"

I laugh at her Italian insult and give her the whole story, from getting the grant opportunity to last night at the club to what just transpired. I'm met by silence.

"Um, Lo? Are you still there?"

"I... wow," she states. "I'm still here. That is a lot to process. I haven't thought about Robby in years. How are you handling this?"

"Fine. Good. Terrible. I don't know!" I exclaim. "It's almost too much. I'm having a much stronger reaction to seeing him than I thought I would. When I see him, my brain goes haywire. I've been a bitch to him, which is not me."

"Not like he doesn't deserve it," she mutters, making me smile. Get yourself friends who hold grudges with you.

"You're not wrong, but now I have to see him every week for this tournament. Maybe... maybe I should drop out. I can try to find another way to get the money for my program."

"No!" Lola shouts. "No, absolutely not. You are not going to let this man take anything else away from you. You're going to go to those games with your head held high and show him that you're doing fine without him. This grant is yours, and nothing stops a Francelli woman from getting what she wants. Nonna would never let this man—any man—win! The patriarchy has taken enough from us!"

"Wow," I remark. "That was quite the girl power speech."

"Yeah, sorry," she laughs. "I watched Legally Blonde last night, and the 'I'm taking the damn dog' scene stuck with me."

"No judgment here, Bunny," I giggle. I've called her that ever since we first watched Space Jam together. She acts embarrassed by it, but she secretly loves sharing a name with the badass rabbit.

After an extended conversation about how the early 2000s were the golden era of rom-coms, I say goodbye to Lola. I decide she is right. I'm not going to let Robby Becker keep me from my dreams. I'm gonna make this charity softball tournament my bitch.

Chapter Ten

"**D**uunnn dunnn... duuuunnnn duun... duuunnnnnnnn dun dun dun dun dun dun dun dun dun dun dunnnnnnnnnnn dunnnn," Kim hums the Jaws theme as we walk into our Monday staff meeting. Today is the day we tell Camila about the tournament and grant.

"Kimmy, I don't think that works when we're the ones moving toward her," Haley chastises.

With an eye roll so exaggerated it's a wonder they remain in her head, Kim pushes in front of us to enter the conference room. "It will all be fine," Haley says, giving my arm a squeeze. "Any money and attention we can get is a good thing."

On a philosophical level, I know she's right. But Camila is such a loose cannon sometimes I am not sure she's going to respond favorably. As I go to take my seat, I peer around at my smiling coworkers.

People often get worn down working at nonprofits—especially when their bosses care more about making connections with the 'right people' than serving the clients.

I am thankful that most of my coworkers are genuinely pleased to be here. When serving our community, they all have a positive and 'whatever it takes' attitude. That's going to come in handy when they hear what I have to ask of them. Luckily, I came into the meeting with a secret weapon: Gibson's donuts. You can't say no when your mouth is full of sugary goodness.

Instead of enjoying one, Camila goes to the diffuser that she insists we need to create a 'productive and inspired environment' in this windowless dungeon of a conference room. She digs through the oils she's so protective of that none of us dare touch them.

"Today's scent is grapefruit. It's known to help reduce stress and balance moods." I gag. I HATE grapefruit. I have strong opinions on the bitter citrus that interacts poorly with a whole slew of medications.

Apparently pleased with her smelly water vapor, Camila turns and faces the room clapping her hands together. "Now that we've gotten that taken care of, we can get rolling! Carina, I understand you have an announcement for us all?" she says, eyeing me dubiously.

"Yes, I applied for a grant to help us fund some new initiatives. Last Friday, we received a callback and were offered the chance to compete in a grant contest hosted by a local organization. I met with them over the weekend and have all the information we need to see what volunteers might be interested in helping us with this opportunity."

I try to keep it vague to avoid Camila's ire, but she must see through that because she has follow-up questions. "Compete? What is this, nonprofit Survivor? And how much exactly are we going to be given if we play in their little contest?"

I swallow hard before answering her. "Uh, yes, compete. The contest is being hosted by the Memphis Blues Birds. Not a survival show, unfortunately—no tropical locale for us." No one laughs at that joke. "It is a softball tournament, and the winner gets $25,000 for their charity."

"A minor league baseball team has $25,000 to give away?" Camila muses. "How?"

"I believe it is a donation made by the team's owners."

"Ah, a tax write-off," she hums. "Well, whatever the case, $25,000 would go a long way for our organization! We could buy more locally sourced food and increase our investment in community gardens..."

Haley interrupts, "Camila, if you recall, at last week's meeting, you told Carina if she found the money to fund her mobile market idea that she could get it rolling. I believe these funds will be earmarked for that."

My face heats as Camila scrunches her nose. "I did say that," she hedges.

"Carina got all the information from the Blues Birds and has already created a preliminary roster and plans to help us win," Kim pipes in supportively.

Seemingly annoyed at the unity among her staff, Camila concedes. "I see. Well, if you're prepared to skip around a baseball field to earn your grant, I won't stand in your way. Don't embarrass the organization."

Not exactly an enthusiastic approval, but I'll take it. My boss's demeanor tells me she is done with this conversation. I slide back into my seat and grab a vanilla sprinkle donut to hide my smile as she moves on to other topics.

After lunch, I call Haley, Kim, and Alex into my office to strategize

"Alright, team, we need to get serious. Winning this grant may be my only chance to launch my program anytime soon. Obviously, the four of us are on the team. Camila is a hard no. Kevin and Brittany both had kids recently, so I don't see them joining either. Maybe Brad might be interested? Kim, what can you tell me about the volunteers?"

"Oh, do I have some superstars for you," she declares with a mischievous glint in her eye. She sets down nondescript manilla folders and pulls out what surely isn't full background checks.

"Jesus, Kim," Alex exclaims. "Did I miss when you became an FBI agent? How, why do you have all this information on our volunteers?"

"I don't play around," she says, ignoring Alex's rebuke as she turns to me. "First, we've got Jim. He's thirty-one, married with no kids, and his Braves hat may *actually* be sewn onto his head." I nod at her to continue.

"Next, we have Doris. She might be sixty-six, but she's a retired gym teacher who mothered four kids that played various sports."

"Those are both super promising. You think they'd be available?"

"They both are. I reached out to my top picks last week when you gave us your news to get an understanding of their interest levels. But I haven't even told you about my crown jewel."

"Excuse me, Mrs. Great Detective, please carry on," I mock.

"Thank you," she curtsies. "You remember Jada Jones, right?"

I shake my head at her because the name doesn't ring a bell.

"Mid-thirties, chocolate goddess? Volunteer/former client? She works in IT at Express Delivery?" I must still have a confused expression on my face because she exasperatedly says, "Jalen's mom?"

"Jada! Yes, I know her. But she works in IT. That doesn't exactly scream sporty."

Clutching her chest in mock horror. "How dare you stereotype her by her job! She can be both a computer science savant and a former D1 athlete who went to college on a softball scholarship. Full ride."

"Well, dang. Hello, Jada. Amazing job, Kimmy!" I acquiesce. Kim beams at my praise.

"Alright, seems we have a good base. Let's get a list together and reach out to anyone else who might be interested, and we'll see who can make it to practice tomorrow."

I blanch at the thought. I almost, *almost* forgot that this team we're putting together means going back to the ballpark and working with our 'coaches.' I shiver thinking about it before tuning back into the brainstorming session at hand.

Chapter Eleven

"Hello, Maleficent," I grouse when I pick up my phone and put it on speaker while I finish prepping for a fresh manicure. Tiffany lets out a quiet giggle before responding.

"It always tickles me that people assume *I* am the dramatic friend. Besides, calling me Maleficent isn't an insult. Have you seen Angelina Jolie's version? I would trade my left tit to look that good in my forties."

"Eloquent as ever, Babs." It's times like these I forget everything that's happened over the last several years. Some days I'm shocked we're not still in our Cali apartment eating our weight in gelato—because "You're Italian, we can't have regular ice cream!"—and dreaming about our futures. Me with Robby and Tiffany in some stuffy marketing job. How wrong we were.

"Anywayyyyy, I did not curse you," she whines.

"Really?" I let out a snort of derision. "Because I hadn't seen hide or hair of Robby Becker in four years until you sent the universe out to deliver me a soulmate. What kind of sick joke is that? The universe couldn't even give me something new? Sure, the packaging was upgraded, but I'm sure what's in the box still suffers the same manufacturer's flaws as the original version."

"Admiring the merchandise, were you?" she teases.

"Do not get any ideas. This is going to be awful, Tiff. I don't know how to act around him. My body sets on fire the second he is close, and my sass cranks up to ten."

"He was always a fan of your sass, if I recall correctly."

"I'm serious! This is a DEFCON 5 level crisis."

"Is DEFCON 5 the worst, or is it one? I can never remember which one is most extreme," she muses.

"That is not the important part to focus on right now," I deadpan.

"Sorry, sorry. You're right. Talk to me, babe. Tell me what you're thinking. I know seeing him again was a shock to your system. Hell, I'm shocked, and I haven't even technically seen him." Like the ride-or-die she is, Tiffany cut Robby out of her life after we ended things. It wasn't hard with him seemingly ditching most of the people he knew back in Cali, but they'd always had a sibling-esque bond similar to what I have with Sean.

I sigh. "I don't know. I short-circuit when he's around. My body hums and is desperate to get closer to him. It's as if it still remembers his aura and wants his touch. He's familiar, ya know? His laugh is the same. The playful gleam in his eye when he's volleying back and forth with me makes me forget the last several years ever happened."

"Okay..."

"But then my brain kicks in and says, 'Absolutely not!' It remembers what he did to us and the shit we went through after he left, the loneliness, the heartache, the knock to my self-esteem, the—"

"The Jäger," she interrupts.

"Oh God, don't remind me," I groan. Jägermeister and I had a very intimate relationship for a while. Did you know that not only does the German-crafted beverage aid digestion, it also aids in numbing all those pesky emotions you don't want to deal with? 10/10 recommend it if you need to forget that the love of your life is too busy to care about you.

"Someone has to remind you. You certainly don't remember those nights."

And she isn't wrong about that. There was a good eight months after my breakup with Robby, where I went a little wild. Between the breakup and turning twenty-one, Tiffany and I made efficient use of all the suck-ups wanting to get or stay in her mother's newest husband's good graces. Why they thought letting his barely drinking-aged step-daughter into wild parties where we downed bottles of Veuve and hooked up with white boy wannabe rappers and B-list teen drama stars would make him like them is beyond me, but we weren't about to look a gift horse in the mouth.

Thankfully, during the spring semester, our friends staged—an intervention is too strong of a word—let's call it a group therapy session at Sean's beach house. It ended with us (the girls) crying in an empty bathtub while the guys did whatever it is that men do when they have big emotions. Project them onto sports teams? In any event, we calmed down and processed our feelings in healthier ways.

Seemingly lost in my thoughts, I am jolted back into the conversation when Tiffany finally responds.

"I don't know why the universe sent him to you, Meatball. Maybe it wants you two to give it another shot." I choke on air.

"Or maybe it wants you to properly heal and move on. We both know you haven't," she says before I can object.

"I know," I admit defeatedly. "How am I supposed to move on now when every time I'm around him, I feel like both the eighteen-year-old that fell in love with him and the twenty-year-old he decimated?"

"First of all," Tiffany voices strongly. "He did NOT decimate you. He *may* have left you marginally worse for the wear, but you didn't let that keep you down. You are a bad bitch. You are the girl who poured a pitcher of beer on Mike Hannigan's head when he needed to learn that just because his daddy has more money than God doesn't mean he can put his hands wherever he wants.

"No two-bit ex-boyfriend can rattle your confidence, no matter how good he was in bed or how much you wonder if he could still play your body like a fiddle."

Leave it to Tiffany to be both inspiring and dirty. Thinking about Robby's bedroom prowess is the last thing I need right now. I certainly don't need to remember the way he knew exactly where and how to touch me to make me see stars.

Robby was always good at reading me—my mind, my emotions, my body, all of me. I hate that he is still the best sex I've ever had. And that's not for lack of trying. During those eight months, I tried the 'you've got to get under someone new to get over someone' method. Total BS.

No hate, no shade to those who enjoy that, but random hookups aren't my style. That's probably why I haven't been with anyone since I moved back to Memphis. Tiffany was right; I did need to put myself back out there. I'd gone on a few dates here and there, but I hadn't met anyone I clicked with. Either my sass was too much for them, or they didn't understand my passion for my work.

I dated many different types of men, but none ever made my heart flutter. I refuse to admit it might have been because the right someone was a few hours away. Nope. Not even going to consider that possibility. Not after what he did. I'm sure *he's* not thinking that.

The next night when I get ready to go to my first practice with the team and our 'coaches,' I remember Tiffany's words. I hype myself up on the drive over with Taylor's ten-minute version of All Too Well and get ready to face my ex.

Chapter Twelve

Robby

Today is the day of the designated weekly family video chat. Why I need to stare at half of my parents' faces or have my sister shove her dog on camera is beyond me, but I gave up that fight years ago.

When I join the call, I see Morgan hanging out in the hotel room of whatever city Ralphie is playing in right now. Linda, my mom, as always, is at my parents' kitchen table. I can picture the stack of slightly used cookbooks her phone is propped up against.

As contentious as some of my last years with them were, knowing that my parents still live in my childhood home warms something inside my chest. After my first year in the majors, I paid off what was left of their mortgage to make sure they never had to worry about leaving there. You'd have thought my dad would be grateful that I was honoring the begrudging sacrifices that allowed me to play baseball, but he was offended instead.

Like many men of his generation, he has trouble showing emotion and has some warped ideas about what a man is. I won't claim to be the wokest guy out there, but I'm not ashamed to admit I cried when my childhood dog, Vader, died after fourteen years of friendship.

The man himself walks into the frame and sits beside my mom as if summoned by my thoughts. It's funny to see them sitting together. It's almost a—hopefully not too close—view into mine and Morgan's future. She takes after my mom with her blonde hair and blue eyes. I got my mom's eyes, too, but everything else: the height, the hair, the bulk, I got from dad. I used my size to my advantage in baseball, while he used his to be the star receiver of his high school football team. Or so I was reminded incessantly when it became clear I wouldn't follow in his footsteps.

My dad, Frank, isn't a bad guy. But he is set in his ways. In his world, nothing is more honorable than taking care of your family and putting in your time at your job. He worked hard and was able to take over the family plumbing company about ten years ago. I am proud of all he was able to accomplish, even though I know this isn't how he saw his life going.

His football career was supposed to extend beyond high school. He got a full scholarship to USC. Unfortunately, as with everything else she does, Morgan decided to make a dramatic entrance into their lives. My mom found out she was pregnant a few months before he graduated. Instead of leaving my mom high and dry like many guys would, he stepped up to the plate and worked for his uncle as a plumber.

After I was born a couple of years later, Dad even supported the entire family while Mom went to nursing school. I respect the hell out of him for the sacrifices he made to support our family and his love for my mom. I wish we could find some common ground about my life choices. By my age he was working sixty-hour weeks supporting a family of four, but that isn't my journey. It's not as if I'm shirking some imaginary responsibilities; I don't have anyone depending on me. I proved years ago that depending on me isn't a safe bet.

"Hi, Daddy," Morgan singsongs. Such a daddy's girl.

"Hi, Princess," he replies. "Rob," with a head nod is the greeting I get. I'd point out the clear mismatch in affection, but I'm used to it.

"Hi, Dad. Hi, Ma. No hockey boy today?" I tease Morgan.

She rolls her eyes. "No," she shakes her head. "He has a game later tonight, so the team is doing whatever it is they do before to prepare."

"Plugged in as always," I joke.

From there, the conversation dives into how everyone is doing and what has been going on lately. As I finish recapping my rehab and progress, my dad chimes in:

"Don't you think it's time you hung up those cleats and tried to get a real job? I've given up hope on you joining the family business, but we didn't send you to that fancy college to spend your life playing a kid's game. Not that you have a real degree, but it exists, so people must be doing something with 'exercise science.'"

Yes, he used air quotes and everything. I pinch the bridge of my nose and try to come up with a response that isn't telling him to go eff himself. I shouldn't have to remind him I got a full ride plus living expenses to play in college. *He* didn't send me anywhere. Apparently, he takes my silence as a license to continue. "It's not as if your job does any good in the world."

Before I can say anything, Morgan comes to the rescue. "Daddy! That is not a nice thing to say. I don't see you saying that kind of thing to Ralphie about his career."

"Ralph played his sport to help him escape to a better life. I can respect that. Plus, he sends money back to take care of his family. Your brother just didn't want to grow up and face the real world. He throws a ball a few dozen times once, maybe twice a week, and he's sitting on millions. What good is being done with that?"

Having enough of my dad's condescension toward my chosen

profession, I jump back into the conversation. "If you recall, Dad, I tried to send money back home, too. You refused it."

"We don't need your money," he grumbles.

"And I am doing plenty of good. I donate a large portion of my salary every year and am on my way to coach a group competing to win a grant for their nonprofit right now."

"That sounds wonderful, honey," my mom remarks, finally making her way into the conversation. "What organization are you working with?"

"It is called Feeding Memphis. It helps those locally who are facing hunger get meals through school lunch and after-school programs, deliveries to shut-ins, and such."

"That sounds familiar. Did you work with an organization like that before?" Mom inquires.

"Uh, yeah. In college, I coached for an after-school program that focused on something similar. It was out in Hawthorne." I swallow down the memories of my time there. I'm sure it's not hard to imagine that a sassy brunette was also involved with the charity. Carina and I spent countless hours with those kids over the two years we volunteered.

As I talk about the league, my gaze shifts to Morgan, who is eyeing me appraisingly, and I know the third degree is coming. The rest of the call goes on as usual, with my mom and sister doing most of the chatting with the occasional comment from me and grunt from my father.

I don't have to wait long for my sisterly inquisition. The second we disconnect from the family video chat, she's calling me to talk one-on-one. Pinching the bridge of my nose, I steel myself for what I know is coming.

"For most people, a thirty-minute call with someone is enough for one day," I drawl.

"First"—she shoves a finger in front of her face—"You and I both know I could talk for hours. The limit does not exist for my preferred call time. Second, I know there is more to this story you aren't telling us. And third, there is no way being in that city and working with that type of charity isn't bringing out some unresolved feelings. Mom may not have remembered the details of your volunteering in college or known about a certain ex's passion for food insecurity, but I do."

This is worse than I expected to get from her. I do not want to talk about my confused emotions around Carina with my sister, but her face says she won't be letting this go. Resigned, I respond, "There is a little more to the story in that points two and three may be connected."

"Explain."

"I'm sure you can imagine I didn't exactly sign up for this charity gig." She nods knowingly. "And I certainly wouldn't have picked this specific one. Not only because of their focus area but also because the ex in question works at that nonprofit and is the team captain."

Morgan gasps.

"Wow," I boast. "I guess you were wrong about your ability to talk forever. You seem speechless to me." Her reaction almost makes the situation worth it. I've never seen Morgan speechless before.

After several beats, she recovers. "This must be what happens to my computer when I have too many tabs open simultaneously. That is... wow. I'm sorry; I just need to clarify. Are you telling me you are spending time with Carina?! Carina Ballerini? Sassy Italian? College and all-around sweetheart? The girl who rightfully dumped your ass four years ago after you shit the metaphorical bed in your relationship?"

"That is what I am telling you, yes. Though 'shit the bed' seems harsh."

"No, it's not... Talk about fate!" she squeals.

"Excuse me, 'fate'?" I repeat.

"Yes, fate. Re: those unresolved feelings I mentioned earlier.

You're getting the opportunity to fix the mess you made and get your girl back!"

I stare up to the heavens for, I don't know, the strength and patience to get through this conversation.

"If you'd have witnessed the ire Carina has been sending my way, you would not be saying anything about us getting back together. It has not exactly been the warmest welcome. This isn't a chance to fix any mess. It is a PR assignment that I hopefully won't even be here for the end of because I'll be back in Nashville with my actual team in a few weeks. She can get back to her life, and I will get back to mine."

Unimpressed, my sister comments back, "Ire? Smart word for such a stupid boy. But maybe you aren't the only one with unresolved feelings. That's a good sign! And the life you built? Please, all you do is play baseball and pine over the one that got away."

"I think hers were fairly resolved when she blocked me and all attempts I made at apologizing."

"Pish posh." She waves her hand in the air. "She knew back then that it was all lip service and you needed time to grow into your new world and place in the league. You know Ralphie and I went through similar struggles when we first got together. It was a big adjustment for both of you, and the timing wasn't right. Now, however..." she says, wiggling her eyebrows at me.

"I'm not sure you're right on this one. She seems not only pissed at me but guarded as hell. You should've heard the sass she was spewing at me the other day. Even if I wanted a second chance, which I'm not saying I do, that option is very clearly not on the table."

Morgan's expression shifts to something I can't put my finger on. "All I'm saying is don't slam the door to the possibility. We both know that Carina is the only girl you ever loved. The only one you were willing to make sacrifices for. Were you a dumbass twenty-two-year-old on his own for the first time in a crazy environment? Yeah."

I go to defend myself, but she is right. I was a total dumbass.

Morgan continues, "You're a better man now, Bobert. Back then, you were still a lost boy trying to make a name for himself. I know if you gave it another try, you could be the man she wants and needs. Consider it. I want you to be happy, and you were never happier than when you had her. I know you won't admit it, but you are still pining for that girl. Promise me you'll think about it?"

"Fine," I sigh. "I'll think about it and keep an open mind, but don't get your hopes up. I hurt something fragile, and I don't know what she did to put it back together, but I fear she made it Robby-resistant."

Glancing at the clock, I notice the time. "Alright, I gotta go shower and get ready for practice."

"Okay, bro," she mocks before turning serious. "Remember, ladies love a good grovel, and you owe her a hell of a grovel if she considers taking your stupid ass back. I'll text you updates from the game tonight. Keep me posted on this situation!"

"Will do. Bye."

While in the shower, I replay our conversation, my break up with Carina, and all that has transpired since. I put the idea of us being together out of my head years ago. She deserves way better than me. That said, no one else I've met has ever sparked my interest like she does. Even with hate radiating in her eyes, she is still the most beautiful woman I've ever seen. I may be the victim of her sharp tongue, but her quick wit and sass were what drew me to her in the first place.

Thinking back, when we first got together, she made me work for it. Maybe I can win her over again. Not that I want to win her back. Probably. Okay, I may not know what I want to do, but I do know if I ever have the chance to call her mine again, there is no way in hell I'd let her go.

In my next relationship, I am going to be all in. I won't screw it up by allowing the woman I care about to think she's anything other than my world—if there is another woman who can make me feel that way. It is certainly different from the approach I took four years ago. I know Carina would be worth the effort, but I don't know if I could handle losing her again.

Chapter Thirteen

Robby

Four years ago...

Well, that was a fucking shit show. After getting off the phone with Carina, I try to forget how the call ended, but it's playing on a loop in my mind. Sure, we've had our fair share of fights, but we were never that couple that would have stupid half-breakups every other weekend. Is this who we've become now?

I was telling the truth when I said this wasn't a party. I go back in and watch my teammates get picked off one at a time by a camper in the game. I'm not in the mood to play anymore. I stew in my thoughts off to the side.

"You okay, man?" Tony says, sliding in beside me and handing me a fresh beer. "You look like you need this."

"Thanks," I say as I run my hands down my face. "Yeah, I'm straight, just dealing with a girlfriend who doesn't understand the pressures."

He nods like he gets it. But I know he doesn't. What I told Carina about baseball needing to be my number one priority was accurate. If I'm going to make it to the next level, I need to work my ass off and stay the course. But does that mean I can't be who she needs? Is it better to cut this now before I miss out on more and keep disappointing her?

We had a plan, but will she be happy living in the B-list cities that minor league teams play in while we wait for my chance to get called up? Even when we end up in Seattle, there is no telling how long we'd stay there. I know they have nonprofits everywhere, but she gets attached to the groups she works with. Moving would be hard on her.

Where are these thoughts coming from? Fuck, it doesn't matter. We love each other; we'll make it work. I'll do whatever it takes to make her happy wherever we are. Hell, I'll start a nonprofit in every city we live in and buy a house for her mom if that is what she needs me to do. All I know is that I love her, and more than that, I need her.

Before leaving for practice the next morning, I shoot her a text apologizing. We both said some stuff last night, but I'm ready to let it go and get us back on track.

I finish practice a few hours later and check my phone to find Carina hasn't responded. That's fair. I was kind of a dick yesterday. If giving me the silent treatment makes her feel better, so be it. When it gets to dinner time, and I still haven't heard back, I call her. When it goes straight to voicemail, I text her. She's taking this too far.

After several unanswered texts, I send one to Tiffany. All I get in response is a GIF of Tyra Banks saying, "We were all rooting for you," and the middle finger emoji. When it hits 2 a.m. Worrying this may be more serious than I thought, and call my friend and former roommate, Sean.

"What do you want, dickhead?" is his greeting. Hostility noted.

"I take it by your tone you're still mad about the charity thing?" I inquire.

"Nah, I'm over that now."

"Okay, then what is your deal?"

"My deal," he scoffs. "My deal is that I've spent the last several hours trying to convince your ex-girlfriend to eat while watching her fall fucking apart over some guy who frankly isn't worth it."

Harsh. "I'm her *current* boyfriend, not her ex. Listen, bro, I know I haven't been the best friend lately, but I've had a lot going on. There is no reason for the attitude. Get out of here with that shit. We had a slight misunderstanding. This will all blow over once she hears me out."

His response is a kick to the crotch. "'Hearing you out' is what got you here in the first place. I don't know what your understanding is, but the fact I know to be true is that Carina is done with you. You made your choice, and now you have to live with the consequences, but I can guarantee you won't have Carina by your side when you do."

"Be serious, bro. Me and her, we're endgame."

"Well, the game is over, *bro*. And you lost," he states as he hangs up.

I frantically call Carina again and then again. I shoot off a couple more texts before calling it a night and having a fitful sleep. When I wake up, I see a message from Carina ending it.

Over the next several days, I call and text her dozens of times to no avail since she blocked me. It's clear that, at least for the time being, she doesn't want to have anything to do with me.

That fact both pisses me off and crushes me. I know she's it for me, but I also can't believe she's giving up so easily. If that's how she wants to be, then fine. I'll do exactly what I told her. I'll focus on baseball and become the best fucking pitcher the Eagles organization has ever seen. If I can't have her, at least I can have the other part of my dream.

Eleven months later, my efforts pay off, and I find myself on the mound in Seattle. It's everything I ever wanted, and I bury the hollow thought that something is missing.

Chapter Fourteen

Carina

Present day...

With music-induced courage pumping through my veins, I walk into Express Delivery Park. Conversations with both Tiffany and Lola put me in the right mindset to take advantage of this opportunity. I refuse to let Robby Becker derail this for me.

I spot him in the tunnel talking to Leo, our other coach, and make my way over. I try not to notice the way his t-shirt stretches perfectly across the muscles or the way his backward hat makes my mouth water. What is it about backward hats that make men look so sexy? Now is not the time, I scold myself. I am a bad bitch on a mission, and the only satisfaction that mission involves is an agreement from Robby to take this seriously. I'll worry about the other kind when I get home later.

"Hello, Leo," I say with a smile. "Robby." I see a flash of something that looks suspiciously like appreciation as he scans me on my approach. I ignore it, and the twinge of joy I feel from him checking me out as I clear my throat and fully face him. God, the hat is even hotter facing him than from behind. Shake it off, Carina! "Do you have a minute to chat before practice?"

After Robby whispers something to him, Leo excuses himself to grab our equipment while the team who practices before us wraps up, leaving us alone.

"Cute nails," Robby comments with a smirk on the manicure I gave myself this weekend that features a gradient of pink to blue polka dots. "What can I do for you, Kitten?"

"Don't call me that." I ruefully narrow my gaze at him, ignoring his compliment and the butterflies it set loose in my stomach. "I wanted to ensure we are on the same page with what this tournament means for Feeding Memphis."

As the other team slowly files out, Robby herds me out of the way. I'm backed against the tunnel wall while his shoulder is leaning against it. As he peers down at me, a familiar softness is present in his eyes. I close mine to stop the distraction his closeness is causing and get to my point.

"You may or may not remember, but helping people dealing with food insecurity—especially single mothers and their kids—is a huge passion of mine. I have this idea for a program that not only gets them access to free-slash-affordable quality produce, meat, etc. but also teaches them how to turn those fresh ingredients into healthy food.

"My boss isn't keen on the idea. This grant is the only way that it will happen. All our current funding is allocated, and since she doesn't believe the program is worth the resources, I have to find them elsewhere. It's the entire reason we're in this tournament.

"I know that you're focusing on healing your injury, and this may not be a priority for you, but it is for me. It's everything to me...professionally. If you're doing this as a PR stunt or because you have to, please, take it seriously. Or at least stay out of the way. I'm sure Leo can coach us if you aren't into it, but please, please don't impede this. I—we need this money to make the FM Mobile Market possible."

"Is that what it's called?" he asks, surprising me.

"What?"

"The program. It would help people struggling the way you and your mom did when you were younger?" He inquires further.

"Oh, um, yeah. You remember that?"

He chuffs. "Of course, I remember that. I remember everything about you."

I stare into the blue pools he calls eyes, unsure how to process his confession as he seems to decide what to say next.

"Couple things, Kitten." His mouth lifts at my shocked expression. "Even if it wasn't you or this cause or hell, any cause, I would never get in the way of my team winning. I'm way too competitive for that. Second, like fuck am I going to let Leo or any other guy coach your team to victory. You and I both know I'm the best coach ever; I've got the mug to prove it." I smile as I recall the day one of the boys on his Little League team gave him a mug saying that.

The expression he gives me says we're reliving the same memory. Then, something else flashes across his face. "If you need a donation to fund your program, I could give it to you," he mentions causally.

"What?!" I sputter. "You can't give me $18,000. That's crazy."

"Why not? You need it. I have it. It's a good cause. I once promised to help you found your own nonprofit, and this has to be way cheaper than that. Plus, my accountant can write it off."

"That was different. We were a couple then. It was a future investment."

"A nonprofit isn't exactly an investment, Care."

"You know what I mean!" I huff, exasperated.

"Not really, but I'll let it go for now. However, in the unlikely chance we lose, the offer stands."

Still dazed by his proposal, I don't notice the body approaching my other side. Robby steps further into my space as if he plans to protect me from the intruder.

"Carina," a familiar voice grates.

"Marshall," I sneer flatly at the interloper. "To what do I owe the displeasure of what is sure to be dreadful conversation?"

Marshall Davison is my counterpart at another nonprofit in town. When I first ran into him at an industry event last year, I thought we could collaborate on some initiatives. He's about my age and obviously passionate about serving others, but he's had it out for me for some reason. While his organization, Restore 901, focuses on strengthening communities by helping them better their infrastructure and giving them resources to help families improve their homes, ours focuses on hunger. There is some overlap regarding food deserts in the communities they serve, but we're mostly doing totally different but complimentary work.

"I wanted to see your face before it's crying in the stands when my team wins this thing. I see you're already getting cozy with your coach. Too bad it won't help you win."

I hear a low growl beside me that goes straight to my nipples.

"Unlikely, Davidson," I retort. "I don't think you even know how to win since you've never done it against me. Maybe you're confusing it with third place? That's where you guys finished in the Giving Tuesday Tik-a-thon, right?"

"You had an advantage for that and you know it!" he spits. "Besides, we have the Blues Birds' star player as our coach, and my team is stacked with former athletes—*male* athletes."

With a scowl that matches my own, Robby shakes Marshall's hand tightly based on the smaller man's wince. "Robby Becker, pitcher for the Nashville Songbirds and coach of her team," he says in a tone similar to his earlier growl. It makes me glad not to be on the receiving end of it.

"We'll have to agree to disagree on who the best coach is. Word of advice: underestimating a woman on a mission is never a good idea, especially this one. I've seen her throw together an A-List gala in twenty-four hours with a $1,000 budget," Robby declares, head tilting to me. I try not to preen at the praise.

Marshall laughs. "I'm not worried. In an athletic competition, we've got this in the bag. I'm just sorry you got stuck with this team. Hope you have a high tolerance for gossip and estrogen. See you on the field Cares Too Much," he snarls. I hate that nickname. We work for nonprofits. If you don't care too much, what are you even doing?

Robby shifts his gaze back to me after staring daggers at a retreating Marshall. "Who the hell was that guy? And what in God's name is a Tik-a-thon?"

"That," I sneer, "is my nemesis."

For some reason, this breaks the tension on his face as he tries to hold back a laugh. "Since when do you have nemeses?"

"You may remember 'everything' about me," I mock in as deep a voice as I can muster, "but I'm not the same girl you used to know. Now, we've got a practice to get to and a smarmy jerk's ass to kick."

As I walk away, I swear I hear him mutter, "Maybe I don't wanna know what a Tik-a-thon is."

I go see the rest of my team and Leo outside the dugout. Studying the others who make up the Feeding Memphis team, I am pleased with the roster.

We've got me, Haley, Kim, Alex, and Brad, our supplies manager, from work. Volunteer-wise, we have Doris, Jim, and Jada, all recruited by Kim. We also have Kelly and Melina, twins who attend the local university and volunteered with us last semester to complete their community service requirements. They brought their boyfriends Curtis and Mike to play as well. We also managed to snag two stay-at-home moms, Angela and Diane. I don't know if they have any softball experience, but they both play tennis, so their hand-eye coordination is at least on par.

I make small talk with the twins and their boyfriends as we prepare for practice. Once Robby joins, everyone huddles up. As somehow the de facto leader of this little endeavor, everyone stares at me. Taking a deep inhale, I speak up. "Thank you all for coming today. I, and the rest of the Feeding Memphis team, appreciate you volunteering your time and skills to help us out in this competition.

Winning this grant will be invaluable to the organization, but more than that, I think the experience will be fun for us all. I'm going to toss it over to Leo Davis, one of our coaches, to get us going."

"Alright, ladies and gents, before we do anything, we need to stretch. Follow my movements. I'm a big boy, so try not to show me up too much with your limberness. Talking to you, Doris," he teases the older woman, who smiles seductively back at him. Go, Doris, go.

We stretch and practice a few drills. I can't help but peek over at Robby. It gives me a sense of déjà vu seeing him in this element. When he catches me watching, he sends me a wink before returning his attention to sorting through our equipment. I let out a small squeak and switch my focus back to Leo.

Chapter Fifteen

Robby

The words she said to me as we joined the rest of the team stick with me. "I'm not the same girl you used to know." I wonder how true that is.

I can certainly tell she is much stronger and more confident than she used to be. She seems to have outgrown some of the insecurities that plagued her. Despite that, I still see glimpses of the feisty Italian beauty I fell in love with all those years ago.

It's why I keep calling her Kitten, the nickname I gave her when we met. She was cute and tiny but also came with razor-sharp claws. It's a combination that my dick and I still can't get enough of if the way he's pushing against my compression shorts tells me anything.

As I'm sorting the equipment, I see her watching me and send her a wink that has her turning a cute shade of pink. Good to know I'm not the only one affected by whatever this energy is between us.

I'm pulling out the bats that will work for the variety of players we have on the team when Trevor rolls up.

"Sup, bro? Mind if I tag along with your practice? Mine was kinda lame. Punk thought he knew more than me because he won state in high school. Prick."

I chuckle. "Sure, man. Leo is finishing up some drills, and we're about to move them around on the field to see where they might be a good fit. Grab that bucket of balls and meet me near the plate, will ya?"

Trevor does as I ask, and the rest of the team finds their way to us.

"Good job on the drills," I commend. "Y'all are doing well. Now, let's get you set up to run through some actual plays so we can see what positions work for you. Trev, do you mind playing catcher while we work out the infield? Leo is already taking some of the team who showed some arm power during drills into the outfield."

"You got it, boss," he salutes.

I have everyone left form lines in the different base positions so we can run through some scenarios and see where they might excel. "Carina," I call out. "Can you stand at home plate? That way, everyone can react as if it's a live game? Throw the balls at first to guarantee where we want, then you can bat."

She gives me a thumbs up as she heads over, and I can't help but see the way Trevor's gaze runs over her. It makes me more agitated than it should. I noticed the fact that her sports bra matched her leggings, too, Trevor, but you don't see me eyefucking her like I can see through them.

Carina sends the ball to each position as grounders and flies while Trevor continues to flirt with her in between each throw. I'd say I'm not a jealous guy, but that would be a lie, especially when it comes to the sexy siren currently smiling at my d-bag teammate.

After running everyone through each line, I place people where I initially think they'll have the most success. I peek into the outfield and see that Leo has his group situated.

I take my spot on the mound. I'm not officially cleared to pitch again, but since this is underhand and at nowhere near my full strength, it's fine, according to Anastasia. I felt like a kid having to ask his mommy for permission to play when we talked about it at this morning's PT session.

I turn to the pair flirting at home plate as Trevor says something that makes Carina laugh, which only adds to my annoyance. "Are we gonna play ball or gab?" I grouse.

"Excuse me, grumpy pants," she responds. "Ready when you are." My pants are something, but grumpy, isn't it.

For someone who presumably hasn't played in years, Carina is doing decent at bat. After she misses a few in a row—mostly due to my throwing, I see her scrunch her nose at something Trevor says. I'm just glad she stopped laughing. I see the bastard stand up and try to put his arms around her to adjust her stance and grip, but she puts her hands up to halt him. I inch closer to hear their conversation.

"I'm only trying to help you out here, sweetheart," he drawls. "I know how hard it can be when you're inexperienced, though you seem to handle a bat and balls pretty well." Does that kind of shit actually work for him?

Before I can make my way over there and smack some sense into him, Carina replies. "I'm good. If you haven't noticed, I've done well up to this point. This isn't my first rodeo."

Stepping back, Trevor challenges, "Then show me what you got, honey. To make it interesting, if you can hit the ball into the outfield on the next pitch, I'll donate to your little charity."

"And if I don't?" She questions.

"If I win, you've got to go out with me." I shoot Trevor a glare that has made greater men cower, but he smirks at me. If I wasn't so mad at the blatant play he was making on my girl, I'd laugh at his foolishness to challenge her.

Wait, my girl? No. Carina is not mine, at least not anymore. I don't know where this protective urge is coming from, except maybe my dislike of Trevor. That has to be it. I saw how he was at the club and heard his comments about women. It's about him, not wanting her to be mine again. The idea tastes like a lie even in my head, but that's the excuse I go with.

Shaking off that train of thought, I catch a twinkle in Carina's eye that says, 'we know something you don't know.'

"This next one's coming in Harry Styles—hot and surprisingly straight," I tell her. I send the pitch straight down the middle and hear the crack of the bat as the ball sails through the air above the shortstop's head. It drops in the outfield between left and center. Slowly, everyone turns and sees a smirking Carina and an open-mouthed Trevor.

"Did I not mention I spent college hanging out with the baseball team? A few of them even taught me a thing or two," she notes primly. Smiling, she skips, yes skips, around the bases as Leo has the outfield scrambling to make a play. I hear heckling from her coworkers, asking why this is new information to them as I turn my attention back to the plate.

"Doris," I yell. "You're up!"

Once practice is over, I gather up all the equipment and take it to the side. Nestled in between two of the tarps that protect the field from rain, I spot a kid. He appears to be about eleven or twelve and is sprawled out like he has every right to be there.

"Uh, hey," I say to him.

Glancing up at me, he gives me a chin lift. I search around for a parent, but I don't see anyone aside from my team, who is doing some sort of post-workout centering with Leo.

"Are you supposed to be here, buddy?" I finally ask.

"Yep," he responds with extra pop on the p. Unsure of what else to say, I decide to take his word for it. It's then I notice what he's doing.

"Hold up, are you playing a Game Boy?" I question, astonished.

"Yeah," he confirms, "I'm playing Super Mario. Ever heard of it?"

"Have I heard of it? Hel-heck yeah, I have. That game used to be my jam when I was your age. I didn't know kids were interested in those games these days." Oh my God. How old am I?

"Most aren't, but one of my friends in the Electronic Club had one from when his uncle was younger, and now we all play them. We play old games there, especially on Nintendo."

I spend the next fifteen minutes talking to this kid until his mom comes up. Jada is her name, I think. "There you are," she exclaims. "I'm sorry, was he bothering you? He was supposed to be playing his game."

"Nah, he wasn't. If anything, I was bothering him."

"Facts," the kid states, drying.

"Jalen Marcus!" Jada shouts.

"Ohhhh, government named. You're in for it now," I tease.

He gets up from where he is sitting and grabs his backpack. Before he leaves, he looks at me and offers, "If you ever want to play, my club meets every Thursday at 10 a.m. White Station Middle School."

"Duly noted, little dude. I'll see you next practice."

On the trek back to my apartment, I reflect on my weird day. Between the call with my family and the conversations with Carina—not to mention the emotions they've stirred—I need a beer and a night vegging out to clear my head. The Central Perk gang usually has the answers to my questions hidden somewhere in their silly plots. Time to find today's message.

Chapter Sixteen

Robby

"Give me two more. That's it. You're doing great. I'm proud of all the work you've put in today. You deserve a massage gun session," Anastasia purrs. If I had a praise kink, I would be loving life right now with all the positivity she is throwing my way. Unfortunately, that isn't my thing—though I do love the reaction a well-placed 'good girl' can get me.

Speaking of good girls, my phone lights up with a text from a number I never thought I'd see again. After our break up, Carina blocked me, and based on all the undelivered drunk texts I sent over the following twelve months, she didn't unblock me for a long while. I thought about deleting her number a hundred different times but could never bring myself to do it.

10:19 AM

I want to pretend it doesn't sting to know she didn't still have it, but it does. What grinds my gears even more, is the fact that she had that shithead's number before mine.

Ah, there is the sass I always loved. Carina has always thrived over text. On more than one occasion, her texts wrote checks her sassy ass couldn't cash once we were back in person.

Her confession brings up something I've always wondered: if she dated any of my old teammates after we broke up. I mean, she's fucking beautiful and amazing, and more than one of those fuckers had a thinly veiled hard-on for her.

At the time, I would have guessed she'd end up with Sean, but they had more of a brother-sister vibe. He and I didn't talk for almost a year until I got my shit together and apologized. We're good now, but we never talk about her. I have no idea what their relationship is like today. I stopped checking up on her by the time Sean and I made up. I thought she'd have cut baseball players out altogether, but the way she was talking the other day makes me wonder if she didn't.

> So you say. As much as I love bantering with you, is there a reason you wanted to talk before practice tomorrow?

> Obviously. 😊 I had some insight and ideas on how to best utilize the talents of the team.

We spend the next fifteen minutes texting about the league while Anastasia uses the massage gun on my back and legs. These things are nirvana on tight muscles—which mine are from sleeping on the discount mattress in my apartment compared to the practical cloud I have at my condo. After she finishes, Anastasia grabs her tablet and video chats Doc back in Nashville for a check-in.

"Becker," the middle-aged physical therapist greets. He may be twice my age, but I would not want to go against Dr. Kurt Mathis in a fight. He's got balls of steel dealing with major league egos all day and fists of steel from the MMA training he does to keep in shape.

"Do you want the good news or the bad news?" he asks.

Ugh, not this again. "The last time you asked me that question, I didn't love either answer," I say dryly.

The man grins at me. "Well, I think you'll be happy about at least one of them this time."

"Alright, hit me with the good."

"You are cleared to practice with the team and integrate pitching back into your routine... at full strength." He eyes me like I'm a naughty schoolboy.

"I was told the softball thing was cool," I defend, raising my hands in surrender. I know that is what he's referring to because, of course, he knows about it. The man has eyes everywhere and knows everyone's secrets.

"I'm teasing. The softball league you're coaching is good. Giving back will do wonders for your temper and your ego." I smile to myself, thinking about how any ego-checking it did was being counteracted by Anastasia's praise earlier.

"If I can practice again, does that mean I can play?" I ask hopefully. It's only been three weeks without pitching, but I am getting antsy.

"Not yet, son. I want you to spend another four weeks seeing how it performs before you jump back into the game. We're aiming for an Independence Day weekend comeback. By then, we'll have done another set of scans, and I'll be positive that you're fully healed. After that, it won't be long until you're called back home, assuming everything keeps going as it is."

That last part is welcomed news. Logically, I know I am one of the best players in the league, the best in my division for sure. But a small part always wonders when you get sent down if you'll be stuck there forever.

Signing off with Doc, I check my phone for another text from Carina, but the conversation ran its course. I sort of hoped she would want to continue talking about non-softball stuff, but I'm not going to let it get me down after the great news I received. There are two hours before the team has practice, and for the first time since I've been in Memphis, I get to take part.

The next evening, the Feeding Memphis team gathers for another practice. After last week's embarrassment, Trevor decided not to stick around, much to my delight. He was trying to punch way above his league with Carina. I'm glad he finally realized it.

Like last time, Leo runs the team through stretches, and we do some ground and fly ball drills. Next, we do some running drills to get them used to sprinting. Many said they're runners, but that style of running is all about stamina. In baseball, it's about exploding to cut the ninety-foot distance between bases. Scanning to my left, I see Carina giving a half-assed attempt at her sprints and take the opportunity to make conversation.

Sliding up beside her, I needle, "That was much more house cat than lion, Kitten."

She rolls her head over to glower at me. "I'd love to see you do better."

Indignantly, I respond, "I could run circles around you, and we both know it."

"Only because you have tree trunks for legs."

"My legs are perfectly proportional to the rest of me. If I recall correctly, you were always a fan of these powerful thighs," I retort while patting my legs.

She blushes but doesn't respond since it's her turn again. With a smile on my face, I notice she runs with more urgency.

Once the team has made their laps, Leo and I set them into position. We rotate between starters and alternates; that way, everyone gets a chance to bat, including the two of us, to ensure they each have base time.

I ground out a single to third and end up beside Carina on first base.

"Fancy meeting you here," I jeer.

"Couldn't have hit at least a double, huh, big guy?" she asks.

"Whoa, shots fired there, babe. I could've, but a single got me here next to you."

She makes a gagging noise. "Gross. Is that how you get ladies these days, with cheesy lines? You're better than that, Becker."

"I don't have any problems in the female department, don't you worry your pretty little head," I scoff. I see something that looks almost like jealousy or hurt flash through her eyes, but it is gone before I'm sure.

"Hm," she hums. "Yes, getting desperate cleat chasers to fall into your bed takes real skill, I'm sure. I just hope they get what they come for."

"Oh, they come plenty."

Before she can respond, Doris hits a fly to short that Kelly misses, and I am on to second.

As we take a water break later, I see Carina frowning at her phone.

"Everything okay?" I ask.

She stares for a second before deciding to answer me. "Everything is fine. I got a text that my grocery delivery was canceled, and I haven't eaten anything since the smoothie I had for breakfast."

"You haven't eaten anything all day? You know better than anyone that isn't good if you're going to exert yourself," I chide.

"Hop off! I got busy and forgot," she clips.

Sighing, I walk over to my bag and grab a Chewy bar I always keep on hand. "Here, eat," I grumble, tossing it to her. She stares at the bar and then back at me, confused. "Problem?" I question.

"No. Thank you. I didn't realize you still carried Chewy bars. Shouldn't a professional baseball player eat something more nutritious?"

My own face heats the way hers did a few minutes ago. "Probably, but I was never able to give them up. They remind me of a simpler time, and old habits die hard, I guess," I confess.

She gives me an indescribable expression as she thanks me again.

She devours the snack, making her way back to the field to finish out practice. I get a weird sense of satisfaction knowing I was able to take care of her, even in such a small way.

Chapter Seventeen

For the third Tuesday night in a row, I make my way to the field at Express Delivery Park. Unlike the other times, there is another team, and half a dozen fans stand waiting for us to play. I'm nervous. One game won't make or break our chances in the grand scheme of things, but I want to start things off on a strong note.

Waving to Jada as she gets Jalen situated, I go to put my stuff down in the dugout. As I'm leaning down to tie my cleats, a Chewy bar, Cracker Jacks, and light purple Gatorade—my favorite—are set down in front of me.

"What's this for?" I wonder out loud as I meet Robby's congenial gaze. Thank God I'm already sitting because the sincerity in his expression and words makes me weak in the knees.

"I wanted to make sure you had something to eat before we play. And I doubt you're hydrated enough. It's not exactly the healthiest, but I know Cracker Jacks and Riptide Rush are your favorite ballpark snacks, so I grabbed some on my way in." He shrugs. He flipping shrugs. As if this isn't the most considerate thing I can remember a guy doing for me in years. Like him, doing something little to take care of me doesn't make my chest tighten, and my stomach flutter.

"Thanks," I manage to murmur as he smiles and walks over to chat with Leo.

"Um, excuse me, Miss Ma'am. Do you have something you want to tell us about you and Mr. Tall, Dark, and Athletic?" I stand up to see Haley, Kim, and Alex gawking at me. Oh good, gangs all here, and they witnessed whatever the hell that confusing encounter was.

"What do you mean?" I feign nonchalance.

"Oh, I do know," Kim exclaims. "How about that hunk of a man bringing your 'favorite' snacks to the game to ensure you've eaten."

"Your use of air quotes is slightly aggressive and unnecessary," I grumble.

"How does he know your sports drink preferences? I don't even know that, and I've been sitting beside your ass for over a year," Alex whines.

"One, I don't usually drink sports drinks unless I'm, ya know, sporting. And two, you guys are making too big of a deal out of this. I must have mentioned it during practice one day."

Haley watches me like she knows the secret I'm keeping while Kim and Alex badger on.

"Is there something going on between you two?"

"Have you taken that man to bone town?" they ask simultaneously.

"Kim!" Alex gasps.

The redhead gives him a glare that says, 'like you weren't wondering the same thing.'

"Of course not! We've all just met him, and he's the coach of our team, and he's only here temporarily," I stammer.

"Right, right. I forgot how hard it is to get a reservation at Chateau de Carina's pants," Kim mocks in a French accent.

"Oh my God, this conversation is over," I say, hiding my face in my hands.

"Alright, guys, that's enough inquisition for now. We have a game to win," Haley states.

I mouth a 'thank you' to her, but she gives me an expression that tells me the inquisition has yet to truly begin. Great.

Intense is not quite the word I would use to describe a competition of this level, but this game has had more going on than I expected. Doris hit a triple in the first to drive Jada home, giving us a 2-0 advantage until the other team scored in the fourth and fifth. Both teams scored matching runs in the sixth with no action again until the eighth when The Humane Society's volunteer coordinator sent a ball beaming deep into center field.

Now we are at the bottom of the ninth, 5-4, and I'm up to bat. We've already got one out, thanks to Alex's fly foul caught by the catcher. Somehow, I manage to get walked by Kendra, their pitcher and resources director. Curtis is up behind me, and I have confidence that we might be able to pull something out.

He manages a hit and rushes toward first as I sprint to second. I make it, but Curtis isn't as lucky and gets tagged out. It's all up to me and Diane. After two consecutive balls, Kendra sends a strike right down the middle. I'm getting nervous.

Robby is standing at third, acting as the base coach. I peer over at him and find him concentrating on the game in front of us. He wasn't lying when he said he'd take this seriously. He shouts something at Diane that has her adjusting her grip. The next pitch seems to happen in slow motion. I watch as it hits Diane's bat with a smack. It sails high toward right field.

The sounds of the small crowd pull me out of my haze as I see Robby motioning for me to run. As I get closer, he windmills his arms, signaling me to keep going to home. I obey. Out of the corner of my eye, I spot the outfielder sending the ball to the cutoff point at second base. I realize she's about to throw it home, and I may not make it. I can't tell you exactly what happens after that since I black out. Next thing I know, I'm on the ground lying on home plate with the umpire calling me safe.

I pop up and stare down at the plate, then a dumbfounded group of friends, and last to Robby. He lets out a loud whistle and screams, "Atta girl! Can't slide my ass!" The pride on his face is evident, and I preen.

I go back to the dugout and watch as Mike hits a double that brings home Diane. As she enters the dugout, we all jump up and down to celebrate our win, cheering even louder when Mike, Robby, and Leo make it in.

"We won!" Kim exclaims. "I've never played a sport before. Is this what it always feels like?! It's a freaking high. I've never been this titillated in my life."

I shake my head at her antics as Leo drawls, "Sweetheart, I'm not sure that's something to brag about. Don't get me wrong; I find base-ball as stimulating as the next guy but 'titillated'? I'm happy to provide you with some experiences way more titillating than this..."

Kim laughs, and Haley jokes, "Honey, you're not ready for all of that. Mama Kimberly would eat you alive and run you ragged."

Leo wiggles his eyebrows back at them with a challenge in his eye, causing them to giggle. "Don't threaten me with a good time."

Deciding to let whatever the hell that is run its course, I turn to go grab my stuff but instead, walk into a wall. Walls don't move or grab your arms to steady you, though. The firm surface my hands are resting on must be Robby.

"Hi," I squeak, gazing up at him.

His perfectly white smile dazzles me, "What happened to 'Robert, stop trying to make sliding happen; it's not going to happen,'" he mocks in a girlish voice.

"Is that supposed to be me? That is not how I sound!" I respond indignantly. Robby wraps me up in a bear hug and lifts me off my feet.

Ignoring my grunts of protest, "You slid! You told me you would never slide in your life, but you did it. You did amazing, Care," he declares without putting me down. I melt at his praise. Such simple words should not have this effect on me, but I know he means them. Slightly embarrassed by my reaction, I push on him to put me down.

"Thank you," I reply after swallowing not once but twice to keep the emotion from bubbling up. God, the look he's giving me. It's so soft. So affectionate, so familiar. Too familiar. "I had a good teacher."

If possible, his smile grows even brighter. "Well, whoever he is would be glad to know his hard work paid off because that was fucking awesome. How did it feel?"

"Honestly, I don't know. My body decided to do it before my mind could put on the breaks, and the next thing I knew, I was across home plate."

He nods his head as if that somehow makes sense. "Jalen got a video of it—you have to see it." He pauses. "I mean it, Carina. You did amazing out there. You should be proud. I know I am."

Robby Becker's praise should not have me swooning the way it does. I shouldn't care what he thinks after the way he threw us—me—away. Yet all I want to do is run out there and do another slide so he'll pet my hair and tell me what a good job I did again.

He heads to find Jalen as I collect myself and catch a knowing glance from Haley. I am freaking screwed.

Chapter Eighteen

I walk into work the next Monday to a group of coworkers who have been replaced by Cheshire Cats, if their smiles are anything to go by. "Hey guys, what's up?" I ask hesitantly.

"Nothing too much, we had a video go viral this weekend, and we were talking about it," Alex responds with a gleam.

"That's incredible, Alex! Good for you."

"No, honey. Good for you." When I peer at him suspiciously, he pulls out his phone and clicks on Instagram to show me the video in question.

The video voiceover says, "When the food industrial complex is trying to keep single moms down," and shows my slide into home. On top of home plate are the words, 'the patriarchy,' and above me, it states, "badass bitches with a plan." Then the scene flips to everyone cheering as I make it back to the dugout and cuts to Robby picking me up in his bear hug. The words, 'even Robby Becker approves,' appear over us, and a link to donate to Feeding Memphis to join the fight against hunger.

Wide-eyed, I peek back up at the group of grinning, unknowing traitors. "Oh my God! What did you do?" I practically scream.

"Made a viral video," Alex scoffs like it is the most obvious thing in the world.

My anxiety spirals. "Why did you have Robby in here? We can't use him in videos! We have to pay him to use him and presumably check with his managers and the team and—" Haley's hand goes up to stop me before I fully succumb to my panic.

"Hon, chill out. Alex sent the video to Robby, who was totally cool with it. I checked with Stacy from the Blues Birds; she was all for it. They both even shared it on their channels yesterday, which helped increase the numbers. We did it all by the book."

For some reason, that doesn't make me any less anxious. "We've already received $2,600 in donations from the video," Kim informs me. Holy crap, that is almost a month's operating budget for all our summer programs.

After watching the video as a group a few more times, Alex and Kim head to her office to discuss the next volunteer recruitment campaign, leaving me with Haley.

"You want to tell me what that was really about because I don't believe for one second it was legalese?" she implores.

"What? Yes, it was," I lie.

"Hmm, not buying it, Care Bear."

"It might have been about me being in a video with Robby that over half a million people have seen," I admit.

"Oh, I got that," she responds. "But why? There must be a missing piece of the puzzle here."

Inhaling deeply, I straighten in my seat. "Do you remember that night a few months into working here when we had approximately four half-and-half margs each from La Casita's? You told me about Kendric, your college boyfriend, and how he cheated on you."

"Yeahhhh..." she puzzles. "And then you told me about the

douchey baseball player you dated until he...SHUT THE FRONT DOOR!"

I shush her as people glance our way.

"Sorry, sorry," she whispers. "Holy crap. Robby was the guy. Mr. Tall, Dark, and Athletic is the college boyfriend that ditched you after going pro?"

Ouch. "Okay, ditched is an oversimplification, but yes, he is the guy I dated in college."

"Wow," she says again. "I have about eighty-five questions I need to ask you about this, but I've got to prep for the staff meeting. Don't think you're getting out of explaining this one, Carina."

"Ugh, okay, fine. But can we keep it between us for now? I don't need everyone knowing and wondering if it had something to do with the competition or grilling me endlessly."

"Fine. But you owe me a lunch gossip sesh."

"Welcome, welcome everyone," Camila singsongs, oddly chipper. "I want to kick off this meeting with some happy news. Thanks to a boost this weekend, we have already met our fundraising goal for June. I knew the people of the East Memphis Country Club were generous, but I didn't realize attending their gala over the weekend would have been quite that fruitful."

What? Yikes. Camila thinks the fancy event she attended over the weekend in the guise of 'networking' is the cause of the donation. That's laughable. People like members of that country club don't donate online, at least not when there is no way to show off their generosity.

Alex clears his throat. "While we did a slight bump in donations from the checks sent over from the gala, most of this weekend's donations came through Instagram and TikTok."

"TikTok? The app for kids? How did they find us? Why would

teenagers be donating to our organization? How do they even have money?" she rapid fires.

"Uh, I can't confirm the age of the donors right now, but we had a video from our game go viral on social media this weekend. Most of the donations came in small increments under $100, but we received the majority of them based on the reach of the video."

"I see," Camila notes gingerly. "Well, that is wonderful. I take that to mean the softball thing is going well?" She turns to me, and I choke on my water, being put on the spot.

"Things are going well. We won our first game. All the volunteers seem to be having fun, and we are clearly spreading some awareness based on the content Alex has created from it."

Nodding her head, she replies, "Wonderful. Keep up the good work, and maybe you'll be able to get that food trailer idea of yours off the ground." With that, she asks Kevin about the summer camp partnership program he is running. I return to wondering how to get out of my lunch with Haley later.

I get out of it, temporarily. I'm able to put Haley off for a few days, but she corners me on Thursday. I wanted to tell her I wasn't hungry, but my stomach growled the second she mentioned splitting cheese fries at Hugo's. And that is how I find myself sitting in a booth in the back of a restaurant with names written all over the walls and toothpicks in the ceiling.

It might be a place many of my former classmates wouldn't find themselves dead in, but it has the best burgers in the city. The cheese fries are worth the after-lunch food coma.

As we wait for our burgers to arrive, Haley has apparently decided she's done waiting for details. "Spill," is all she says.

"What do you want to know?" I ask, hanging my head in resignation.

"How about we start with when you guys reconnected and how

112

long you thought you could keep this a secret. Why wouldn't you tell us?"

Grabbing a fry, I twirl it until the cheese breaks. "I thought I could keep it a secret forever. And I didn't tell you because I didn't want to broadcast that the hunky baseball player everyone was lusting over dropped me like a sack of rotten potatoes. I don't exactly want to advertise that I'm unwantable."

"You are not a sack of rotten potatoes or unwantable! I don't know everything that happened between you, but in no world does that man not want you. He practically drools every time you come near him. This week he brought you presents like a kindergartener with a crush," she gushes.

"I would hardly call Gatorade and a couple snacks a present." I insist while rolling my eyes.

"Pssh, we both know gifts and food are your love languages," she teases.

Mock offended, I reply, "How dare you! Everybody knows I am a total words affirmation girlie."

"Mm, that explains why you practically liquefied when he congratulated you on your run the other night. But back to my point: you are not unwantable. I can name five guys I know personally who would fall at your feet if given the chance. I mean, Terrell from the food bank is practically ready to fill you with babies at any moment."

"Ew, and no thank you. That man gave off total seahorse energy anyway. Let him carry them," I joke.

"I don't know what that means, and I don't care to find it out. What I do want to know is when you reconnected with Robby and how you're feeling about it," she voices as our food comes.

While we eat, I go into the details about our interaction at the club—the parts she didn't see and then talk about my emotional well-being. "This is all surreal, Hales. One minute Robby is this mythical ex, the villain in my story. The next minute, he's helping me win a grant and bringing me my favorite, hard-to-find drinks because he's worried I'm dehydrated."

She smiles at me softly and covers my hand with hers. "I'm sorry, babe. It's got to be confusing."

"He hurt me," I mumble. "And here he is calling me 'Kitten' and acting like the sweet boy I used to know, but I don't know him—not anymore. And the version of himself he was at the end is not one I am interested in getting to know again."

"I get that. He didn't treat you how you deserved, and you can't just forgive that because he spent $5 at Walgreens on you," she acknowledges. "I'd say he wants you, and I think he does, but I don't know him well enough to make that assessment. Maybe he's trying to be nice and make the most of the situation. He's in a strange city, and the only person he knows is you. Maybe he is aiming to stay on your good side so it doesn't blow up in his face, and the snacks were a peace offering."

"Maybe," I admit. "And the innuendos?"

"Well, those are just hot," she remarks slyly. "But in all seriousness, maybe they're part of a flirty persona he's adopted. I mean, you said you don't know him anymore. He could be a total flirt now. For all we know, he has a girlfriend in Nashville."

Oh my God. I haven't even thought about that. Here I am wondering what all his nice gestures mean, and he probably has a girl or three waiting for him back in Nashville. I'm an idiot. Of course, he wants to keep the peace; he's always been Mr. Chill. I can't believe I fooled myself into considering he might be interested in me. He made what he thought about me crystal clear all those years ago. I need to get it together.

"You might be right," I concede. Haley leaves me alone with my thoughts for the rest of the meal. On the drive home, we blessedly change the subject to work stuff. As we get back to the office, I make myself a promise to stand strong and not get sucked back in by Robby Becker's charm. Been there, done that.

Chapter Nineteen

Robby

After several weeks of easy rapport with Carina, something shifted. I don't know what it is, but I don't like it one bit. Being in Memphis has been more enjoyable with us getting along. It gives me a sense of nostalgia I didn't know I was missing.

We haven't hung out, but we talk at the field, and she sasses me, which I am not ashamed to say is one of the highlights of my week. It's nice; frustrating with the way my body still reacts to hers after all this time, but nice nonetheless. It's easy and fun, two things I haven't had with a woman since her. Fun, yes? But easy? In some ways, yes. But nothing is easy when you're always on guard for people's intentions.

Yesterday after she hit a line drive through the second baseman's legs, I had to physically stop myself from sweeping her up in my arms again. Sneaky little Jalen didn't let me know he got our hug on tape last week. Imagine my surprise when Alex sent me the edit.

I asked Jalen about it while volunteering at his school the next day. "If I told you everything I took a video of, we wouldn't have time to talk about anything else," he deadpanned. Fair enough.

I thought the video was why she was upset since she texted me apologizing if they overstepped. I don't know why she thought I'd care about that. Sure, if she worked at a for-profit company, my manager and PR rep might not want me giving away my pretty face for free, but it's a charity. If anything, it's good for my image.

It can't be the video that is unsettling her, because I saw her at the next game, and she was her same sassy self. Something was different last night, though. She was standoffish and formal. There were no sneaky, lust-filled glances. If she did look at me, it was with an expression of almost dejection.

Maybe she was having a bad day? But she would've mentioned that wouldn't she? That's a silly thought. Why would she mention her bad day to me, of all people? She doesn't owe me anything after the way I treated her. I can't help the constriction in my chest at the thought of her having a bad day and me not being able to fix it. The tightness is now as familiar as the boner I sport whenever she's around or on my mind, which is practically all the time.

I'll text her to see if it was a one-day thing or if maybe I did something to upset her.

11:34 AM

Good afternoon, Kitten.

KITTEN

What can I do for you, Coach Becker?

Hmm, more formal than expected, but tone is hard to tell over text. Maybe this was a bad idea. I decide to call her instead, might as well double down. I can't get her vibe over text. After a couple of rings, she answers. "Hello?"

"Hi, Carina," I say lamely.

"What's up, Robby? Is there something I can help you with?" Her tone tells me she is not thrilled to be on the phone with me.

"Is everything okay?" I question.

"Everything is fine. Why?"

"I don't know, you sound grouchier than usual," I respond.

I hear her take a deep inhale before responding more brightly. It might fool most people, but I've spent years of my life studying this girl. And even more years reliving memories of her. She may have changed a little and grown up since college, but she is still the same at her core. She still wears her heart on her sleeve and her feelings on her face—and voice apparently.

"Nope, everything is great, just working. Do you need something from me or the team? I'm happy to help."

Shit. This was clearly a bad idea. She's at work. It's not exactly a good time to get into why she's mad at me. Scrambling, I ask, "I don't need anything from the team. I was hoping you could recommend somewhere to get a gift for a thirty-year-old who buys herself everything she could want but deserves a gift nonetheless?"

She coughs to cover her gasp. "You want recommendations on where to buy your girlfriend a present? Wouldn't it be easier to order her something from a place she shops at in Nashville?" She pauses. "Um, but if you want it to be local, there is this great gift store in Saddle Creek and another in Southaven—"

"Girlfriend? No, this is for Morgan," I blurt with a laugh. "Her birthday is later this month, and I wanted to see if I could find her something here. I don't have a girlfriend," I add quickly.

Girlfriend? Did she think I wasn't single? Is that why she was mad? We haven't talked about it, but surely, she didn't believe I would be flirting with her the way I had if I was in a relationship. Does this mean she cares if I'm single or not? I'd be annoyed that she thought I was disloyal to my non-existent partner if this wasn't such an interesting development.

As my thoughts spiral, I hear her exhale the breath she must have been holding. "Right, I remember her birthday was close to mine. What were you thinking? Clothes? Jewelry? Something for her house?" She almost sounds relieved. Interesting development, indeed.

"She and Ralphie moved into a new place, and art might be nice. You know how loud her taste is. Are there any local places you know of that would match it?"

"She's still with Ralphie?" she asks in a small voice.

"Yeah, they got married last year. They're in Tampa now."

"Wow, good for her. That's great. He was a nice guy."

"He's the best," I affirm.

Carina gives me the list of a few artists to research and a couple of shops that carry work she believes will fit Morgan's taste. She seems to have softened as we talk about her.

Preparing to end the call, I thank her for her help. "And you're sure you're okay? Don't need help with anything? Need me to kick someone's ass?"

She lets out a half-giggle. I'll take it. "I'm good. If I needed someone's ass kicked, I'd send in Kim, anyway. She may be small, but she's scrappy."

"I believe that. Okay, well, thanks again. I'll see you Tuesday. Call me if you do need anything, though, anything at all."

"Okay. Bye, Robby," she states before hanging up.

I had no fucking intention of getting Morgan art for her birthday, but I am now. I usually book her a spa package and call it a day. She must have enjoyed it because I haven't heard any complaints. Sorry, sis, you're paying for your own mani-pedi this time.

Later that night as I'm running on the treadmill, I think back to my call with Carina. Something was obviously up with her, but I have no idea what. All I know is that I have this innate need to fix it. To make everything perfect in her world. I don't know why. The last time I had this feeling was when we were together. I always tried to be her rock, her safe, quiet place in a chaotic world.

Is that what I want now? That would be crazy, right? Trying to be with her again would surely be a mistake. It didn't end well for either of us last time. The flirting has been fun, though. Her sass is the biggest fucking turn-on and makes me desperately want to fuck the attitude out of her. She was always so agreeable when moaning my name. Wanting to sleep with her doesn't mean I want to date her again. Although, I've wanted to sleep with plenty of people. I've never wanted to cocoon them from the harshness of the world the way I want to with her. I assume it's because a small part of me never got over her, but that doesn't mean there is anything to pursue here.

I'm no less confused when my phone lights up, and I see my Songbirds' teammate, Brady Miller's name.

"Sup, Papa Bear?" I greet. Miller may not be a dad himself, but he is definitely the dad of the team. As captain, he keeps all the younger guys in line and ensures we're all doing what we're supposed to. The nickname also came about because he is supposedly a Daddy, but I can neither confirm nor deny that. I do know he is part owner of a sex club in Nashville, though. I wouldn't be surprised if he is a Daddy. The dude is a natural caretaker.

"Hey, man. How ya doing? I heard you got cleared to pitch in next Saturday's game. Congrats. You feeling good?"

While him checking up on me doesn't surprise me, it still makes me feel good. I had coaches and teammates that cared about me at other levels of ball, but nothing beats support from Papa Miller. "I'm doing well. Arm is great. I've been back to my normal pitch count and strength at practice. That's all I can ask for."

"That's great, man. We can't wait until you're back up here with us. Although, the dugout has been much better behaved," he notes.

"Whatever, man, I am arguably one of the tamest guys you've got. Besides, life isn't nearly as interesting without me. I know it isn't here. Aside from practice and hanging out with the few guys I find tolerable, all there is to do is sit and reflect."

I hear him hum on the other line. "Thinking about anything in particular?"

Because I'm not a man who is afraid to get real with my friends, I dive into my thoughts the last few hours. I recap everything that happened the past few weeks with a quick interlude into my past relationship with Carina.

"Damn, that's heavy stuff, buddy," he says when I finally finish.

"You're telling me," I mutter. "I don't know what to do. I've spent the last four years solely focused on the game. Sure, I've had a few chasers warm my bed here and there, but nothing serious. I haven't even had the slightest interest in a relationship until she popped back into my life... or I guess I popped back into hers."

"Let me ask you this. You told me how you feel when she's around, but what about when she isn't?" he asks.

After a minute of consideration, I sigh, "Like I wish she was. Like I wish I knew what she was doing—how she was doing. Like I wish she would tell me all about it. But that could be totally platonic. We were friends before we dated."

"Could be," he muses. "How would you react if you knew what she was doing and it was spending time with someone else? Talking to someone else, flirting with someone else, touching someone else, letting someone else take care of her problems."

I let out an audible growl.

"Well, that answers that question," he remarks cheekily.

"So, I don't want her to touch anyone else? That isn't that weird to think toward an ex."

"True, but you have another ex, right. Mary or something."

"Marissa," I reply.

"Right, Marissa. And the idea that Marissa might be touching another guy right now?"

"Best of luck to him," I huff.

"Exactly. Based on what you've told me about your previous relationship and what I'm hearing now, I'd wager you're still hung up on this girl, man. I've been with my fair share of women, and I have that protective instinct you mentioned with all of them. It's woven into my DNA. But it hasn't typically extended past the duration of our time together. I've never cared about seeing them with another man after me. In fact, I'm glad they found someone who fits their needs in a way that I couldn't."

Taking in his words, I know he's confirming what I have been afraid to even admit to myself. "Holy shit," I rasp. "I want to get back together with her."

"Afraid so," he commiserates.

"I think I just convinced myself I was done with her because she was done with me—that we were better off apart. It's hard to have a relationship in this career. After we broke up, I didn't see a point in attempting to get back together once I was stable enough to put down roots. This life can be crazy and far from normal."

"Do you still believe that? That she's done with you?" he asks.

"Honestly? I don't know. Last week, I would've said no, but this week I'm not certain. I've seen the interest in her eyes. I know I affect her, at least on a physical level. I just don't know if she is happy about that. I know I hurt her before, but I'm not that dumb kid anymore."

"And do you think a quote, unquote 'normal' relationship is what she wants? She hasn't found one while y'all were apart. Maybe she is waiting for something extraordinary. We may not live that nine-to-five, picket fence life, but that doesn't mean you can't have a great relationship. Lots of guys do it."

"I guess you're right," I concede.

"You know what you have to do then."

"I do?"

"I swear to God, you boys are helpless," he mutters. "Yes, you do. You've got to win her back. Prove that you can be the man she needs, a man worth wanting, a man she can build an incredible life with. Get yourself another chance."

Nodding my head, I wonder out loud, "How do I do that?"

"That's all on you, Becker. You know the girl. You should know what would speak the most to her. Sounds like you've got her body on board. Now you've got to convince her mind that her heart is safe with you. Don't fuck it up."

With his last declaration, we end the call, and I go to bed brainstorming ways to prove to Carina I'm now the man I should've been all those years ago. I decide on the perfect idea. I need help pulling it off; I know just the people for the job.

Chapter Twenty

Today is my birthday. I am officially twenty-five. It makes sense that I'd be twenty-five years old when my quarter-life crisis hit. I wake up to a barrage of texts from friends and family. My college group chat has blown up with birthday wishes from all my college friends. The longest one is from my honorary big brother, Sean. He's the epitome of Golden Retriever—sweet, loyal, and eager to please—although, he isn't afraid to rip someone apart to defend those he loves. He was always taking care of everyone. I haven't seen him since graduation over two years ago. I miss him. I also haven't told him about Robby, which laces me with guilt.

Robby was always a weird topic between us. They had a friend breakup at the same time we had our couple breakup. Robby had been as shitty a best friend as he had a boyfriend, and Sean hated seeing me hurt. Before we graduated, though, I overheard Sean talking to another friend, and he mentioned Robby had reached out and apologized to him. They were working to make amends. I can't blame him. They grew up together, and now they're both living out their dreams of playing professionally.

After I respond to the group and to my family, my phone lights up with a call.

"Good morning, birthday girl," Tiffany singsongs.

"Wow, that's a lot of pep for 6 a.m., babe. Even for you."

"Well, lucky for me, I am in New York and it is 9 a.m. I am doing makeup at a showcase for an up-and-coming designer ."

"That's amazing, Babs! You go, girl!."

She flips her long hair and gives me a face that says, 'They're lucky to have me.'

"Loving the birthday, mani. Is that sprinkles or confetti?" she comments.

Scanning my festive, glittery nails, I smile. "It's whatever you want it to be. I just wanted something with a little dazzle for today."

She nods in approval. "Do you feel more refined now that you're officially out of your early twenties? What are the plans for today?"

"I feel the same as I did yesterday. No big plans today. When you work in the exciting world of nonprofits, you spend your birthday in the office. As far as birthday celebrations, I'm sure we'll have cake and maybe go out to lunch, but that will be it. I celebrated with Mom and Steve at dinner on Sunday. Lola FaceTimed me last night and sent me some beautiful flowers. Have you talked to her lately? Something is up. She was acting weird and got cagey when I asked about Phil."

"Hmm, not for a few weeks," she replies thoughtfully. "I'll give her a call later to check in. What about tonight? Plans with the girls?"

"No, tonight I have a softball game."

"Oh, right," she says with a glimmer in her eye.

"What's that look?" I question.

"There is no *look*," she emphasizes with an eye roll. "How is that going? Boned 'dick who must not be named,' yet?"

I bark out a laugh. "God, I forgot about that nickname. No, I haven't. That isn't my style."

"Hm, too bad," she hums. "Someone has to give you a birthday orgasm. Why not him? Wouldn't be the first time."

I gasp. "Oh my God, you are the worst. I'm not going to jump into bed with some guy because it's my birthday. Besides, he doesn't even want to."

Now it's her turn to laugh. "Please. He's not some stranger off the street, and he so does want to. I doubt there is anything that man wants more than to bone you until you forget what a douche he was."

"How would you know? You haven't even seen him since he left for the minors."

"I don't have to see him," she replies. "I've seen the two of you together. Your chemistry is grotesquely electric. The fact that you don't know if he wants you means he does. If he didn't, he would've made it clear. Guys are terrified of clingy women. He'd make it known from the get-go it was off-limits if he wasn't interested.

"And to your earlier point, he's not 'some guy.' He's the love of your life and the best sex you ever had. It's no brainer to me."

I know she doesn't mean anything by it, but her assessment stings and hits close to home. The fact that he did let me know I was being too clingy is part of the reason we broke up. And the fact that Robby was the best lover I've ever had, hands down, is rude on the part of the universe. It's not as if I've given him much competition, but still. Also, 'love of my life?' Depressing.

"*Was* the love of my life," I say with more force than necessary. "As stimulating as this conversation has been, I have to get ready for work."

"Wait!" she yells, sensing my agitation. "I'm sorry, I didn't mean it that way. All I'm saying is that if you have a master mechanic on hand, why not let him spend some time under the hood."

"You're too much," I chastise. "My engine is running fine without a tune-up, thank you very much. Having sex would make things more complicated than they already are."

"And how complicated are they?"

"Too complicated," I respond with a sigh. "I don't understand what he's doing. He's being incredibly nice to me."

Tiffany snickers, "The way things ended between you two aside, Meatball, he was a nice guy especially when trying to woo you."

I scoff, "he isn't trying to woo me."

"No?" she questions. "What is he doing that's nice then?"

"Well, he keeps bringing me snacks and drinks to our games, and he even offered to donate the money I needed to fund my program. That's crazy, right?"

"I don't know how crazy it is; the man brings in tens of millions a season. $25k is a drop in the bucket for him. And as far as the snacks go, isn't that the same thing he did when you two had that class together in college? Before you started dating, ya know, when he was wooing you?" she recalls. "Geez. The man's moves haven't changed since making it big."

She's right, though. He did do that. Before we got together, he would bring me coffee and a treat to class and study sessions. He always seemed to have my favorite candy on hand whenever I wanted something sweet. When I asked him about it, he said he "couldn't let me get my sweetness from anywhere else." Is that what he's doing now?

"A few Gatorades and snacks aren't going to make up for basically throwing me away and making me out to be a distraction to his career," I grit out. "Maybe he was right, though. Look what happened when he gave baseball his sole focus."

"Oh, honey, I know he hurt you big. He was a stupid boy. I'd hope he's grown up over the last few years. As a now twenty-five-year-old, I bet you think back at some of the things we did at twenty-two and cringe. I know I do every time I remember those five minutes when I dated Aaron Zapos." She shudders.

"Aw, Aaron was pretty, though. I know you're right. I hope he has changed, but he hasn't even apologized for how he treated me. The last time when he wanted me, he was one hundred percent clear on his intentions. Until that happens, I won't even go down that road."

"But you'd be open to his advances if he did those things?" she presses.

"I-I don't know. I haven't even let myself consider it. There are so many unknowns and so much work he'd need to do to show me he was serious. I'd have to see that he genuinely regretted what went down between us and how he wouldn't let it happen again. You were with me, Tiff. I barely made it through. Getting over him was the hardest thing I ever had to do. I don't know if I could do it again."

"I know, sweetie," she coos. "I just don't want you to close yourself off from something because you're afraid to get hurt again."

"I have every reason to be afraid," I murmur. "But it's a moot point anyway. He doesn't want me."

With a shake of her head, she speaks, "Alright, alright, I'll drop it for now, Meatball. I hope you have a magical day. Let's catch up more this weekend."

This morning, I was greeted at work by an iced lavender latte and macarons from my favorite bakery, courtesy of Alex. He even bought me a bottle of their lavender syrup so I could make my own lavender lattes at work.

Kim and Haley took me to La Casita's for lunch though we skipped the margaritas since we have a game tonight, and it's a work day. They made me promise to drink with them this weekend at the Blues Birds game we're attending. They also gave me some small gifts even though I hate people spending money on me. Kim gave me a cookbook filled with recipes from my favorite celebrity chef. Haley gave me a collection of fun nail stickers and wraps to feed my manicure addiction.

All in all, it has been a good day. We won against the YMCA of Memphis, moving us up in the standings. I hate competing against other organizations knowing they need the grant as much as we do, but it isn't like we're taking it from their pockets. Plus, everyone I've talked to who is participating has seen an increase in donations from the publicity, which I suppose was part of the point anyway.

As we're packing up, Robby walks up to me. "Hey," he says nervously. "Can you wait up a few minutes? I, uh, have something to give you for your birthday."

"Oh, wow. You didn't have to get me anything. Helping us win is enough of a present, and I didn't expect anything from you," I stammer. "I mean, thank you."

He smiles at me warmly, my reaction calming his nerves a bit. Glad stuttering and embarrassing myself makes him more comfortable. He doesn't say anything and leads me back out to the field. Kim and Haley, who are waiting for me off to the side because we rode together, eye us curiously. I shrug because I have no clue what is happening.

"Up there," he finally says, pointing to the Jumbotron.

At first, it shows the game's stats, but then the video flips. I turn to him wide-eyed before turning back at the screen and seeing three faces staring back at me: the Ryder Brothers. They were the stars of my favorite show as a kid. They went on to become one of the biggest country groups of our time. What is happening?

"Why? How? What?" I shriek, looking between the screen and Robby. Before he can answer me, Declan, the unspoken leader of the group, speaks.

"Carina, we heard from a friend of ours that today is your birthday. Happy twenty-fifth!"

"Ah, to be twenty-five again," Grayson, the oldest brother jokes. "So fresh, so young."

"You're only twenty-eight," Jack, the youngest brother, says.

"Yeah," Grayson responds. "But those three years have felt like a lifetime when I've been stuck recording and touring with your hyper ass."

"Boys," Declan interrupts. "Bicker later. We're supposed to be serenading a lady."

"Right."

"On it, boss," they say simultaneously.

Picking up guitars, my mouth opens impossibly wider as they begin to sing my favorite song of all time *When I Make You Mine*. It's a beautiful ballad about the future a guy envisions if his love would give him a chance. Peeking at Robby through my periphery, I wonder if the choice has a hidden meaning or if he remembered it was my favorite.

They follow that up with a special performance of a song from their yet-to-be-released album. I am DYING. I can't believe I got a sneak peek!

When they finish singing, Declan speaks again. "We're honored that we got to play for you on your birthday. Our agent told us about all the good work you're doing with Feeding Memphis, and you've inspired us to give back as well. We've sent a donation to your organization and one in our home of Nashville doing similar work feeding the hungry."

Grayson chimes in, "Well, we've taken up enough of your time. We hope you enjoy however much of your birthday is left. Have fun!"

"Don't do anything I wouldn't," Jack says with a wink.

"That is a short list," we hear someone say off-camera as the video fades. It takes me a few beats to collect myself, and when I do, Robby is studying me sheepishly. "Well?" he asks.

"Oh my gosh!" I squeal, jumping into his arms for a hug. Thankfully he caught me despite my lack of warning.

"You're welcome," he chuckles sexily. I didn't realize a chuckle could be sexy until this minute, but somehow it is. "There's more. Can I put you down and give it to you?"

"More? Hearing them say my name was more than enough," I sigh dreamily.

"Geez, Kitten, don't make me jealous of my present," he jokes. "Here."

He hands me an envelope. I must be looking at it like it's a snake about to bite me because he nudges me. "Open it."

When I do, I am flabbergasted. Inside is the printout of an article from a paper in Los Angeles dated tomorrow that says, *Hawthorne Middle School announces Ballerini Food Fund.* It details how an anonymous sponsor gave the school an undisclosed donation to fund a breakfast and lunch program for students. I tear up as I read quotes from students on what it will mean for them to get breakfast and lunch every morning. It also includes accounts from parents on the burden it takes off their shoulders to know their kids are getting quality meals at school.

"Did you, are you? What?" I stumble over my words again as he watches me kindly.

"Did I make the donation? I made an initial one to help launch the program and set up a smaller ongoing one. I also talked to some old contacts at MSC. They are going to use the Fund as one of the organizations the nonprofit class supports and create a position for it in the internship program."

I stare at him as he continues to explain the gift. "I know how much those kids and that school meant to you. I can only imagine how sad you were when you left them to move back here. I figure this way, a small part of you will stick around and do some of the work you did when you volunteered there."

I am full-on ugly crying now.

"Shit, babe. I didn't want to make you cry." He reaches down to cup my face and wipes some of the tears away with his thumb.

Staring into his eyes, I confess, "This is the most amazing gift I have ever been given. I don't know how I can ever thank you."

His cheeks pinken at the acknowledgment. "Nah, it's nothing compared to all the good you do. You've always had the biggest heart."

"It is everything," I interject meaningfully.

With the tension mounting between us, Robby breaks away with one final, reverent swipe to my cheek. "There is one more gift, but it won't be here for a few weeks."

"All of this was more than enough. I can't—"

"Holy crap," Kim shouts, running up to us and killing the mounting tension. "Robby, that was incredible! How did you manage to get the Ryder Brothers to record that?"

His eyes tell me he has a million more things he wants to say, but instead, he indulges my over-animated friend. Robby explains that they're all under the same PR firm, and he had the reps connect them. They were more than happy to record the video in exchange for some home plate Songbirds tickets. Once they learned about Feeding Memphis, they were moved to make some donations of their own.

As our group heads toward the exit, Kim chatting Robby's ear off with questions about the band, Haley loops her arm into mine. "That was something," she states.

"Yeah." I gulp. "It was."

We don't say anything else as we venture to the parking deck. Clutching the news article to my chest, I spend the drive home trying to process everything that just happened.

Chapter Twenty-One

Robby

Entering the locker room, there is usually familiar sense of anticipation. Even with the triggering smell of leather and chalk, I can't help but recall Carina's reaction to her present earlier this week. I hoped she would love it. I knew she would die over the Ryder Brothers part. She'd been obsessed with them since she was fourteen.

It's the lunch program I was nervous about. It was a great idea. Conceptually, I knew she'd be into the Fund, but her reaction to my suggestion of giving her the money for the mobile market program made me anxious it would be a step too far. Thankfully, it was a hit. I know it doesn't even come close to making up for everything I did to her. It is the first step in showing her I know what is important to her; I support those passions the same way she always supported mine. Her happiness and fulfillment are a priority to me, as it always should have been. It's a small way to show her I've changed and am trying to be a man who deserves her.

Lost in thought, I take a seat at my cubby. Leo claps me on the back, and Justin asks, "How ya feeling, man? Ready to get back on the horse?"

"I'm ready," I say assuredly, more for me than him. "It's like riding a bike, right? My body remembers how to do the job. I just gotta let it do the work."

That's partially true. My body does remember how to do this, and I've been practicing for weeks now. It's about getting in the right headspace mentally. Now that I'm here at this moment, I'm glad Head Office sent me down. I can't imagine the pressure of having my first game back in front of a major league crowd where the stakes are higher.

"You're gonna kill it, dude," Leo comments, joining the conversation. "We've all seen how hard you've been practicing and have total faith in you."

"Thanks, man," I choke out. The amount of support I've felt from the team here is matched only by the guys back in Nashville. I thought you only got that in majors when people weren't fighting to claw their way to the top. However, I've found the guys here genuinely care about one another's success.

It still jars me to get support. My parents were always working when I was growing up. As soon as I was able to go to the games myself, they took extra shifts. Morgan would tag along a lot and even drive me once she got older, but her interest was limited. She came to as many games as she could and cheered me on, though. It's part of the reason she's such a good partner for Ralphie. She'd already put in the time with me that she knew what she was getting into with an athlete.

Even though she did come, Morgan wasn't interested in the game. She spent her time flirting, talking to friends she dragged along, and playing on her phone. She'd watch me but never understood the complexities of what I was doing or the implications. She didn't get the mental side of things. The only person who ever did was Carina.

I remember the first game of mine she attended. I gazed up in the stands assuming I'd see her chatting it up with Tiffany and the other girls, but she wasn't. Her gaze was glued to mine as she sat there in my jersey. That's not to say she didn't have fun and eat an ungodly amount of cotton candy. I'm only on the field for part of the inning, but when I was, her attention was solely on me. She wasn't the most knowledgeable, but her questions after the game showed me she paid attention and wanted to learn more about this sport I loved. By the end of that first season, she knew my stats better than I did.

Smiling at the memory, I remember that she's here today. The Feeding Memphis softball team decided they needed to be here to support me because it was my first game back. They called it "team bonding." A corporate partner has a suite and let them use it for the night. I won't be able to hear them cheering, but I should be able to spot them. Express Delivery Park isn't huge, especially compared to the MLB stadiums I'm used to.

Everyone starts gathering their stuff, and we head to the dugout. After a quick pump-up speech from our coach, warm-ups, and all the pregame festivities, I approach the mound to prepare for my first pitch. As I get situated, I scan the stands and the suites. As I hit the last section, I see a familiar silhouette staring down at me. I smile to myself at the sense of rightness and, after a moment to savor it, launch a slider right to Leo.

"Strike one," I hear the umpire yell. And so, it begins.

Chapter Twenty-Two

My birthday was four days ago, and I still don't know what to think about what Robby did. It was so freaking thoughtful it still makes my head spin. I have no idea what it means. I try to tell myself he was just being nice again, but that was too big a gesture for even me to buy it.

The video from my favorite band was enough within itself, but the food fund? I'm still reeling over that. Robby was right that leaving Hawthorne was hard for me. I'd worked with some of those kids since they were sixth graders. Luckily, we were still able to stay in contact over TikTok. But to now have a legacy at the school I held dear, beyond the kids who knew me then? That is an indescribable honor.

I ponder these thoughts and more as I make myself a hotdog and grab a bag of Cracker Jacks. The team decided to come to the Blues Birds game tonight. All of us except Alex, whose husband took him on a fancy anniversary getaway to the beach. The cheeky bastard teased us about it all week in the office.

Everyone is excited to be in a suite with snacks and A/C instead of sweltering in the Tennessee heat. I don't know how enjoyable I'll find it, though. I'm a wreck. I haven't been this nervous at a game since watching the Pelicans play in their first College World Series.

I take a seat next to Jada and Jalen. "Hey, buddy," I say.

"Hey," he says in his toothy grin. "I'm excited to see Mr. Robby play a game in real life and not just on a screen."

"What do you mean?" I question.

"Robby has been volunteering at Jalen's school," Jada answers.

"I'm the president of the Electronics Club. It's a club to help us learn how stuff works but mostly we play vintage video games and take apart old stuff like DVD players and VCRs. Do you know what a VCR is, Miss Carina?"

Laughing, "I do, bud. It was the only way to watch movies when I was a kid."

"Wow." As if considering something, he taps his finger on his chin before he asks, "Are you as ancient as my mom?"

I gawk, and Jada chokes on her drink. "Jalen, you can't ask women their age, and I am not ancient, by the way," she scolds. "If I recall, I smoked your butt in Street Racer last night."

"It's fine, Jada. I wear my MySpace days as a badge of honor. What were you saying about Robby volunteering at his school?"

She then goes on to explain that once a week, Robby goes to Jalen's school and helps supervise his club as they play games or play with electrical components. She also confirmed that a teacher was present, and he was not responsible for them not electrocuting themselves, thank goodness. But the information shocks me nevertheless. He has experience working with kids, but mainly on the baseball field and not with electronics.

Robby has never mentioned volunteering with Jalen to me. Though, to be fair, I haven't given him the chance. I wonder what else I don't know about. I wonder if he would have told me if I hadn't been keeping my distance recently. He seems to keep that stuff to himself. Even with the Ballerini Food Fund, he gave his donation anonymously. It would've been a great PR move to announce his initial investment in the fund. I would've considered it an amazing gift, even if it was named after him. Knowing the kids were getting hot, healthy meals is enough for me.

The sound of the announcer pulls me from my thoughts as we all stand for the National Anthem. I stay standing when I see Robby make his way to the pitcher's mound. I forgot how good the man wears a baseball uniform. Those pants should be illegal... or everywhere. I wonder who I need to talk to about launching a campaign to normalize men wearing baseball pants off the field the way women wear leggings. It's a cause a lot of people would get behind.

After taking the mound, Robby scans the stands as if he's searching for something. When his gaze lands on me, he stops. It's too far away to read his expression, but I know he locked in on me. I see his chest expand as he inhales deeply and prepares to throw out the first pitch. Play ball.

The Blues Birds won their game 2-1. Robby only allowed two hits, and the run scored was on the relief pitcher. Ryan scored the final run in the eighth inning. It was quite the exciting display, with him taunting the pitcher with a big lead from third. He ended up making it home without stealing it, but you could tell he wanted to.

Jalen wanted to see the guys after the game, so Robby and Leo invited the team to meet them outside the locker room. The little guy is bouncing around the hallway taking everything in as the players slowly file out. I get a major sense of déjà vu as they pass me. How many times did I wait outside a locker room in college waiting for Robby? Too many to count.

I see his large form make his way out the door, and my breath hitches. He's wearing blue gym shorts that hit a couple inches above the knee and a Dri Fit shirt that you can't convince me wasn't painted on. His damn backward baseball cap makes another appearance, and I can't help but appreciate how hot he is. He was attractive in college, but this version of Robby is all man. His arm and back muscles are more defined, and his butt is fuller and tighter, if that is even possible.

He ambles up to me with a smile. "Fancy meeting you here," he greets.

"Mr. Robby!" Jalen shouts, pulling away his attention. Thank God, because I was about to swoon like a school girl.

"Hey, little man. Enjoy the game?"

"Yeah, it was awesome. My mom even let me have space ice cream. But I don't know why the astronauts can't eat it in a cone like Earth people do."

Robby's eyes shift to me questionably. I mouth, "Dippin' Dots," and he nods. We talk to Jada and Jalen for a few minutes about everything the eleven-year-old did and did not enjoy about tonight's game. Spoiler alert: not a fan of the Kiss Cam.

One of the coaches comes by to check in with Robby about his elbow as Leo, Kim, Haley, and Justin come join our little group. "We thought it might be fun to go to our apartment to celebrate the big man's first game back," Leo drawls.

"Why would you call him the big man when you're as tall as him?" Jalen asks, puzzled.

"It's a nickname, Jay. Say goodbye to your friends. We gotta get you home and ready for bed. We're going to church with Grandma in the morning," Jada states. With that announcement, they bid us farewell.

"What do you think, Care Bear?" Haley asks me. I see her concern that they're pushing me too far. I take a second to consider it. I haven't spent any time with Robby outside of softball. Do I want to? Maybe. I want to understand this energy that is between us. Am I scared? One thousand percent. But after my birthday, I owe it to myself and him to hear him out if he has more to say. There are still unresolved issues between us. I know getting it all out in the open would go a long way to helping me heal.

Coming back into the fold, Robby asks, "What are we talking about?"

"We're all heading back to Leo's place to drink and hang out. We don't typically go out the night before a Sunday game, but it isn't until later due to the holiday weekend. Some of the other guys are meeting us there," Justin answers.

"You're all coming?" Robby questions, and I nod.

Grinning wide, he remarks to the group, "Alright then, let's see how many drinks it takes for Justin to get shut down by Kim." The redhead laughs while Justin appears embarrassed. Seems like someone has a crush. Good luck, Justin.

I smack Robby in the chest for the comment, which causes him to let out that sexy chuckle that gives me goosebumps. He throws his arm around my shoulder as he leads us out of the stadium. I try not to revel in his closeness, but his body is warm and familiar; I don't have much success. As the group journeys across the street to the Ballpark Alley Apartments, I wonder if I am starting something that I don't know if I can finish. That's not true. I know I can. I just don't know what will be left of me after he moves on again.

Chapter Twenty-Three

Carina

After a few minutes, we all make it to the guys' apartment building and head up to Leo's unit. It is honestly way cleaner than I expected a bachelor pad to be. I don't know what it is about Leo, but I didn't expect a guy built like a linebacker to be so... tidy. Not only tidy, but his place is also filled with personal touches, throw pillows, art, and a bar that goes beyond whiskey bottles.

The apartments are so close to the stadium that the view from his balcony is of the outfield. "Doesn't it defeat the purpose of having a view of the field if you can't watch any games?" Kim asks.

"Nah," he answers. "I've seen the soccer team play a few times. Plus, I much prefer the view behind the plate than from up here." That makes sense, considering he's a catcher.

A knock at the door draws Leo's attention while Haley and Robby disappear into the kitchen to grab drinks for us. Justin hooks his phone up to the speaker and puts on a playlist that he calls, "the shit everyone should be listening to." It's a mix of off-brand top forty and Memphis artists, but it's nice background music.

The apartment fills up, and someone sets up beer pong on Leo's ostentatiously large island. The group that came in heads over there and immediately starts a game. I spot a few of the guys on the team and what I assume are their girlfriends because they aren't giving off cleat chaser vibes. This night is going to be as low-key as advertised.

Haley returns and hands Justin a beer and Kim a Jack and Coke. When I'm about to ask her where mine is, a glass appears in front of my face as Robby hands me a drink. I glance at him questionably because I never told him what I wanted.

"Sprite and Cherry Limeade vodka. He may look like a grown-ass man, but Leo has the alcohol selection of a sixteen-year-old," he says, nodding to the drink. "He didn't have peach. It was limeade, plain, or Ruby Red, and I know your thoughts on grapefruit."

The shock that he remembers my drink preferences must show on my face because the side of his mouth lifts. He leans in and whispers conspiratorially, "I also threw in a shot of Malibu, but I won't tell if you won't."

"Th-Thank you," I manage to stammer out. "It sounds perfect."

"Told ya, I remember everything, Kitten." With those parting words, the man has the nerve to give me a panty-dropping wink and walk away and leave me awestruck.

I manage to make my way over to Haley, Kim, and Justin, where they are talking about the latest Marvel movie, which releases in a few weeks. I'm more of a rom-com girl, myself, so I just nod along and pretend I understand what they're talking about.

I'm really watching Robby, though. He's working the crowd, talking to everyone as if he's been here for years, not a few weeks. He's always had the ability to breeze through any room he is in with easy confidence. It's one of the things that attracted me to him in the first place. As an introvert, I appreciate a partner who can take the lead in socializing. Maybe it's the Italian in me, but I love to host a party. However, I'd much rather be in the background making sure things are running smoothly than playing ringmaster. We were a perfect pair in that way. Anytime I have had to MC a charity event, it has been a nightmare.

A while later, as the conversation turns into Paul Rudd's believability as a superhero, the hair on the back of my neck stands up. I glance over to see Robby staring at me from where he chats with Leo. His eyes on me feel like a physical caress. When our gazes lock, everything else disappears; it's just the two of us having some silent conversation we can't put into words.

The slam of the door causes me to break eye contact, and I realize we are back to our original six-some. Having enjoyed her fair share of Leo's bar, Kim exclaims, "Let's play a game!"

Kim decides she wants to play Never Have I Ever, and the look on her face dared anyone to argue with her over it. We all refill our drinks and filter into the living room to get comfy. Our redheaded ringleader kicks us off with, "Never have I ever gone streaking." Robby, Justin, and I all drink.

Kim stares at me in shock, "You've gone streaking?!"

"What? You consume as many drinks as I have on the beach, it's bound to happen. I'm more shocked that you haven't gone streaking."

"As if I would ever take my clothes off to run," she scoffs. "That is reserved for fun activities."

Leo is up next with, "Never have I ever been arrested," which causes Kim to drink and then shrug in response. Not surprised. Haley comes in with, "Never have I ever had sex outside." This has Leo and Kim drinking and eyeing each other appreciatively, which makes Justin's jaw tick. Interesting. On his turn, Justin says, "Never have I ever had multiple orgasms."

I don't realize I'm the only one drinking until Kim gapes at me.

"Lucky bitch," she mutters. "We're going to need you to share more with the class on that one."

I blush. "What's there to tell?"

"How about who, what, where, when, and why?" she states.

"Seriously?" When her pointed look tells me to keep going, I answer. "Um, who: an ex-boyfriend. I don't know what 'what' means in this context, the orgasms? Where: a lot of places? Mostly our dorms/apartments. When: when we were having sex? Why: because he wanted to put his anatomy knowledge to the test, and I wasn't about to stop him."

"*Mostly* at your dorms/apartments? We're talking more about that later. Also, it was a common occurrence?! Is he single now? I low-key hate you, bitch. Where do I get one of those?" Kim asks, disgruntled.

I have to be tomato red at this point. "Sorry? I'll put some feelers out for you."

"If you want, I can help make sure you get to drink for this one next time we play, Red," Justin whispers to Kim more loudly than I think he meant to.

Haley chokes at my response and from the obnoxious smirk on Robby's face. Real subtle. Thankfully, no one is looking at him. I avoid eye contact because I don't need to add any fuel to the fire with the way things have been sizzling between us this week.

"Okay, my turn," I say. "Never have I ever had sex in a hot tub." And the game goes round and round.

A few turns later, things have gotten targeted, especially between the guys and the girls. Leo hit us with a, "Never have I ever played with my nipples during sex." Obviously, not something many men do.

And then Haley came in with what she thought was a guy-focused answer, "Never have I ever fooled around in a dugout."

Everyone gawks at me as I take a sip. Robby's lips are practically invisible, tucked so far into his mouth, trying not to laugh at my embarrassment after he takes his sip. "I'm not the only one drinking," I whine when everyone won't stop staring.

"I'm surprised you two haven't hooked up with a girl in a dugout," Haley says to Leo and Justin, trying to shift the focus. A true friend.

"Not all of us can be major league studs," Justin mutters as if he is upset he hasn't.

"Hey," Robby states, "my dugout hookup was in college. You can't credit the major leagues for that. It was one hundred percent genuine Becker charm."

I snort. I know exactly the situation that led to that hookup because it was with me. Sure, his charm played a role, but I'd give a little credit to a sudden rainstorm.

"Plus, a sexy and adventurous partner," Robby adds, shooting me a secret smile and biting his bottom lip. Gah. Who taught men how powerful a well-placed lip bite can be? I'm going to melt into the carpet if this goes any further.

Chapter Twenty-Four

Robby

We are all decently tipsy after a few rounds of Never Have I Ever. This buzz, though, is nothing compared to the one I experienced walking over here with my arm around Carina. She is fucking edible in her sundress. The white dress gives her an innocent vibe, but my thoughts of how I want to wrap her ponytail around my fist are anything but. And hearing her talk about the orgasms I gave her in college got my dick's attention as he relived the memories himself.

We agree to one last round before switching to a new game, and Kim is the last to go. "Never have I ever drank so much Jäger, I ended up naked in a sauna with an Olympic hockey player."

Carina gasps. "I told you that in confidence!"

"Whoa. That doesn't sound like the responsible, bleeding heart, sunshine girl we've come to know and love," Leo teases. "At least you were showing your patriotism."

"He was Canadian!" Kim supplies before Carina can say anything.

"Traitor!" she yells at her coworker before responding to Leo's comment. "Never underestimate the capabilities of a woman scorned, broken-hearted, and newly twenty-one, my dear boy."

"I never do," he says solemnly with a mock salute.

The idea of Carina being broken-hearted makes my skin crawl. I want to strangle the guy who did that to her, but then I'd have to strangle myself. Based on the timing of her story, that guy was me. She turned twenty-one a month after we broke up. From the social media stalking I did of our old friend group, I didn't see her with anyone else during that time and I'd like to think she'd take longer than a month to get over our yearslong relationship.

Logically, I know I hurt her, but hearing it out loud makes my throat constrict. Not only did I hurt her, but I caused her to act of character in response. The girl I fell in love with and the one in front of me right now would never find herself in that situation.

After that admission, we decide to switch it up and play a round of truth or dare. I get dared to shotgun a beer, Haley has to perform the *Cups* song, and Leo has to tell us how he lost his virginity—in a barn, so Iowa. When it's Carina's turn, it is no surprise to me that my girl picked truth. She was always risk averse, at least when she wasn't heartbroken, apparently. It didn't shock me at all when she chose to take on Haley's "What is the best date you've ever been on?" What did surprise me was what she responded with. It was balm to my soul after her last answer.

Carina glances over to me sheepishly before answering. "Well, when I was in college, there was this guy trying to win me over. After losing a bet, I had to go on a date with him to watch the *Lord of the Rings*. But when we walked up to the drive-in he had DIYed with the help of some friends, it was *Bridget Jones's Diary*—the movie he would've had to watch if I won. He also had a picnic with my favorite snacks. We talked and watched the movie until rain forced us to take shelter."

"And then he banged your brains out with multiple Os?" Kim asks hopefully.

"Um, no. He didn't 'bang my brains out,'" she says demurely. "But I will say I left the date more than satisfied."

"Nice," Justin mutters.

"That is fucking adorable." Haley swoons, and I puff up a bit, proud that I'm the fucking adorable planner behind that date. Carina shakes her head at my reaction before I arch an eyebrow at her.

As the game continues, Leo is forced to show us the most embarrassing picture of himself on the internet, and Haley recounts her worst date ever. Daredevils of the group Kim and Justin have to prank call an ex and perform an awful rap song from the nineties, respectively.

When it's my turn, Justin hits me with a whammy: "What's the worst thing you've ever done to a date or girlfriend?" Because he needed to, and I quote, "balance the choir boy vibes I put out on Tuesday" with Carina's present. If only he knew that present was to balance out the worst thing I've ever done.

Exhaling a breath, I sneak a glimpse over at Carina before continuing. All the color has drained out of her face because she can tell where this is going. I wish I could lie and say something else, but she needs to hear that I recognize what a shithead I was.

"When I first got drafted into the minors, I was focused on earning my spot. I forgot all my other responsibilities and neglected my girlfriend until she got fed up and dumped me," I admit.

Carina shifts uncomfortably, but after a beat, Kim, Justin, and Leo break out in collective boos.

"That's a lame ass story, bro," Justin insists. "There has to be more to it than that. We need details."

I exhale harshly and close my eyes before continuing. "Alright, fine. More detail it is. When I made it to the AA team in Houston faster than anyone else in my draft class, I thought I was hot shit. When I got there, I started spending all my time practicing or partying. The only problem with that was I had a girlfriend back home. I treated her as if she was an obligation and not a treasure—ignoring her calls, waiting forever or forgetting to text her back, and rushing her off the phone when I did answer. Even when she came to see me for her spring break, I didn't alter my schedule at all to spend time with her.

"I was supposed to fly home to attend an important event with her. Instead, I got too drunk the night before and missed my flight. She had told people I would be there, and I embarrassed her by not showing up. I hurt her by making her believe she wasn't a priority to me. Then when she rightfully called me out on my shit, I implied she was a distraction and that my responsibilities were more important than hers. I said I couldn't give her the commitment she needed.

"I realized my mistake after she broke up with me, but it was too late. She didn't want anything to do with the guy I had become, and I don't blame her. Most of our friends were still in Cali. I lost touch with them and created a new path for myself playing ball without the only girl I ever loved—the girl who was supposed to be my forever."

When I finish my story, everyone stares at me with either pity or disgust. Carina looks like she wants to crawl into a hole and hide. Same.

It's Leo who breaks the tension. "Damn, bro. That is dark as hell. Compared to Carina's story about her college ex, you're a real d-bag, but I also feel sad for you. It would suck to lose the girl you want to be with and not realize until it's too late."

I laugh humorlessly at that. "Yeah, it's too bad that guy wasn't there to remind me what my priorities were."

Drunk Kim decides the game has taken a dark turn and wants to lighten the mood. She does this by forcing us all to answer the same question, and whoever has the worst one has to do the dare. We all write down some questions and dares and throw them in bowls. We draw for a few rounds, and it's a good time. We learn everyone's body counts, Carina: 4, Haley: 6, Kim: 9, Leo: 8, Me: 13, and Justin: 26. For being the "man-whore of Tuscaloosa," as Kim dubs him, Justin has to chug some hot sauce. It goes about how you'd expect.

The next question has Haley smelling Leo's gym bag after we learn everyone's celebrity crush.

"Oh, this is a good one." Haley giggles. "What's the pettiest thing you did after a breakup?"

Answering first, Haley talks about egging a guy's car. Justin tells us he spread a rumor that his ex was secretly an Auburn fan who didn't get in and had to go to Alabama instead. Nice boy Leo surprised us all when he says he ran against his ex for class president, won, and then abdicated it to his VP, that girl's nemesis. Kim upped the ante by saying she had a threesome with her cheating ex's best friend AND sister. I admitted to posting my ex's number online with an ad for free puppies.

Carina is beet red and squirming in her seat when it's her turn. This has to be good. I know she can hold a grudge. I'm excited to hear what she did to some poor scrub.

"Oh, come on. This is the one you're going to chicken out on? Not what's your most embarrassing bathroom story? It's not like we're going to tell anyone. Don't be embarrassed if it's low, babe. I quite enjoy this wilder side of yours." Kim laughs.

She totally avoids glancing at me while answering. Uh oh.

"Okay, after going through a bad breakup in college, I went through the six stages of grief. Denial, anger, bargaining, depression, acceptance—"

"There are only five stages of grief," Haley interrupts.

"Not according to my best friend, Tiffany. At least not with breakups. The last stage is revenge." Double uh oh.

"Oh my God, tell us already! I'm dying to know," Justin shouts.

Carina gulps. "I can't believe I'm admitting this. After the acceptance, there was still some resentment left, so I kinda sorta loggedinto-hisxboxaccountanddeletedtheinfo."

"You what?" Kim asks.

She squeezes her eyes shut and repeats, "My ex was into gaming. I knew his password. I logged into his Xbox account and deleted all his history and game info."

"You did what?!" I bark as she opens her eyes and grimaces at me with the decency to appear ashamed.

"He deserved it?" she says more like a question than a statement.

"Damn girl, that is cold. So cold that I deem you the winner/loser of this round," Leo says, and everyone agrees. I'm still staring at her jaw on the floor. I remember when that happened. It was four months after we broke up. I thought someone had hacked into my account. It never once crossed my mind that it could've been her.

"Ugh, fine," Carina murmurs petulantly. "What's the dare?"

"You have to... go jump in the pool."

"Seriously? Who wrote that one?" she asks.

Leo slowly raises his hand. "Sorry?"

"Fine, let's get this over with," she retorts.

Our group makes our way down the elevator and to the complex's pool area. It's empty, which isn't surprising considering it's 1 a.m. Haley declares that I, too, should have to jump in because my breakup story was awful. When I point out we weren't doing dares yet, she says, "That girl deserves justice for you being a dumbass. You're lucky it wasn't me." The twinkle in her eyes is unsettling.

Carina and I count down from ten and jump in at opposite sides of the pool. Resurfacing, I see her a few feet away and swim over to her as the others go inside to grab us towels and bring out more drinks.

"I can't believe that was you," I mutter in disbelief. "I spent hours on the phone with Xbox trying to get that data back."

"I'm sorry," she says from under her lashes.

"It's okay. I deserved it. I just didn't know you had it in you, Kitten."

"It may have been fueled by a night of champagne and mostly Tiffany's idea."

I laugh. "Now, that checks out."

When a shiver runs through her, I grab her waist and pull her into me. She's treading water because the pool is five feet deep, and she's barely 5'2". Since it only comes up to my shoulders, I'm able to stand. Fuck, her body feels incredible under my hands. Her white dress is clinging to her like a second skin. I swallow harshly as her body presses against mine, and our eyes lock. Grabbing the backs of her thighs, I hoist her up, forcing her legs to wrap around my waist. I move one hand up the outside of her leg up her lower back and use the other to push the wet strands out of her face. Gazing down at her, I see the girl I used to love, the one I still probably love and don't fully know yet but fuck do I want to.

As I'm about to lean in and kiss her, a wave of water crashes over us. I jerk up and see our friends joining us in the pool. I glance back down at her to see questions swirling in her pretty eyes. We need to talk—about the past, the electricity flowing between us now, and what it all means. It will have to wait until we're, though, because Justin is boosting Haley up on his shoulders and yelling, "Let's play chicken!"

An hour later, we get out and dry off. Even though it's July, the water was cold, making the girls shiver. We decide to split up in order to all get warm showers. Justin volunteers to take Kim back to his place, and Haley heads up with Leo.

Neither man offered to let Carina go up to their place. Smart. I'm fond of Leo and Justin, but there is no way in hell I'm about to see my girl in their clothes. Yeah, *my* girl. After everything we shared tonight, I can't *not* want to make her mine. I hope she feels the same, but if she doesn't yet, that's okay. I had to work hard to win her over the first go around, and I have a much bigger hole to dig out of this time. I'm up for the challenge.

Because I'm a gentleman, I give Carina first dibs on the shower. While she's in there, I hang a t-shirt and boxers on the door. If she wants me to take her home, I can get her some pants, too. I'm hoping she wants to stay, though.

When I hear the water shut off, I hang out in the bedroom area. It's the only spot that would offer her any privacy. My place is a studio with the bathroom opening to the kitchen and living area. After getting dressed, she rounds the corner, smiling brightly. The caveman part of me thumps his chest at the sight of her in my clothes again. This primal switch has flipped in my brain, and I'm having trouble thinking, let alone speaking full sentences. So, I don't. I smile back at her and take my turn in the shower.

Chapter Twenty-Five

Carina

I use my time in the shower to sober up and go over the last few weeks in my head. Ever since that first night at Paula's when I ran into Robby, my world has been off-kilter. I'm at the weird precipice of making one of my dreams come true while being confronted with an old one.

I've had an unfavorable opinion of Robby Becker for the last four years. But the man I've seen the last few weeks reminds me of the guy I loved for those three years in college. Who am I kidding? I loved him longer than that. Honestly, I'm not sure I ever *stopped* loving him, just how he treated me.

When I get out of the shower, I find a pair of boxers and a Songbirds shirt hanging on the door. After putting them on, I walk into the main living area and see Robby sitting on his bed through the cubby wall. He gives me a smile as he passes by me and enters the bathroom to take his shower.

Surveying his place, I try to decide what to do. I see my purse on the counter. Robby must have gone to Leo's to grab it while I warmed up. I should go home, but I'd need some pants to do that. I'm not getting in an Uber without them. And, also, a part of me wants to stay here. There is a lot unspoken between us, but I think I want to give him a chance depending on what he has to say.

I poke around his studio apartment while I wait. It has definite hotel vibes. He told me earlier that it's staged and often used for guys who are here for short stints. It makes sense considering there is hardly any personality in this place. Glancing around his bedroom, I pick up the book on the nightstand.

That fact that he's reading in bed isn't what's shocking. What's surprising is his bookmark. It's me. Well, us. It's a strip of pictures we took in the photo booth at the draft. I can't believe he still has this. Not just has it but still actively uses it. Holding it, I notice something else on the shelf by the window. Beside his Albert Pujols bobblehead is the snow globe I gave him on our first Christmas together. It's a scene from the ski lodge where we became official.

I jump when I hear his voice behind me. "I don't usually travel with the globe, but I knew I'd be here for a while; it only seemed right to bring it along. The picture is always with me. Reminds me of where I come from and the type of man I should be."

I turn to face him. Apparently, we're only allowed one outfit between us because while I'm not wearing pants, he's shirtless, standing there in only grey sweatpants. I can't help but gawk at how freaking shredded he is now. He was fit before, but he's definitely added another pair of abs, and I would have remembered the Adonis belt. Opening my mouth and closing it a few times, his lips tilt at my obvious speechlessness.

"Come on," he says as he holds out his hand. "We should talk."

I put the photo strip back in the book and take his hand as he leads me into the living area. He sits on the couch and settles beside me. He shifts until he is fully facing me.

"Hi," I say shyly.

"Hi," he chuckles back. "I'd tell you not to be nervous, but the truth is, I'm nervous as hell. I don't exactly know where to open this conversation other than the most important part: Carina, I am so fucking sorry."

I suck in a breath. He apologized over text, but this is the first time I'm hearing the words out loud and they seemed genuine.

"I royally fucked up our relationship," he continues. "I took you for granted, belittled your accomplishments, and didn't cherish you like I should have. You deserved better, and I'm glad you broke up with me."

That statement hits me like a ton go bricks. "You're glad I broke up with you?" I parrot. That is not what I expected him to say at all.

"Don't get me wrong, I wasn't at the time, but once I got over myself and realized what a dick I'd been, I was glad," he responds. "You were—are—a treasure, and I didn't treat you like one in the end. If anyone else had hurt you the way I had, I would've decked them. I shouldn't have gotten a free pass just because I was your boyfriend."

"I-wow." I don't know what to say back to that.

"There is no excuse for any of it. The fact is that I was immature. I had growing up to do. And to be honest, I don't know that I would have done that if we'd stayed together. You breaking up with me was the wake-up call I needed to realize how self-centered I'd become.

"I was away from all my family and friends, everyone who kept me grounded. I was surrounded by a bunch of guys in the same position as me: desperate, hungry, alone. We fed off each other in an unhealthy way. I wasn't able—or maybe willing—to volunteer the way I had during college. I didn't have anything to put in perspective that there was a world outside my bubble, outside my dreams.

"You choosing yourself when I couldn't was a hard lesson to learn. In a way, you breaking up with me saved us both. It gave us a chance at one day still having a future."

"What do you mean?" I ask. "How did dumping you keep a chance at a future? Wouldn't it be the opposite?"

Robby releases another of those sexy chuckles and grabs my hand running his thumbs over my knuckles. "You'd think, but the way I see it, you nipped my behavior in the bud early. If you hadn't left, I don't know how long I would've continued to take you for granted, and even one second was too long. You would've grown to resent me even more than you did, and there wouldn't be any hope for us today."

"Is that what you have now?"

"Hope?" he questions. I nod.

"Yeah, pretty girl. I have hope. Hope that I can prove how sorry I am. Hope that I can show you I became a man who deserves you. Hope that we can still have the future we always talked about.

"I know you're scared. I am. But I know it's worth it. You were always the endgame for me. No one I've met has ever held a candle to you. If you give me the chance, I'll work my ass off to prove it."

With that last declaration, he lets go of my hand, and his slides up the side of my neck to cup my face. He searches my eyes for permission. When I give him a small nod, he leans in and takes my mouth with his. His lips move softly against mine.

While he's being gentle and sweet, this kiss is awakening something in me that is anything but. My body has been aching for Robby since we were first reunited at the club, and now that she'd had a taste of him, she wants more.

I return his kiss with furor. He grabs the nape of my neck and my jaw to angle my head how he wants as he deepens the kiss. And God, what a kiss this is. What started out slow and sweet has become intense and frantic. It's as if we're both afraid that if we stop kissing, we will wake up from this dream and realize it wasn't real. Robby kisses me until the last possible moment before pulling away long enough to suck in some much-needed air.

Feeling too far away from him, even though we are literally touching, I move to straddle his lap. I nip at his bottom lip, eliciting a groan. Desperately needing friction, I squirm with my legs framing his hips as his tongue battles mine for control. Grinding against him, I notice the impressive length I haven't had the pleasure of being reacquainted with yet settle between my thighs. I didn't realize until now how little fabric separates us.

There is still too much fabric, though. I rip my shirt over my head, and he checks out my breasts like they are his long-lost best friends. He dives back in to kiss my mouth once more before trailing his lips across my jaw to right below my ear. "You're fucking beautiful, Carina," he moans as I continue to grind on his bulge. I answer with a moan of my own when he rubs his thumbs across my painfully hard nipples.

His hands settle on my hips to stop their motion. "Care," he rasps against the spot on my neck he has been lavishing attention on. I wouldn't be surprised if there is a mark tomorrow. "You don't stop grinding on me, I can't promise to continue to be the gentleman I intended to be tonight."

I grin and resume my movements with an increased determination. I don't want him to be a gentleman. I want him to ravage me. I want him to show me how much he missed being with me because I sure as hell missed being with him. I've been with other guys since our break up, but none of them have ever been able to read my body the way he did. No one was ever able to rile me up the way he has at this moment. God, I hope it's like riding a bike because I have never wanted someone this badly.

Abruptly, his hands land on my ass, and he stands up. He quickly makes his way to the bed and lays me down. Finally disconnecting our kiss, he gazes down at me with mirth in his eyes. "I've been without you for four years," he says. "There is no way in hell I'm embarrassing myself by letting you dry hump me to completion. Now, there is another set of lips I've missed almost as much as the ones I've been kissing, and I need to make up for lost time."

With that proclamation licks his way down my body, giving each of my nipples the attention they desperately want. He sucks one into his mouth while rolling the other between his fingers and thumb. He alternates between the two for what feels like forever.

"Didn't you say you were going to spend some time somewhere else?" I whine.

He lets out a chuckle. "Aww, baby, is someone needy and impatient?"

I don't dignify his question with a response. Instead, I squirm against him, causing him to laugh even more. The vibrations of his laugh against my nipple cause me to grow impossibly wetter. I'm sure the boxers I'm wearing are soaked.

Deciding I've had enough torture, Robby gives my breasts each a final chaste kiss before he resumes his path down my body. When he gets to the waistband of the boxers, he grabs onto them with both hands and slowly peels them down. I lift up my hips to assist in their removal.

Once they're off, he runs his hands up my legs to grab my thighs and slowly pins them back. He licks his lips and stares back at me with a smirk. "Seems someone missed me almost as much as I missed her," he teases as he kisses my thighs.

"Yes," I pant. "Show her what she's been missing."

"Oh, baby, I will. Hold on." With that declaration, he runs his tongue up my slit. When he reaches my clit, he starts to lap at it lightly before circling it with his tongue.

I arch my back, pushing to get closer to him. He groans into me, causing the vibrations to zing across my nub as he continues to suck and taste me. Keeping one hand on my thigh to hold me open, he brings the other to my center and circles my entrance with his fingers. He slowly pushes one into me and then a second. He sets a languid pace pushing in and out of me as he flicks my clit with his tongue.

"Robby," I moan.

"That's it, baby. Moan for me. You taste so fucking good. I want you to come all over my face and fingers before you come all over my cock."

Mewling, I writhe under his ministrations. As I get closer, my hips buck, and he uses his free arm to press me into the bed. "Fuck, that's it, Carina. Come for me. Show me how good I make you feel. Show me how much this body missed me."

With those words, he doubles his efforts, and my body coils tightly. He sucks my clit into his mouth as his fingers toy with my G-spot, and I detonate. I cry out and pull on his hair hard as my thighs try to shut. His broad shoulders keep me from clamping down on his head when he eats me through my orgasm, giving me soft licks and gentle kisses as I come down.

Once my legs stop shaking, he peers up at me with a feral grin and asks, "Ready for me, Kitten?" Hell yes. I may have just had an orgasm, but my greedy body wants more. I need him. I need him inside me.

Chapter Twenty-Six

Robby

I slide my way up Carina's body and take her in a hard kiss letting her taste herself on my tongue. She tasted even better than I remembered. Her moans are sweeter than any in my dreams. If I wasn't gone for this girl before, I know I would be after sinking into her.

Reaching over to the nightstand, I grab my wallet and pull out a condom. I quickly roll it down my length as she takes a few seconds to recover. I try not to smirk in satisfaction at leaving her breathless. Running my hands down the outside of her thighs, I settle between them.

I tap her overstimulated clit with my length a couple times, loving the way she twists beneath me, before lining myself up with her entrance. She tilts her hips pulling the tip in further, and peers at me with pleading eyes. That's all the permission I need. Thrusting forward, I pause once I'm fully seated to give her—and me—a second to adjust.

"Fuck, baby. You're so tight," I grit out. I need to pull myself together. I don't want to come too soon. It's been a while since I've been with anyone, and this could get embarrassing quick.

"Robby, move," she whimpers. Move. Yep. On it. I slowly pull out and push myself back in. Christ, she feels good. I thrust in and out slowly a few more times before picking up my pace. I pull one of her legs up and wrap it around my hips to deepen the angle. The hands roaming my arms clutch me tightly, nails digging into my skin hard enough to leave a mark. Seems my pretty girl enjoys that.

"Mmm, that's it. Taking me so deep. You feel so good wrapped around me. So tight, so wet for me. God, I missed this pussy so fucking much. Did she miss me?"

She's too lost in her pleasure to answer.

I slow down, which causes her to make a keening sound. "Robby, baby, please."

I lean down and suck on her neck. "I asked you a question, Kitten. Did this pussy miss me?"

"Yes," she pants.

"Good," I reply as I pick up speed and swivel my hips, hitting a spot that makes her back bow. I do it again as I feel her body tense.

"Is this perfect pussy going to come for me again, Care? Gonna grip me in your velvety heat? Gonna let me feel you shatter around me?" I punctuate each question with a hard thrust.

"Don't stop, don't stop," she chants.

"Never," I promise, moving my hips faster. The pressure is building inside me. I need to push her over the edge if I want her to come with me. I lean down and suck on her neck as I snake a hand between us and thumb her clit.

"Come for me, baby. Be a good girl, and come on my cock." That encouragement is all it takes for her to tremble underneath me. Her walls cramp down on me so tightly that I can't help but explode inside her with her name on my lips.

I must blackout for a few seconds because the next thing I know,

I'm panting and staring into her beautiful brown eyes. She gives me a blissed-out smile, and I softly kiss her lips and then her forehead as I go get us a washcloth.

When I come back from the bathroom, she's exactly where I left her. Chuckling, I clean her off with the warm cloth and throw it into the hamper before I crawl into the bed and gather her in my arms.

This is what has been missing from my life, I think to myself as I fall into a peaceful, dreamless sleep.

The next morning, I wake up from what has to be the best sleep I've had in years. Carina is still snoozing in front of me. I take a minute to soak in the sensation of her wrapped up in my arms again. She's so soft and peaceful like this. Burying my face into her, I bask in the slight scent of coconuts from her shampoo before laying lazy kisses on her neck and shoulders.

As she stirs awake, she turns in my arms to face me. I shift onto my back, letting her lay her head on my chest. Her hand splays over my abs and traces them as she rouses.

"Good morning," she says shyly, avoiding my gaze.

"Morning, pretty girl." I use my hand to tip her chin back and capture her lips with mine. "Sleep okay?"

"Mhmm. This bed is more comfortable than I expected."

"It's got nothing on my bed at home," I muse before I realize the implications of that statement. Home. As in, this isn't my home. I don't live here, and my time in Memphis is temporary. Shit. Intellectually, I knew that, but we probably should have talked about it and what it means for us last night.

Seemingly remembering the same thing, I watch Carina's features harden as she builds some of her walls back up. I get it. She's protecting herself, but she doesn't need to do that from me. Not anymore. I want to be the one to protect her, not the one she needs protection from.

She hums in response, but I can tell if I don't act fast, I'm going to lose her to the spinning anxiety in her mind. She moves off the bed to physically distance herself from me and the thoughts in her head.

"Hey, don't do that," I plead.

"Do what?" she asks.

"Shut me out. I know we have things to talk about, but I am in this. We'll make it work."

She huffs out a laugh. "I don't see how. We couldn't make it work when you were playing Double-A. Now you're in the big leagues with more pressure and responsibilities."

"Things are different now," I promise. "I'm different. I know what my priorities are, and I won't forget again. Sure, figuring out a balance will take time and work, but I'm up for it."

"And I can't get over you again," she whispers. "It was the hardest thing I ever had to do."

Pulling her back into me, I draw her into my chest. "You won't have to. This won't be like before. We were young. We didn't know the realities life would throw at us. We know now. Plus, we lived fifteen hundred miles apart. Now we can get to each other in less than three hours. It's gonna be okay, baby. I'll make sure of it."

"What if you get back there and change your mind? You return to your fancy life and realize there isn't a place for me in it."

"That won't happen," I assure her. I grab the book on my night-stand and pull out the photo strip. "I've taken this picture with me everywhere. I told myself it was to remember the day my future started, but really it was to remember the man I wanted to be. One worthy of the girl in this picture. She's always had a place in my life. And now that I've met the woman she's become? I'm surer than I've ever been."

"Promise?" she questions with apprehension in her voice. I nod my head and kiss her temple.

"What does that mean in practicality?" she asks. When I give her a confused expression, she goes on. "I mean, like, what are we? Are we a couple? Dating but exclusive? Fuck buddies who call each other for late-night romps? Part-time lovers and...."

I cut off her rambling by rolling her onto her back and hovering over her. "First," I say, kissing her neck. "You're not now, nor will you ever be a 'fuck buddy.' To call what we did last night just a fuck cheapens how meaningful and incredible it was."

"Second," I rasp against her collarbone as I kiss lower. "Call us whatever you want—dating, a couple. Call us soulmates bound together in this and every lifetime for all I care. But we are absolutely exclusive. Now that I have you again, I don't plan to ever let you go. If another man so much as *thinks* he can touch you, I will go absolutely feral on his ass."

She whimpers as I move my lips to her breasts and twirl my tongue around her nipple. "Do I make myself clear, Kitten?" I ask before sucking it into my mouth.

"Yes," she moans, and her body writhes under me.

"Good girl. Now, let me remind you how nice it is to be mine." I spend the rest of the morning doing just that.

Chapter Twenty-Seven

Robby

After leaving Sunday afternoon, Carina has been busy catching up on her weekend to-do list and then working today. Because I pitched on Saturday, I won't play again until our game Thursday. I know rest is important for longevity, but I am itching to get back in the saddle after being out for almost eight weeks. The same could be said about spending time with Carina.

She wasn't able to come to tonight's game, but she is coming over afterward to stay the night because tomorrow is a holiday. Mid-week holidays are dumb, but in this instance, I'll take a weekday sleepover when I can get it. While we haven't talked more about what we're labeling this relationship since this weekend, I know she wants to keep it quiet until we feel more settled. With our history and how much is up in the air about my time here, I can respect that. It stings that she isn't ready to shout it from the rooftops, but I get it. I'm sure everyone will have questions considering what they know about me and how things ended all those years ago.

That being said, I don't understand why she feels the need to sneak into my condo like she's 007. None of the players who live here are going to think anything of seeing a woman hanging around. Paparazzi isn't a concern here, thankfully. I haven't seen any during my time in Memphis. Her secret agent routine is cute but unnecessary.

Fifteen minutes after I get back to my place from the ballpark, there is a knock on my door. I bust out laughing when I see Carina with a cap pulled down and her hair in a low bun, scanning the hallway. I lean against the doorframe and ask, "I'm sorry, ma'am. I'm waiting for my girl to show up, and I don't think she'd appreciate it if I let a completely unrecognizable stranger into my apartment."

She shoves passed me and mocks, "Ha, ha, ha. You're so funny, Bobert."

I grin at the use of the nickname my sister gave me. The two grew close when we were together. Morgan didn't talk to me for a month when I told her we had broken up and the events surrounding it.

"Careful with the sass there, Kitten," I warn. Lust flashes through her eyes, and she licks her lips. As much as I would love to jump her bones right now, I also want to spend some time with her out of the sheets. We haven't had a chance to do that since deciding to give this a go.

"Drink? I've got water, soda, beer, and seltzers," I offer.

"I'll take a berry seltzer, please."

I grab her drink and a beer for myself before settling on the couch. She laughs when she sees what I'm watching. "How many times have you seen the show, a million? Still part of your post-game ritual?"

"There is no such thing as too much of this show," I scoff. "Besides, you love it as much as I do, and you know it."

She settles into me, letting me wrap my arm around her shoulders and drag her closer. We watch a few episodes, and I play with the hair she set loose from her ridiculous incognito bun while her hand runs innocently up and down my thigh. The longer we sit there and chat, the more aware I am of how close that red, white, and blue manicured hand is to my dick. He seems to be thinking the same thing because he's growing harder with every pass. The tension around us is ratcheting up with every dumb thing Chandler says.

"I remember something else that used to be part of your post-game routine that should maybe make a comeback," she suggests.

All my innocent intentions fly out the window. Before the words are even out of her mouth, I have her over my shoulder and I smack her ass as I carry her over to my bed. "You asked for it, baby."

A few days pass when I roll up to the Feeding Memphis office, coffee in hand. I send Carina a selfie of me out front, and five minutes later, she's creeping outside with a weary expression on her face. Well, that won't do. I walk up and kiss her until she's pliant in my arms, then pull away and look down at her.

She is fucking adorable in a white t-shirt and pink polka dot skirt that goes past her knees. It amazes me how she can take my breath away in her sexy club attire and something as simple and casual as this. She's wearing canvas sneakers for Chrissake.

"Hi, Kitten."

"Hi," she greets. "What are you doing here?"

"I can't stop by and see my team captain? Maybe I want to see a tour of the charity I'm working with." That answer seems to surprise her.

"I guess we could do that? It's a mess inside, though. We host a lot in-house when school is out for the summer."

"I'm kidding, beautiful." I laugh. "I was on my way to Jalen's school for the Electronics Club meeting and thought I'd drop a treat off to my girl. It was on the way." I grab the takeout bag she apparently didn't notice sitting on the retaining wall and hand it to her.

Her eyes twinkle in delight. "You didn't have to do that."

"I know," I say as I wrap her up in my arms again and kiss her forehead. "But I know you ran late this morning and thought you might have skipped breakfast. I also got some extra for Haley, Kim, Alex, and whoever else might want some."

She smiles at me like I gave her the fucking moon and not chicken biscuits. This girl is good for my ego. If only she knew how much I was willing to give her to make her smile like that.

"Thank you!" she exclaims. "I was going to have to work through lunch thanks to an impromptu donor request. You're saving my life."

"Such a drama queen." I tease, kissing her forehead. "I am happy to be of service. Text me later?"

"I will. Thanks again, babe. You're the best."

"You've been awfully chipper lately," Leo comments as we hang out in the dugout during Friday night's game.

"What's not to be happy about?" I reply. "My recovery is going well, I had a killer game last night, and our charity team is dominating the competition. I am winning at life."

"Are you positive it's got nothing to do with the brunette bombshell sneaking into your apartment earlier this week?" he teases.

Good, I'm glad he saw. I want all these fuckers to know Carina's mine—not that I was worried about Leo. "I don't know what you're referring to." I smirk over my bad of sunflower seeds.

"Hmm, I bet you don't. Are you ever gonna tell me what the deal is with you two? Cause I know you didn't meet for the first time at the club."

Leo is a good dude, and we've become actual friends at this point. He deserves the truth. "You remember during truth or dare when she talked about the drive-in date? That was me."

"Nice, dude. I'm assuming she's your dugout girl then, too?"

I smile and shrug at him. I'm not gonna blow up her spot by kissing and telling.

"What happened with you two? From what I have observed, you seem good for each other. Your sexual tension alone is enough to get me pregnant," he jokes.

I sigh. "Do you remember my story about breaking up with my college girlfriend?"

"Duuuuuuude," he laments after making the connection. "You let *her* go? I'd have cut off my left nut for a girl like that to commit to me during this crazy ride."

"I know, I know. I was young, dumb, and immature as hell. I learned that lesson, don't worry. I won't be making that mistake again."

"Does that mean you two are getting serious?"

"Hopefully," I confess. "She's understandably a bit skittish, but she's always been it for me. I never thought I'd get a second chance. Now that I have one, I'm not about to fuck it up again."

"What happens when you go back up?" he questions.

I pull off my hat and run my hands through my hair. Sometimes I miss my long hair. I wonder if Carina misses it. I've still got plenty for her to grab onto when I'm between her legs devouring her, but not nearly as much as I used to.

"We haven't worked out all the details, but I'm not worried about it. I'll do whatever she needs. I'm hoping I'll be able to convince her to move there before next season. We'll see how that goes. She loves her job here, but I know her dream is to run her own nonprofit, and with my connections in Nashville and funding, we can make that happen. I have eight years left on my contract with a no-trade clause. That means I'll be there long enough to get something set up before the risk of moving is on the table."

"You've thought about this," he remarks.

"Yup, now I have to figure out how to convince Carina to jump in with both feet."

"You know, I might have an idea on something that could help turn the tide in your favor."

Leo spends the next few minutes explaining his date night idea, and I gotta say, it's pretty fucking brilliant. He will make some lucky lady an amazing partner when he finds the right one.

I tug on my shirt, trying to smooth out any wrinkles as we walk up the path to Carina's parents' house. "Would you relax?" she asks, amused.

"I am relaxed," I lie. I'm not. I am totally nervous. Carina's mom is amazing, but she can be scary as hell. Steve is a big ole softy, but I saw him in court once, and that guy can be a real hardass when he needs to be.

"You are so not relaxed," she chuffs. "I know 'meeting the parents' can be stressful, but you've met them before, several times. Hell, you've stayed at this house before when visiting them with me. It's not exactly a scary scenario."

"I'm not scared. I just want to make a good new first impression. I'm sure they weren't thrilled with me after our breakup, and I don't want to give them any more reasons to dislike me."

"Please," she says. "My mom has always loved you. She even suggested I look you up when I graduated and try to rekindle things."

"She did?" That is surprising. "Why didn't you?"

The eyebrow raise she gives me says it all. She smiles while wrapping her arms around the one of mine that isn't carrying an insanely expensive bottle of wine. "It's cute that you're nervous. It means you care. Plus, I enjoy seeing you off-kilter."

Right before we approach the door, I spin around until her back is pressed against the house, and she's caged between my arms. Bringing one hand to her face, I pinch her chin between my finger and thumb. "You are loving this," I muse. "Don't worry; I'll get you back later tonight by teasing you until you're squirming as much on the outside as I am on the inside."

Her breath hitches, and I smile, diving in for a hard, quick kiss. Against her lips, I say, "And I care more than you can imagine. Now, let's get this over with. I want to hurry up and get to my dessert."

After taking a second to collect herself, Carina sends me epic side-eye as she pushes open the door. "Mama, we're here!" she shouts.

"*Mia bambolina!* Roberto, welcome. It's good to have you here," a carbon copy of Carina says. The two Italian bombshells in front of me could pass as sisters. They say if you want to know how a girl will age, you should look at her mom. If that is the case, I hit the fucking lottery.

Movement catches my eye, and Steve enters the foyer. He sends me a knowing glance as if he is reading my mind. My ears heat being caught thinking about his wife. "Robby, nice to see you, son."

"Thank you, Mr. Shaw. It's good to see you again as well. Mrs. Shaw, you are even more radiant than last time I saw you."

"Oh, stop it! Steve and Teresa, please! You've slept with my daughter. You can call me by my first name," she quips. Yeah, not only did Carina get her beauty, but she also got her attitude. Her mom isn't quite as sassy as my girl is, but she may keep that side hidden. Who knows how she acts when no one else is around but her and Steve.

"Mom!" Carina gasps as Steve snickers.

"Let me take that," he says, grabbing the wine from my hand. "This will pair great with what Teresa made for dinner. Let's go give it time to aerate."

We walk into the kitchen, and I am hit with a strong sense of nostalgia. It's been four, maybe five years since I was in this house, and it is exactly how I remember it. It's crazy how little some things can change when other things change completely.

"It smells incredible," I compliment.

Carina and her mom both beam. "Thank you," the older of the

two replies. *I remembered how much you loved my chicken parmesan. I hope that fits into your fancy baseball diet.*

I laugh. "Almost nothing delicious fits into my fancy baseball diet, but I won't tell if you don't."

And delicious it is. Teresa's cooking is some of the best I've ever had the pleasure of eating. And I've been to Michelin-star restaurants. Her food is somehow complex and intricate while never tasting pretentious. With two working parents, I didn't eat a lot of home-cooked meals growing up. I appreciate one whenever I can get it.

As Steve brings dessert out, some layered fruit magic in a glass dish, Carina excuses herself to the bathroom. A few minutes later, my phone dings. The good guest I am, I ignore it. But when Teresa asks about my sister's wedding, I pull it out to show her pictures.

I notice a Snapchat from Carina and open it immediately, hoping everything is okay.

I almost choke on my tongue as I am greeted by a picture of Carina's bare, glistening pussy and the caption, "Don't fill up ;)."

Yeah, she added a winky face. That saucy little vixen. She is in so much trouble when we get home.

"Everything okay?" her mom asks.

"Uh, sorry. I had a weird text from a buddy," I respond, showing her the pictures. While we're talking about my family, Carina comes back into the room with a teasing smile. The four of us continue chatting. When Steve and Teresa debate about which of his nieces had a nineties band at their wedding, I lean over to my girl and whisper in her ear, "You think you're funny, Kitten? Sending me naughty pictures and getting me hard when I'm at dinner with your parents? I think someone is angling to get their ass spanked later." Her eyes dilate as she bites her lip. Interesting.

Then she shrugs and smirks as she asks Steve a question about work. Okay, two can play this game. I drop my napkin between our chairs. As I lean down to pick it up. I trail my hand up her ankle and calf to her thigh. She shifts under my hand and inadvertently, or maybe totally on purpose, widens her legs.

I discreetly start rubbing my pinky higher and higher up her thighs until I reach the edge of her panties. Slowly, I push my fingers under her silk thong until I reach her wet lips. She's barely able to smother her gasp when I finally make contact with her clit.

Under the tablecloth, Steve and Teresa have no idea what's going on as the family continues their conversation. I chime in every so often. Carina is biting her lip as I continue to gently pet her swelling nub. It's not nearly enough to get her off, but it is plenty to get her needy.

"You okay, *mi mini?*" her mother asks suddenly.

"Yes, a little tired," Carina replies quickly. "We should get going soon. Robby had a game earlier today, and we've both got busy days tomorrow."

"Of course, *bambolina,*" her mother agrees. I wash up in the bathroom before we leave, mainly to avoid looking her parents in the eye while shaking their hands, knowing where mine has been.

"It was wonderful to see you," I tell them both.

"It certainly was," Teresa says with a smile. "We better see you more Sundays to come."

"Count on it. My nutritionist may hate it, but it's worth it."

With that, we walk to my car. Carina attacks my mouth as soon as we're out of the front door's line of sight. "You're a jerk," she mumbles against my lips.

"I don't know what you're talking about," I remark as I open the passenger. "I was warming up my dessert." With a smug grin, I round the car, get into my seat, and pull out of the driveway, hoping we don't hit too many red lights.

I need her home, spread open on my bed, and I need it now. The lustful glint in her eyes tells me she isn't going to mind if I ignore a few traffic laws on our way.

Chapter Twenty-Eight

Robby

I pull up to Carina's apartment before sunset and pop out of the car to get her. It's not an apartment as much as it is a classic Midtown-style house that has been split into multiple units. It looks like a duplex from the outside, but she says the top level was closed off to make a third unit accessed from the back.

Before I have the chance to knock, she opens her door with a bright smile on her face. I haven't told her what we're doing, but I did mention she should dress comfy. As always, she nailed it. She's cute and comfortable in a grey cotton dress and sandals. Her style has always been more neutral than bright and bold. This is giving me college-Carina vibes. Honestly, with how beat up the sandals are, she may have had them then.

"Hi, pretty girl," I coo. "Ready to go?"

"Yep," she replies. "You sure I don't need anything?"

"Nope, just your sexy self. C'mon. Your chariot awaits."

I help her into my Bronco and give her a quick peck before rounding it and getting in on my side. I plug in my phone and throw on the latest country hits. My girl sings along happily until we get closer to our destination. "Are you ever gonna tell me where we're going?"

"Nah, what fun would that be?" I muse cheekily. She hates surprises. She is a major type-A planner, so I know this is driving her crazy. That's okay, though. She's been driving me crazy for weeks now. It's nice to get her off balance.

When we reach our destination, she turns to me and squeals. "The drive-in?!"

"I take it you approve?" I ask. She nods enthusiastically.

I pay the entrance fee and then navigate over to our spot. As I'm fiddling with the radio to get the right station, she's taking it all in.

"What movie are we seeing?" she asks.

"They're having a nineties classic night. We had a few options," I explain.

"What were the choices?"

"*Never Been Kissed*, *The Goonies*, *Edward Scissorhands*, and the one we're seeing: *Clueless*. How'd I do?"

"You did great," she beams. *Clueless* is one of my favorite movies, and *Never Been Kissed* makes me cringe."

"I remember—your secondhand embarrassment is strong. You cringed through most of *Bridesmaids*; we almost had to turn it off."

"Well, she was such an awkward mess!" she defends.

"I think that was the point."

"Perhaps... Is it too much to hope you've got a hidden dinner compartment somewhere in this fancy car of yours?"

I bark out a laugh. "No hidden compartment, but I do happen to have a warming bag magically stashed in the back. As if I'd ever forget to feed my girl. This isn't my first rodeo or even my first drive-in date with you." I boop her nose and grab the bag I always keep in my car because I'm bougie and love a hot meal.

She reaches toward me with grabby hands. I swear she drools

when she sees it's cheese pizza from Aldo's. The moan that slips out of her mouth is fucking erotic; my pants immediately tent.

"Geez, if I knew pizza was all it took to get you to moan like that, I'd have brought it to our first drive-in date."

She rolls her eyes, retorting, "You didn't have any trouble pulling moans out of me that night."

"Mmm, you are right about that, pretty girl. Maybe if you're lucky, you'll get a repeat performance tonight." She blushes at the statement. "Oh, now you blush? I didn't see you blushing this weekend when you screamed so loud the neighbor's dog barked."

"I don't remember you complaining about my volume level," she quips.

"Trust me, I'm not. There is nothing hotter than hearing my name on those sweet lips as you come for me. I want the whole damn world to know how good I make you feel."

The radio crackles and announces the previews will begin momentarily. I give Carina a grin and a quick kiss before grabbing some pizza for myself and settling in to watch the movie.

Halfway through, the pizza is disregarded, and she slides beside me when I lift up my console. "Does Cher remind you of someone?" I wonder out loud.

"Absolutely. When I first got to MSC, I thought she and Tiffany could be twinsies."

"Yes, that's it!" I reply. "How is FSB doing?"

"Well, she certainly isn't missing that nickname," Carina laughs. "But she's doing good. She's a makeup artist now doing all fancy things. She was in New York a few weeks ago, working with an up-and-coming designer. She's got a few celebrity clients, too. I don't know how much she loves all the egos, but she loves the craft."

"Wow, good for her," I remark. "I imagine changing career paths was a hard conversation to have with her mom. She was about as supportive as my dad."

"It was rough there for a few months," she says. "It happened around the same time as our breakup. We commiserated together.

Luckily it wasn't long until her mom was preoccupied with husband number four." Her gaze goes hazy as she sinks into the memories of that time.

It fucking cracks my heart that Carina went through something hard, and I wasn't there for her. Logically, I know I caused it, but it still hurts. I hate that Tiffany was going through something hard, too, and I couldn't support her. We had a special bond that went away when I screwed everything up with Carina—not that I was a good friend to anyone at that time.

"I'm sorry she went through that. I'm sorry you went through that, and I wasn't there," I admit.

Peeking back at me, she gives me a sad smile. "It's okay. I think you were right about what you said the other night. We needed the time apart to grow. You spent that time maturing, and I did, too. We both had some growing up to do if we wanted a real shot at making this work. That time strengthened the bond between Tiffany and me and cemented us as besties 5ever."

"5ever? You mean forever?"

"No. Five. Because forever isn't nearly long enough," she scoffs like that should have been obvious.

I couldn't agree more. Forever is not nearly enough time to get with this girl.

Chapter Twenty-Nine

Carina

It's the first weekend I haven't had plans in a while, and I'm loving it. I am savoring all the time I've gotten with Robby, but I haven't had much me-time since we got back together. I am barely keeping up with my manicures!

When he isn't at practice or a game, he is usually with me. Thank goodness his games are after my work hours; otherwise, I don't know when I'd get anything done aside from working and hanging out with him. Not that I mind, but I do still have to adult a little.

I spent this morning grabbing a delicious smoothie from the new food truck by my place and attending a Pilates class with my favorite instructor, Savannah. Her bubbly encouragement is the perfect way to start the day.

I'll go see my mom Sunday night for family dinner, but other than that, my weekend is all about me. Robby is out of town for a series of away games, and the girls both have other plans. I'm not mad about it. I have a few errands to run and some tasks at home I've been neglecting due to spending all my time with my boyfriend.

It's weird to call him my boyfriend again. On the one hand, it's super familiar and gives me warm fuzzies. On the other hand, we feel a step beyond boyfriend/girlfriend territory.

I check my phone before switching my laundry and see a few new notifications. The first is a text from the man in question. It's a picture of him, and Leo eating BBQ in Charlotte captioned, "Doesn't hold a candle to Central."

Charlotte makes me think of Seany. That's where he's playing these days. I wonder if he and Robby will see each other outside the ballpark. I know they made up, but I don't know how close they are. I shoot Sean a "good luck and miss you" text before replying to Robby.

12:14 PM

> Traitor! And you're going to make a mess all over yourself.

I see a text from Tiffany telling me to check my IG for a video she sent me. It's a funny spoof on what it's like to go to MSC. I send her an "lol" back in my DMs before pulling up my last notification, a text from Lola. I reached out to her this morning. I feel like she's been distant lately.

10:42 AM

> Hey, Bunny! I miss you.

11:56 PM

LOLA 🐰

179

Hey, ballerina. I miss you, too. How are things going?

12:15 PM

They're going well! My program is one step closer to being funded, and I kinda, sort of have a boyfriend.

WHAT?! Who??

Um, it's someone you know…

Noooo. You got back with Robby?!

I am totally happy for you, but it's a shock.

Yeah, I'm a little shocked, too. But he's grown up a lot and says he's in it for good this time. I'm trying not to get my hopes up, but it's been amazing so far.

Wow, well, if you're happy, I'm happy. I could use some good news about love still existing in the world these days.

Cryptic much? What's that supposed to mean?

Nothing, sorry. PMS-ing.

I don't buy that for a minute, and I tell her that. When she doesn't respond immediately, I return to my laundry. Once it is all put away, I work on deep cleaning my apartment while rocking out to VOILA's latest album. Before I know it, a few hours have passed.

I realize Robby texted me while I was in the cleaning zone. He'll be at the stadium talking with coaches and teammates as they prepare for tonight's game against the Kings. He pitched last night, though, so it should be a chill evening for him. Since he doesn't have to have game-day level focus, I decide we can have some fun, especially when I read his response.

2:36 PM

BEST COACH EVER

> You know I love a good mess, Kitten. Though, I prefer making it of you than a sandwich.

Damn. Is it hot in here? I was not prepared for that sexy of a comeback.

3:23 PM

> Someone is feeling spicy before his game.

I'm always spicy when it comes to you.

> Better behave, or you'll be hanging out in the dugout with a hard-on.

Nah, I'll blame it on the cup. Besides, haven't you seen the gossip sites ranking Baseball Bulges? It could move me up on the list. Rambo Rivera is currently #1.

> Yeah, that's what your ego needs, more validation. Don't get enough of that at home?

4:13 PM

Oh, I get plenty from hearing your sexy lips telling me how good I feel, how deep I'm getting, how I'm hitting the right spot, not to stop. Ring any bells?

I'll ring your bell

Awfully sassy when I'm hundreds of miles away and can't do anything about it, aren't you, baby?

Don't worry; I'll fix that when I get back Monday. We'll see how feisty you are with my fingers holding your orgasm hostage.

Don't you have warmups to get to?

Heading out soon. Talk after?

If I haven't melted into a puddle of goo by then, sure.

I'm sure my pretty girl will make it through. Don't play with yourself.

Excuse me?

You heard me, baby. I've got to go cheer on the guys, but if you're a good girl, I'll take care of you later.

I am both put off by his demand and turned on. Holy hell. He's been so sweet lately that I almost forgot he had this bossy side to him. Not one to take orders sitting down, though, I decide to fight fire with fire. Because I'm about to hop in the shower, I pile my clothes up and pull out my recently neglected, battery-operated friend. I snap a few photos of them together on the bed and then an audio message of the buzz.

I smile to myself as I think about riling Robby up, surrounded by his teammates. He'll have to school his reactions because I know he won't want to share this with them. He's one of those 'no one gets to hear or see you but me' types. For some reason, his impending discomfort delights me.

4:41 PM

BEST COACH EVER

> Kitten, trying to tease me?

> Fuck, I listened to the audio message. It doesn't sound like you're being a very good girl.

I don't know what you're talking about, babe. I'm always a good girl.

> Hmm, I think right now you're being a bit of a brat. Is someone needy without her man there?

Instead of responding, I send him a selfie of me in a silk nightie with my hair mussed from my shower bun. My nipples are hard and visible, poking through the thin fabric. In the mirror behind me, you can see the bottom of my ass cheeks since the nightie is short.

4:54 PM

Damn it, baby. I was joking about Baseball Bulges. Fuck you're sexy in that. Bring it to my place next time you come over.

I should be back at the hotel in about five hours. You better be ready to answer your phone.

Hmm, we'll see. I might be sleepy and that is past my bedtime...

Don't test me, pretty girl.

Seeing how worked up he is, I will absolutely be awake for that phone call. But it's too much fun to tease him when he can't do anything about it.

Almost exactly five hours later, my phone rings. Smiling, I answer it with the sexiest voice I can muster.

"Hello, my little Kitten," Robby grouses. "You think you're funny, don't you? Sending me hot as fuck pictures of you when I can't do anything about it? I've got a long memory, baby. I'll get you back."

"I don't know what you're talking about, babe. I was keeping you updated on my evening's activities," I reply innocently.

"That's all, huh? Tell me, baby, did you touch yourself, or were you a good girl for me?"

Hearing him say it out loud makes me clench my thighs together and suck in a breath.

"I think you were a good girl for me because you knew I'd reward you. Did my texts earlier turn you on, Care? Did my girl get turned on thinking about me using my fingers and tongue to tease her and eat all the sass out of her? You're always so sweet after I've made you cum. Do you need that tonight? You need me to help you get off?"

"Robby," I choke.

"Mmm, that's right, baby. That's the name you'll cry when you come for me in a few minutes. Where are you right now?"

"I'm in bed," I respond.

"Good. Is your toy nearby?"

"Yes?"

"Grab it," he demands.

I want to sass him, but this conversation has gotten me all hot and bothered again, and I need to take the edge off. Who am I to say 'no' if he wants to help me get there.

"Got it," I murmur.

"Good girl. Look at you listening. Now, turn it on, low. I want you to tease yourself with it. Rub it lightly on your clit but don't put it inside, not until I say."

Whimpering, I do as he says. I let out a keening noise as the vibrator rubs against my clit.

"That's it, pretty girl. Rub that vibe up and down your needy pussy. It misses me, doesn't it? Wishes it were me playing with it?"

Falling deeper into the moment, I don't respond. "Carina," he cajoles. "If you want me to keep going, you have to answer me."

"Yes," I blurt out.

"Yes, what, Kitten?"

"Yes, I wish it was you touching me."

He groans at my admission. "Me too. I wish it was my face between those toned thighs. I wish it was your hand stroking up and down my cock. I'm so hard picturing you playing with that pussy. Put the phone on speaker and turn your toy up higher."

I follow that command, too. Apparently, he was right about me being compliant when there is an orgasm on the line. I moan as the vibrator hits my clit at its higher setting.

"That's it. Put it inside just a little. Pretend it's my fingers pushing into you."

"Shit," I whimper.

"Feel good, baby? I know my cock feels so good with my hands running up and down pretending it's your hot, wet cunt. You're so fucking sexy, Carina."

"Yes, yes. It feels amazing."

"Keep going, fuck yourself harder," he rasps. "I wanna hear you come for me. I'm close. Get there with me."

"Ah," I moan. "Shit, Robby, close."

"That's it, Kitten, such a good girl. Come for me. Come with that toy in your pussy, listening to me stroke my rock-hard cock for you. Come on, Carina, you can do it for me. Come!"

With his last command, I combust. I've never come so hard unassisted before, and holy hell, was that hot as fuck. We're both panting.

"That was amazing," He huffs. "You okay?"

"God, yes," I reply, making him chuckle.

"Damn, it's been a while since we've done that," he comments. He's not wrong. We've had our fair share of phone sex when the team traveled in college, but I don't ever remember it being that good. I hum in response.

After a few minutes, we both clean up and crawl into bed.

"I wanted to ask you," he hedges, almost sounding nervous. "Would you come to my game on Thursday?"

"Of course," I say.

"Will you sit in the family suite?" Oh.

"You want me to sit in the family suite with, like, the families?"

I can hear the amusement in his voice when he responds. "Yeah, Care. You're my girl, and I'd love to know you're up there. Plus, I have a surprise for you."

"What kind of surprise?" I question.

"Well, if I told you, it wouldn't be a surprise, would it? You're going to love it, though."

"Okay, yes. I guess I can sit in the family suite."

"Thank you, baby. You won't regret it," he promises. "Now, tell me about your weekend."

Chapter Thirty

The "family" suite at Express Delivery Park is similar to the suite I was in a few weeks ago with my colleagues. If anything, it's less nice because the people in it aren't paying customers. It's for wives, girlfriends, and other relatives of the players. It has a homey, comfortable feel. The toy box in the corner and a block set that a little boy is playing with give it a slight pediatrician's office vibe.

When I walk in, several faces turn to study me. It's clear there are some cliques among the residents of this suite. Most glance at me curiously, but one group of ladies gives me major side-eye. If it weren't for my access badge, I think they might ask me if I was lost or who I knew here like some pompous frat party bouncer.

Eventually, one of the women saunters over to me in sky-high heels. Her outfit is more Rodeo Drive than a minor league baseball stadium.

"Hi," she says, eyeing me up and down. "I'm Madisyn, Turner's wife."

"Um, hi," I answer, not knowing who Turner is. "I'm Carina, Robby Becker's girlfriend."

"We know," she states, glancing back at her girl gang. "He hadn't had anyone come to see him all season. Color us surprised when he reserved space in the suite tonight. Players are usually discouraged from inviting their flavors of the month into the *family* box. Sends a bad message to the kids. I'm sure you understand. But I guess with a fancy Big Leaguer down here, they're bending the rules."

She gives me another once-over before she continues with her speech. "It's been a while since we had a cleat chaser in our midst. They usually sit down in the stands. A word of advice, having you in this suite doesn't mean he's going to commit. Don't take it personally when your time is up. The single ones go through women like they do bats. Enjoy the ride while you can; it won't last long."

I gape at her. First of all, she said "family" as if I'm here to corrupt the children. If anyone is going to traumatize them, it's her with how hard her boobs are trying to escape her tube top. Second of all, how dare she? There is nothing about me that resembles a cleat chaser. It disrespects me and Robby to assume he's out here banging girls and inviting them to his games. Other players could be doing that, but rude to assume he is one of them. He's never been that kind of guy.

"Listen," I retort in my hoity-toitiest voice. "I don't know who you are, and I don't know who your husband is, but I can assure you that I'm not a cleat chaser nor a 'flavor of the month.' You don't need to worry about me taking anything personally. My self-esteem isn't tied up in the man I'm attached to. I have far too many other things going on that validate my worth. I'll take a pass on the advice. Now, if you'll excuse me, my man is pitching, and I came to support him, not hold court with the head of the witchy WAGs welcoming committee."

With that, I grab a Pepsi—because what is it with stadiums only carrying Pepsi products—and sit out on the balcony to watch the game. I don't know when this promised 'surprise' is supposed to show up, but it can find me out here. It's chilly inside, and I'm not talking about the A/C.

We get through all the pregame festivities, and I settle in to watch the first inning. Robby is pitching, and I don't want to miss anything. After he successfully strikes out Lincoln's third batter, I hear some commotion in the suite. Loud whispers and fake-girl ass kissing catch my attention, but I don't turn around to see what all the fuss is about. Then, I hear a familiar voice yell out, "Holy hell! Tini Rini, it's really you!"

Next thing I know, a blonde blur has pulled me into a hug so tight I can hardly breathe. That nickname and hair can only mean one thing, the woman squeezing the life out of me is Robby's sister. Gazing over her shoulder, I spot Ralphie, her husband, which confirms my suspicions. I also see the mean girl wives' faces of shock that I know his sister. Yeah bitches, I'm the real deal.

"Alright, *zlatíčko*, let the woman go so she can talk," Ralphie says with a grin.

Morgan pulls back and blinks down at me. Yes, I say down because not only does she have a perfect face and hair, but she's also 5 '10", which makes her almost a head taller than me. "I'm sorry, I just missed her, and my dumbo little brother didn't tell me she'd be here tonight!"

I smile at her and squeeze her forearms. "Yes, your dumbo little brother didn't tell me you'd be here either, only that he had a surprise for me."

"A good one, I hope," Ralphie suggests.

"The best one," I answer. "Now, it seems we have a lot to catch up on. You're married now! How did you finally manage to tie this one down, Nokavik?"

"It took getting traded and some major groveling, but she finally let me make an honest woman out of her," he replies in his heavy accent. He may have been in the US for over a decade, but the Czech accent remains strong.

"Oh, you two!" Morgan chides. "I've missed having another girl around. I'm glad Bobert got his head out of his ass and won you back. I was secretly hoping this would happen when he told me where they were sending him."

"You didn't warn him I lived here? He seemed shocked to see me in my own city."

"And give him time to overthink?" she scoffs. "Not a chance. Clearly, it worked out in my favor. Now. I have a zillion questions to ask you, but I need to freshen up first. We came straight from the airport after our flight was delayed."

As Morgan leaves, Ralphie slides into the seat next to mine. "She really has missed you. She's made some friends in Tampa, but it's hard to find genuine friends in the circles she runs in. Many of my teammates' wives aren't the most welcoming to her big personality."

"You don't say," I deadpan. "If they're anything like the women inside that suite, I'm not surprised."

He laughs. "WAGs aren't known for being warm and fuzzy, especially when you've landed the big kahuna."

I roll my eyes. "'Landed' is a strong term."

"That's true; you can't land something that was yours to begin with." He smirks at my skeptical expression as he continues. "He may have acted the part, but I don't think Rob ever fully got over you. As I'm sure you know, he keeps his feelings close to the chest. He spends most of his time pretending everything rolls off his back. He never fooled me, though. I could see the tension oozing from trying to prove to his father that he was making the right choices. That weighed on him, even more so after losing you."

"You make it sound simple," I say. Talking to Ralphie has always been easy. He has this calming presence and an old soul. I've never met someone less judgmental and more able to mind his own business. "I want to believe that things will work out, that they'll be different this time because we're different, but I'm scared. Scared, I'll be the foolish girl who lets the same guy play her twice in the exact same way."

"I can see why you would fear that, but you could miss out on something great by not trying. A relationship was the last thing I was looking for the night I met Morgan, and she didn't want anything to do with me at first. But now I can't see a version of my world without her in it."

I sigh. "I believe you. But knowing the pressures he was dealing with doesn't change the past and doesn't change the fact that most of the issues that plagued us then will plague us now, even if on a smaller scale."

Ralphie nods his head knowingly before speaking. "My grandmother used to tell me, '*Odvážnému štěstí přeje.*' It means luck favors the brave. I can't tell you whether it will work out. But I can tell you that you won't know unless you try. I've had the privilege of watching him grow and mature these last few years. He's become someone worth taking a risk for. Plus, Morgan might kill him if he messes this up again. She's already planning sister-in-law trips for the two of you."

"Rob never let his loneliness show, but having slaved to make a name for myself in hockey, I know what those years were like without a partner." He peeks over at Morgan, who has made her way back to the suite and is talking to some of the WAGs with an energy and charisma I'll never possess.

For a brief second, the couple locks eyes as Morgan returns, and I swear I would crumble to have a connection as beautiful as theirs. The entire world disappears when they're together. He is her rock, and she is his sun. Is that what it could be if we gave it a shot? I know these two struggled with the schedule and temptation of professional sports. Morgan had her pick of men, but Ralphie proved himself repeatedly as the man who wanted her for her, not the trophy she could be. He treasures her above all else.

That's how Robby has made me feel since we got together again. It's how he made me feel in college. Maybe Ralphie is right. Maybe he's done the work to be able to handle this relationship. I won't know if I don't give us a shot.

By the final inning, Morgan and I have caught up on everything we missed the past few years as if no time passed at all. She can be a bad bitch when she wants, but deep down, Morgan has a heart of gold and a sensitive soul. I hate that she's struggling in Tampa.

"I knew you were behind the artwork!" she squeals. "He would never get me something like that on his own. He usually gets me a gift card to a spa or pays to have someone clean my house. I absolutely love it."

"I don't want to take all the credit. I gave him the name of some artists and stores. He picked it out himself," I defend.

"Well, either way, it fits in my house perfectly. It's clearly a sign."

"A sign for what?" I ask.

"That the two of you are meant to be! Fate brought you two back together"

"Okay, *zlatíčko*, I think you've had enough girl talk and seltzer tonight. Let's go say 'hi' to your brother, then get to the hotel and sleep," Ralphie cajoles, wrapping an arm around her waist and pushing her long blond hair out of her face. My insides are melting.

"Fine, fine," she says. "But first, we need a selfie! I have to document this magical reunion."

He shakes his head at his wife's antics and grabs her phone to get the best angle for us with his long arms. Morgan wraps her arms around me and smushes our faces together as Ralphie's other hand goes behind our seats.

"Perfect!" she shouts when he hands it to her. "We are on for dinner tomorrow night before his game, yes? We leave Saturday. I want to get in as much sister time as I can."

"Of course," I promise.

Chapter Thirty-One

As I enter work the next day, Kim and Alex are scrutinizing me expectantly while Haley is holding back her best shit-eating grin. "What's up, y'all?" I ask suspiciously.

"As you may recall, I have an affinity for sexy men wielding big sticks," Alex states.

"Okay..."

"And one hunky stick wielder I follow was tagged in an interesting picture last night. It featured a certain Italian imp who HAS BEEN HIDING HER CONNECTIONS TO HOCKEY HUNKS FROM HER COWORKERS."

"Huh?" Seeing my confusion, he shoves his phone in my face, and I see the selfie Morgan took of herself, Ralphie, and me at the game last night. "Oh."

"Oh? Oh?! That's all you have to say. Where did you see them? How did you see them? Why are you this chill about meeting them?

Unless... Was this not your first encounter? Carina 'I don't know your middle name' Ballerini, do you know them?"

I cringe equal parts, guilty and amused by his antics. I respond with nowhere near his energy, "I've known Morgan and Ralphie for years from back in my California days."

"HOW?!"

"Cool your jets, shouty pants. Morgan is my ex-boyfriend's sister, and Ralphie is obviously her husband. They were dating when my ex and I were together. I ran into them last night at the Blues Birds game, and we reconnected."

Alex clearly has more to say, but Kim cuts him off. "Hold on, we're not about to blow by the subtext of what you just said. Why were you at the game last night? In what I'm guessing is a suite based on the background."

"Robby invited me," I shrug.

"And Morgan was there to see...." Alex probes.

"Her brother," I answer cautiously.

"Wait," he says, throwing a hand up.

He scrolls for a few seconds and then pulls up a picture of Morgan and Robby with their mom for Mother's Day. It's clearly not from this year, but it is evident they're siblings.

"You dirty, little sneak!" he screams, showing the picture to Kim, who gasps and glares at me. Haley bites her lip to keep from laughing.

Kim jumps back into the conversation after getting over her shock. She wags her finger at me. "Are you telling me, Carina Adriana Ballerini, that you and our hot, MLB-playing softball coach dated in college? That he is the man from your stories? That you are his one that got away?"

I turn to Haley for help, but she is too busy laughing at my circumstances. "It is possible," I acquiesce. "That the he is him and the she is me."

"OMG! Pics or it didn't happen," Alex exclaims.

"Fine." Rolling my eyes, I pull out my phone. For obvious reasons, I don't have any pictures of us on my social media accounts, but my friends might still have some. I pull up a pic with Sean and Robby from a beach day we had the summer before their senior year.

"Wow, that is a flow he's got going," Kim comments.

I bark out a laugh. "It was. Imagine having a boyfriend with prettier hair than you."

She scoffs. "No one has prettier hair than you. I bet it was fun to grab onto, though."

I sputter, and she shrugs gleefully. "Anyway, to fill in the blanks I am sure you are wondering about. We met through my best friend, Tiffany. Her boy toy at the time was also on the team. We dated for two years, he got drafted, and then we broke up. He filled Haley and Kim in on those details a few weeks ago," I say to Alex. "Long story short, he struggled to balance the pressures of trying to make it to the MLB with a long-distance relationship, and I needed more than he was giving me.

"The club earlier this summer was the first contact we'd had in four years. He's made his intentions evident the last month, and we decided to try again after the party at Leo's. I don't know where this is going, but I am giving it a shot with an open mind. Now, everyone is all caught up."

They all peer up at me with warring emotions of sadness for my past, excitement for my presence, and curiosity.

Breaking the tension, Alex asks, "So, have you seen the Czech checker shirtless? Is he as beautiful in person as he is online?" Leave it to Alex to ask the hard-hitting questions.

Saturday, Haley, Kim, and I decided to have a girls' night out at karaoke. The Blues Birds have a game, but it is an early start. The first pitch went out at 6 p.m., meaning Robby and some of the guys may join us when they're done.

We had dinner at La Casita's, our usual haunt, to pregame our evening with carbs and margaritas. We then headed to The Shipyard

—a pirate-themed dive bar—to get on the list to sing our hearts out. We typically sing together as a group, but sometimes we dare one another to sing solo.

That is how I ended up on stage now, doing my best T. Swift impression featuring a surprising amount of audience participation considering the demographics of this crowd. As I get to the chorus, I spot a familiar form in a backward ball cap. Moving down to his face, I see his eyes sparkling as he soaks me in. It's a miracle I don't fumble the words.

Robby makes his way in front of the stage with two figures by his side—Leo and Justin, I assume. I can't find it within myself to break our eye contact as I finish my song. The crowd is clapping, but all I see is him as I put my mic on the stand and take his outstretched hand. His smile is wide as he grips my hips and slides me down his body onto the ground.

"Great job, Kitten," he says into my ear. "A little disappointed not to hear Carrie, but excellent song choice,"

"Thank you," I reply. "The girls chose it. Kim said that performance was my punishment for being 'Sneaky Bear—the least favored of all the Care Bears.'"

He laughs and nods his head. "Morgan's post gave you away, huh? I had my first pap sighting since I got here this morning. I guess living in anonymity was always on a clock. You need a refill, baby?"

"Yes, please," I answer. Robby and Leo go to the bar to get drinks for the group, and I join Haley, Kim, and Justin at the table. A terrible rendition of *Pour Some Sugar on Me* plays in the background as I tune into the conversation.

"Come on," Kim whines. "You have to sing at least one song."

"And what do I get if I do?" Justin challenges.

"As much as you can handle," Kim volleys back.

The other guys come back, and Leo replies, "Oh, we're definitely going up there."

I laugh as the color leaves Robby's face. "Good luck getting this one up there," I remark, pointing to him. "I tried for years and was only successful after a couple Jäger Bombs and an immense amount of peer pressure."

"I think you've got everything you need to persuade him this time," Kim retorts.

Robby glances at me shaking his head as I turn on my puppy dog eyes. "Please, RobbyRob. It would make me so, so, so happy."

"Care, you know I don't sing."

I push out my lip into an exaggerated pout. "Pretty please with peaches on top," I beg. Everyone else starts chanting his name.

After a few chants, he finally caves and agrees, but only if he gets to pick the song and Leo takes the lead. Thirty minutes later, the three hunky baseball players make their way to the stage and queue up their music. The girls and I get another round from the waitress and settle in for the show.

I am delighted when I hear the opening chords to *Girlfriend* by *NSYNC. Memphis loves it some JT. As promised, Leo takes the lead and serenades the crowd. Justin hams it up in back up, but his gaze keeps darting back to our table and a certain redhead, eyes are full of mischief and unspoken promises.

As the song reaches the bridge, I am gobsmacked to see Robby take over lead vocals. Staring right at me, he sings the bridge of *NSYNC's *Girlfriend*.

Is it possible to internally combust? Because I am going to. The timber of his voice, the smolder in his eyes, and the sensation of being his sole focus are revving me up in all the right ways. I am going to melt into a puddle of tension before he gets back over here.

He winks at me as he finishes his part. That m-fer knows the affect he as on me. I fan myself as they complete the song to a round of uproarious applause. I wonder how long we have to stay before I can drag Robby out of here and back to my place? I will be counting down the minutes.

Chapter Thirty-Two

Robby

I can't believe I let myself get conned into singing karaoke. If I'm going to do this, I am going to do this right. I submit our song choice and down some liquid courage as I remember how Carina glowed on that stage. Her butterfly two-piece outfit was showing off her beautiful tan skin and petite frame, and giving her an ethereal appearance.

She's always had a good voice and frequently subjects me to mini-concerts in the car. But damn, something about seeing her up there being admired by others does something for me. It takes my mind back to another time I found myself in a similar situation.

Sean, Blake, Taylor, and I walk into the tiki bar, scanning over the crowd. We see Tiffany and Kelsea at a table. "Where is Carina?" I ask as I roll up.

With a smirk, Tiffany points to the side of the stage where an emo kid is currently screaming some song by The All-American Rejects I vaguely recognize. "She's up next."

The music ends, and I watch the emo guy exit the stage to mixed reception. A visibly nervous Carina approaches the mic and takes a deep breath. As the music plays, Carina transforms before my eyes into a country vixen singing about the revenge she'd get on a cheating boyfriend. She is gorgeous up there in the stage lights.

Gaining some swagger, she saunters down the stairs and walks toward our group. I try not to boil over with jealousy as she serenades a few guys along the way. She stops right in front of me and puts her hand on my chest as she sings, eyes locked with me.

Present day...

I'm pulled out of my memory as Leo slaps me on the shoulder. "We're up, Big Leaguer." Great. Let's get this over with.

I hardly remember any of the performance; I might have blacked out for it. I may or may not have hallucinated Carina fanning herself during the bridge. Good. I'm glad I affect her half as much as she affects me because I'm on fire every time she's around. As the guys and I return to the table, I smirk at the lust in her eyes. Soon, baby, my gaze promises. Soon.

I can't remember the last time I had this much fun at a bar. Usually, my Nashville teammates and I spend our time in VIP sections where we won't be bothered. Recently, we've mainly been hanging out at our apartments. Most of us live in the same building or at least share a crash pad for late nights/early mornings.

Going out was a lot of fun in the early years, but it got tedious the longer I was in the majors. Most nights were full of women trying to get close to us for all the wrong reasons or fans hoping for a picture. Despite the pap outside the airport this morning when I took Morgan and Ralphie to catch their flight, it's quiet here—interruption-wise, anyway.

Part of my apathy for the bar scene is probably because I haven't been out with a girl I genuinely enjoy spending time with for a while. Being around a woman who doesn't want something—money or clout typically—from me has been rare. Most of the teammates I hang out with are single. Kent had a steady hookup for a while, but they were never as serious as she wanted to be. It's nice to hang out with a group of women, knowing none of them are with you for status. It's even nicer hanging out and having your girl by your side. I forgot what this was like.

I envision how it could be if I can convince Carina to come to Nashville with me. Being around professional athletes won't phase her. She's used to the types of personalities that make up a team. She spent years hanging out with my buddies in college—even without me, apparently.

I know she'll get along with Miller. He is a big softie and one of the chillest dudes I know. She'll even find Kent delightful. He has a playboy persona, but only with the gold diggers who try to use him, never to someone's partner. His mother would beat him if he was disrespectful. Filipino mothers are not to be messed with.

I loved having her in the family suite earlier this week. Knowing she's there cheering me on gives me an extra boost to play well. Getting to come home to her from road games would make it that much sweeter. The idea of waking up with her in my bed—my real bed—causes tingles in my chest and my crotch. I've got to convince her to come back with me. I know it's the right choice for us. It could be a great opportunity for her career as well. I have connections in the city through the team and friends that could help her create any nonprofit she wants.

Before I can get too lost in planning details, I notice the girls giggling over something Leo said. Carina's face is flushed, and the way she's watching me tells me her mind is somewhere entirely more wicked than mine. It doesn't take much for mine to join hers. We've been here for a few hours already, and they've been drinking since 7 p.m. We'll need to call it a night soon if these ladies want to be functional tomorrow.

Carina slinks over to where I'm sitting and wraps her arms around my waist, kissing me before turning back to the group. Shifting forward on my stool, I slide my leg out and settle it between hers, giving her a perch to sit on. She's not one for heels, so I bet her feet are killing her. I feel the heat radiating between her legs when she grinds down on me slightly and peeks over her shoulder at me. Yep, that's our cue.

I turn to the guys and say, "I think it's time to get my girl somewhere more private. Can you make sure Haley and Kim get home okay?"

Justin nods, wrapping his arms around Kim and caging her against the table as he whispers something in her ear. I need to make a note to ask Carina what is up with those two. Haley and Leo down the rest of their drinks and gather our things.

"Ready to go, pretty girl?" I coo. Carina nods at me and slides off my leg, and wraps her arms around one of mine. Using my free hand, I pull out my phone and book an Uber back to her place.

Ten minutes later, we pull up to her apartment and say goodbye to Jerold, our driver. He was kind enough to keep the karaoke going so Carina could sing the whole way home. When I lock her door and turn to see my girl staring back at me. She's already ditched her shoes and is just wearing the sexy two-piece set.

"What's that look?"

"What look?"

"The one you're giving me right now that says you want to eat me alive."

She sashays her way over to where I am and runs her hands up my arms until they clasp together behind my neck. Pushing up to her tiptoes, she kisses my jaw and trails her lips along my neck. "Maybe I do," she whispers.

"Me first," I reply. With that, I grab her thighs and force her up my body. Her legs lock around my waist. I spin us around and push her back against the door as I descend on her mouth. I grind my hard length against her warm heat until I tear a moan from her body. I smile as I keep devouring her mouth. My tongue licks in and out battles with her until she concedes. Once I decide she's good and ravaged, I walk us back toward her couch. Resting her ass on the back, I pull back and gaze down to her.

"You're so fucking gorgeous, Care. Have I told you that?"

"Not today," she sasses.

"Cheeky little thing tonight, aren't you?" I ask. One hand travels up her throat to grip her jaw while the other squeezes her hip in warning. "Careful, baby. You remember what happens when you're sassy. Is that what you want?"

"Yes," she exhales.

"Mmm, of course, it is. You love when I run my tongue on your body and orgasm you into submission," I say right before nipping at her lip and giving her another punishing kiss.

"I dig this little skirt, babe. It's going to make getting to your pretty pink pussy that much easier," I comment, toying with the hem of the garment. I slowly push it up, and she lifts her hips to help.

"Someone is eager." My teasing causes her to make a mewling noise into my mouth. "Aww, does my Kitten want something? What's wrong, sweetheart? What do you need?"

"Please..." she moans.

"God, I love when you beg. Tell me what you need, and I'll give it to you. Say the words," I coo.

"Please, Robby, make me cum. I need you."

"Fuck," I hiss. That was hotter than I expected it to be. "Don't worry, baby. I got you. I'm going to eat that needy pussy until you can't think straight."

With that, I drop to my knees and rip off her panties. I kiss my way up her thighs giving little bites with my ascent. I spread her thighs back, and her hands go to my head to help her balance on the back of the couch. My face is the perfect height to stare straight into her glistening cunt.

Deciding I've teased her enough already tonight, I unceremoniously lick up her seam and start swirling circles around her clit. She immediately squirms, causing my hands to tighten on her thighs. She may end up with bruises tomorrow, but I am too swept up in giving her pleasure to care about that right now.

I lick, suck, and toy with her sensitive nub as she trembles. "That's it, Kitten. You're so close. I can feel it. Give me what I want. Come all over my face. Come on my face so you can come on my cock next."

She lets out a loud moan. There is no doubt her neighbors heard, but damn if it didn't make my cock impossibly harder. I bring my thumb down to toy with her clit while I fuck my tongue in and out of her, wiggling it against her quivering walls. I hum into her, making her feel vibrations everywhere.

Rubbing my thumb faster, it doesn't take much longer for her to totally fall apart. Gazing up at her, head thrown back, mouth open, I swear there is no more beautiful sight in the world. Giving her a few more licks for good measure, I rise from where I was kneeling and take the rest of her clothes off. Before I can pull off my own, she bats my hands away, and hers shoot to the button of my shorts. Shucking them and my boxers both down my legs, she maneuvers us around so I'm sitting down on the couch.

Her perfect tits are level with my face as she unbuttons my shirt. Like any red-blooded, straight man, I suck them into my mouth, causing her to buck. I peer into her eyes and give her a playful nip as I continue to toy with her. As she finishes my buttons, she pushes my shoulders back further, forcing me against the back of the couch.

She grabs my wallet from my pants and takes out a condom which she ever so slowly rolls down my shaft. She then moves to straddle my lap and seats herself right above my hard-as-steel cock, teasing herself with the tip.

"Kitten..." I warn. She hums in response as she slowly lowers herself down. We both let out groans when she is fully seated. She wiggles her hips to find an angle that she rubs her all the right ways, and then lifts back up, slamming herself down until I see stars. God, this girl. We're in for a long night.

Chapter Thirty-Three

As I bounce myself up and down on Robby, I can't help clawing at his shoulders. I swear his dick imprinted itself on my pussy all those years ago because it feels like it was made for me. Neither of the other guys I was with after him ever made me feel this. Sure, that isn't a long list, but I doubt there is a man out there who can master my body the way he does. It hits every spot inside me perfectly. I wanted to go slow and tease him, but why punish myself?

His mouth is still toying with my nipples as his hands land on my hips to help me balance. It seems he's done giving me full control because he is now meeting me thrust for thrust, and I can't get enough. My legs tremble as I clench around him, but I'm not ready for this to be over yet. Sensing that, Robby slows down my rhythm and brings my face to his, and plants a soft kiss on my lips. "You ride me so well, baby, but I'm nowhere near done with you."

He guides me up and down his hard cock at a leisurely pace that is driving me crazy. I have no idea how he maintains such control, but I'm determined to make him lose it. I clench around him, causing him to falter and allowing me more room to move. I grind my hips down on him and lean backward, adjusting our angle. He fills me up even more this way. His hands move to my ass, and he swats it hard enough to sting before grabbing both cheeks.

"You want it deeper, baby? I can give it to you deeper," he says.

"Yes," is all I am able to moan out.

With that confirmation, he lifts me off him and flips me over to my knees with my chest leaning against the back. He gives my ass another slap and pulls my hips back before slamming in. I let out a gasp at the intrusion before my entire body shutters. Yes. This is what I needed. He's using his powerful legs to thrust into me over and over again.

"Fuck yes, baby, that's it. You feel so good. You're taking this cock like it was made for you."

"Yes," I answer. "Mine."

"That's right, Care. It's yours, all yours. You gonna come on your cock, baby? You gonna clench around it so hard you mold it to your pussy? I know you want to, baby. Show this cock who it belongs to."

His dirty words do it for me, and my vision goes white as I come around him. I'm vaguely aware he pumps a few more times before following behind. As he pulls out, I let out a soft hiss and collapse onto the arms. I sense his warmth leave me as he goes to dispose of the condom.

When he returns, he carefully wipes me clean and scoops me up bridal style. As he carries me to my room, I ask, "How can you carry me? My legs are Jell-O."

"My whole job is to hone my physique. I got stamina for days."

"For days, huh? Isn't most of what you do standing around and then sitting in between? That doesn't require that much stamina," I quip.

"Oh, Kitten, you're asking for trouble tonight, aren't you? And here I was gonna tuck you in and spoon you until we both pass out."

"Was?" I question.

"Was," he replies, "Now I'm going to have to show you exactly how much stamina I have. Let's see how many times my pretty girl can come until she taps out, hmm?"

With that, he tosses me onto the bed and proves that despite all the standing, he does indeed have the stamina to match his claims.

Chapter Thirty-Four

Robby

After a leisurely morning sleeping in, we make our way to brunch. I have a game this afternoon, but when I complained about the quality of guacamole in Memphis, Carina declared I hadn't been to the right place. She insisted we get "the best guac she's ever put in her mouth" before I leave for the stadium. That is high praise from a girl I know has had authentic guacamole in Mexico.

As we eat, I ask Carina how her job compares to what she thought she would be doing when she got her degree. Boy, did that open the floodgates, but I think it may help me better develop my plan to bring her home with me.

"My job is fine. I am helping those in an underserved community and making a difference. That's all I can ask for."

"But..." I prod.

"But there is more we could be doing. Camila has such an 'if it ain't broke, don't fix it' mindset that she is missing the forest through the trees. There is more we could be doing to serve our clients—other ways we could be making their lives easier. She is rarely willing to try new things for fear of 'wasting resources,' but she also doesn't want to try new things to bring in donations."

Dipping a homemade tortilla chip in the heavenly guac—yes, she was right, this guacamole rivals any I've ever had—I ask her for an example.

"Google has this grant program that gives you free money to run search ads if you're a local nonprofit. Literally free advertising. But she won't let Alex set it up because she is afraid it will attract too many people needing our services, and we'll get overwhelmed. We tried to explain that you can tailor it with whatever messaging you want, and we could target donors, but she won't listen."

"Is that what happened with your food trailer?"

"Yes and no. Yes, she absolutely shot down the idea because it isn't something we've seen in the area before, but, in this case, she isn't wrong about the money. There is a hard cost associated with the truck's purchase, plus ongoing fuel and maintenance costs. Ideally, I'd want to hire a client to staff it instead of a volunteer, which would be additional money. I understand it's a risk, but there are programs similar to what I'm proposing in other markets. Case studies show they can raise the quality of life in some of these food deserts and eventually self-fund."

"You know," I mention casually, "the offer still stands for me to fund your program. Or I could buy the truck for you."

She shakes her head. "I can't take your money, Robby. You worked hard for that."

"Eh," I tease playfully.

That gets her to roll her eyes. "Fine, your agent worked hard for that."

Grabbing her hand, I say to her seriously, "It's not you taking my money, Kitten. It would be a donation to a worthy cause. Now, if you want to be the one who shows gratitude to me for my donation, I wouldn't say no to that..."

"You are too much," she smiles. "For now, I want to stick with seeing how this tournament goes; if we lose, we can discuss a sponsorship."

"You got it, baby. Although, with how good I've heard your coach is, I think you got this thing in the bag."

"He does seem to know his stuff. Plus, he's easy on the eyes."

"Handsome, is he?" I ask.

"Mhmm," she confirms. "Handsome, strong, too bad he's got an ego the size of a bus."

"You brat," I chuckle, tossing a chip her way.

We slip back into casual conversation, but what she said has my wheels turning. Volunteering with Jalen has awakened this drive in me to do good that has been dormant for years. When I was with Carina, she always pulled it out of me. She brings out the best in me. She makes me want to be a better man, a better human.

I would love to help her more, but I know she won't let me. She's proud. Don't get me wrong, she asks for help when she needs it but trying to take something off her plate without her asking? You better wear a helmet.

I wish I could tell her how brilliant her ideas are and that she should branch out on her own, but she's too practical to hear that right now. This is still too new to remind her that I promised we would form a nonprofit together when I made it to the big show. That doesn't mean I can't get the wheels in motion, though.

While Carina runs to the bathroom, I email my agent and my PR rep, Molly. I ask them to research ways I can plug into the community and get guidance on creating my own nonprofit. I ask for information on the market because I want any organization I am a part of to make a real impact on the community. This isn't a publicity project; this is part of my plan to bring my girl home with me.

Later that afternoon, it's family with FaceTime with the Beckers. Morgan is gushing about the vacation she and Ralphie went on now that his season is over. He adds in a grunt or affirmation when prompted by his over-enthusiastic wife.

Mom's favorite doctor is retiring, and she is going on and on about how the young ones 'weren't trained how they used to be' and 'don't understand what nurses do.' She also provides an update on my Aunt Gail's garden and the midlife crisis currently gripping my Uncle Bill. Personally, I believe he's living his best life after Aunt Janine left him for her yoga instructor.

Per usual, my dad had little to share.

When it's my turn, I talk about how the season is going and the moves I'm making to found an organization in Nashville. Morgan sees right through that motivation and mentions how wonderful it was to see Carina and how she's making all these plans for the two of them, such as couples' trips for the four of us in January. Mom is thrilled for me and happy to potentially reconnect with Carina as well. They weren't super close because my parents were always working, but they got along when they did see each other.

My mom elbows Dad as he has noticeably not said anything. "Frank isn't that great? Carina is back in Rob's life. You always loved her," Mom prompts.

"She was a nice girl. Way too good for this one, that's for sure," he comments.

"I agree with you there, Dad. She's way too good for me, but I'm not going to tell her if she doesn't already know."

"C'mon, Bobert! You're a good guy. You've been doing great things since you got to Memphis with the softball league and volunteering at that middle school. I could tell you made some strides for the better when I saw you last week. Not that there was anything wrong with you, but it is nice seeing you focus on something outside of baseball for a change. I can tell how much happier and lighter you are. I'm proud of you," Morgan praises.

A snort comes out of my father before he remarks, "I won't hold my breath that this 'new leaf' doesn't get blown over again the second he's back in Nashville. All those old haunts and temptations. That kind of girl won't put up with being second best to your 'lifestyle.'"

I've never seen air quotes be so aggressive. What Dad says has my blood boiling. He doesn't know me. He didn't have the time growing up to guide the boy I was. He sure as hell hasn't tried to get to know the man I've become. I've worked my ass off to get where I am in my sport. I'm working hard now to be a man that deserves a sweet thing like Carina. But I'll be damned if he'd know that either since these weekly family calls are the only time we talk.

I've been silent long enough. I don't need to take his belittlement anymore. I've done everything I can to be a good son, a good brother, a good person. Sure, I've screwed up along the way. But I've grown from every mistake I've made. I've never been arrested, never been caught in a scandal. My life is tame compared to most guys in the league. Fuck him for not giving me credit for the work I've put in.

"You know what, Dad," I say. "I don't know your problem with me, but I am getting tired of your lack of faith in me. I've been nothing but respectful toward you my entire life. I've tried to pay you back for everything you invested in me and worked to try and be a man you can be proud of. I played in the fucking All-Star game last year, for Chrissake. What more do you want from me?"

"I don't *want* anything from you," he spits. "Your mom and I don't need your money. We didn't pay for things growing up to give you a tab. We did it because that's what parents do. What I wanted from you was to make an honest living and be an honest man. I don't see how you can be either of those things running around the country chasing a dang ball. Won't last."

"I'm sorry that being a professional athlete is such a disappointment for you. Most parents would be thrilled their kid was able to make his dream a reality and support himself doing it. You're right. It won't last, but lucky for me, I manage my money well and can move into other areas of the sport whenever I retire. I'm sorry my success is upsetting to you, but I am done trying to get your approval. It's clear I'm never going to get it."

"Rob..." my mother interjects.

"Don't bother, Mom. I'm done with this conversation. I've got to get ready to go chase around a ball."

With that, I hang up, grab my shit, and go to the field.

While I'm in the locker room doing my pregame prep, I get a text from Miller in our group chat. I swear that guy has a sixth sense of when our emotions are volatile.

4:46 PM

PAPA 🐻

> Becker, I hear you're pitching again tonight. Feeling good?

> Hey, man. Everything is feeling amazing. It's as if the sprain never happened.

> That's great. Think they'll be bringing ya back up soon?

My chest tightens. On the one hand, I miss my teammates in Nashville and the life I've built there. I worked hard to get to that level and want to get back to the top of my game. On the other hand, the idea of not seeing Carina all the time makes me want to puke. In only a few short weeks, she's already embedded herself so deeply under my skin, I'm not sure I could function without her. I know we'd figure it out, but it's smooth and easy right now.

> Not sure. It should be soon, based on the timeline Doc gave me.

> How are you doing with that?

I should have known he'd want to talk about the hard topics. He knows this will be a harder transition for me than originally anticipated.

> Hopeful, excited, and like I want to puke, not being a short drive away from my girl.

> I get that. You two will figure it out. It will be tough, but if she's as gone for you as you are for her, there's no other option.

> I hope you're right, Cap.

Seemingly tired of our touchy-feely conversation, Kent pipes in.

CASANONO

> You see the big trade news this morning? *Miss Honey lowering glasses GIF*

> Damn, I forgot how fine she was. That movie is seriously underrated.

That doesn't sound good. Ignoring his text comment on the beauty of the teacher from *Matilda*, I shoot off a message before scouring through my email for team updates.

> Nah, I was with Carina and then battling it out on the weekly family call. What news?

> Front office traded Sanchez for Jones.

> Derrick Jones?

> Yup. Ain't that a shot to the nuts. *Michael Jordan "and I took that personally" GIF*

> WTF.

PAPA 🐻

Sorry, man, I thought you'd heard by now. Don't let it get in your head. They don't always consider team chemistry and the big picture when making these deals.

I know, but shit. Of all the fucking guys to trade for, it had to be him.

CASANONO

Don't worry. We'll hide some smelly shit in his locker before he gets here so he has a nice welcome.

PAPA 🐻

I get it. But like I said, just focus on your game and doing what you're doing. We're all excited to get you back in town and meet the girl who managed to rile up your chill exterior.

CASANONO

Who knew Becker was such a softy on the inside?

Whatever, man, I can't wait for a girl to knock you on your ass. Don't be so shocked when the one you want won't put up with your shit.

CASANONO

Unsubscribe GIF I'll pass on that. Chasers and Broadway bridesmaids keep me plenty busy. Go show those little leaguers what you got and get your ass back up here. The commune is lonely without you.

PAPA 🐻

It is so lame that you call our condos "the commune." It makes no sense.

CASANONO

Sure, it does. It's the place where we all live together and share things.

As they continue to bicker in the group chat, I shove my phone in my locker and get my head ready to play some ball.

Chapter Thirty-Five

Carina

It's the eighth and final game of the charity tournament. We are currently 6-1. The team we're playing is only one game behind us at 5-2. If they win, we'll be tied. Since they would have beaten us, that would be the tie-breaker. Winning means we automatically make it to the championship game. Losing means we have to 'play-in,' which would be risky because we barely beat some of the teams as it was. There is no guarantee everyone would be able to make it to all the games as the they would be on a condensed schedule.

It's the top of the fourth, and the score is 1-3. Melina struck out, but Alex is on first, and Jim is up to bat. He hits a nice single that sends him to first and Alex to second. It's my turn up, and to say I'm nervous is an understatement.

After four pitches, the count is 2-2. My heart is hammering in my chest as I prepare for the next throw. I let out a sigh of relief when it, too, is a ball. This next pitch decides my fate in this inning. I'm either on base with a ball or hit, or I'm heading back to the dugout, giving us two outs with two potential scorers.

I watch the pitcher survey the field and wind up their pitch. It's almost slow motion as I see the catcher have to stand to grab it. Ball. Thank goodness. I should probably wish I hit it, but I will take what I can get. Not that I was afraid of having to hit it, but I'll take an easy on-base if I can get one.

The bases are loaded as Curtis heads to the plate. It seems as if the pitcher got all the balls out of her system because the first two throws are strikes. Eek. "Come on, Curtis! You got this!" I yell.

When I peek over to Robby at third, I see him give Curtis a signal. Curtis nods and shakes out his shoulders. He must have been telling him to loosen up. As the next pitch heads straight down the middle, I hear Curtis bat before I see it. I freeze, watching it fly toward left field.

"RUN!" Leo is yelling beside me. Oops. I see Curtis barreling toward first, and I take off. When I get close to second, Robby motions for me to keep going. I stop at third and survey the scene. Alex and Melina both scored! The game is now tied.

I beam at Robby. "We tied it!"

"We sure did. But let's not count all our chickens yet, Kitten. We need to get you and Curtis home and hold on to the lead."

"Such a Logical Louie," I sass, rolling my eyes.

"I call it like I see it, babe. We've still got half a game to play. And that's assuming you can get home and secure us the lead."

"Yeah, yeah."

He gives me a chastising look. "Diane is up, babe. Get ready to run. Curtis doesn't have to necessarily make it to third. It isn't a force out. Watch me for a signal."

I nod. When Diane's bat hits the ball, I take off running. Unfortunately, she didn't hit it far, and now the pitcher has it. Instead of throwing it to first, he tosses it to the catcher. Uh oh. I turn to run back to third, only the ball beats me there. I turn again toward home.

I'm in the middle of a game of keep away with the catcher and third baseman, except I'm trying to keep away from them.

Deciding to go for it, I burst toward home. Except all the turning created a divot in the ground. My left foot gets caught, and down I go. Holy crap on a cracker, that hurt. My ankle feels like it was ripped off. I almost look down to see if it is still there.

Before I can spring back up, the catcher is there, tagging me out. Well, that sucks. I try to hop back up, but my ankle gives out under my weight, and I begin to tumble back down. Before I can hit the ground, strong arms grab my waist and keep me up. I peer up and see Robby's concerned gaze staring at me.

"Are you okay, baby?"

"Yes," I cringe. "My ankle hurts, but I think I tweaked it." Glancing around, I see people staring at us. We aren't hiding our relationship anymore, but we don't exactly flaunt it all over town.

"Robby, I'm out. I've got to get back to the dugout," I say, struggling to get out of his arms.

"You're not walking on that," he replies as he scoops me up bridal style and carries me to the dugout. When we get there, he sits me down on the bench and grabs his bag.

"What can we do?" Haley asks.

"Go get some ice from the concession stand," he directs.

"It's fine. You're overreacting," I exclaim.

Giving me a stern expression as he rolls up a towel and puts it on top of his bag, he replies, "It's not fine. I'll text the trainer and have her evaluate it after the game. Don't. Move. Keep your ankle elevated and keep ice on it until I get back from finishing out this inning. You're out for the rest of the game."

"But..."

"The only 'but' I want to hear anything about is yours sitting right here until I get back," he huffs. He gives his best, 'this is not up for discussion' face.

I do as he asks—demands, really, but who's counting. I sit there and watch Curtis and Diane score two runs to give us a 5-3 advantage. Then, I sit the rest of the game while putting ice on my ankle every other inning. Overkill if you ask me, but Robby isn't leaving much room to argue.

Thankfully, we pull out the win at 6-4 and are in the finals! As much as I'd love to celebrate, the adrenaline has worn off, and my ankle hurts like a mother. Not that I'd say it out loud, but it may be more serious than I initially thought. Ugh.

As soon as the game ends, Robby whisks me off to the PT room. We are greeted by an overly bubbly blonde who is giving Robby a sultry look as we enter. Absolutely not. Is she blind? The man is literally carrying me.

"Becker," she purrs, batting her eyelashes. "I didn't expect to see you today? Miss me already?"

"Hey, Anastasia," he responds. Barf. Of course, that's her name. And of course, she resembles a Russian supermodel. "I was coaching my softball team, and Vince Coleman here got tripped up."

"How nice of you to bring her." She rubs against his arm as she passes by the table. "How's your elbow? Carrying her in here didn't aggravate anything, did it? We hadn't discussed you adding weight training to your routine yet."

Um, excuse me. Is she calling me fat? Because hell, no. As much as I say I am not, I am the pipsqueak Sean claims. Robby can bench double my weight on a bad day.

"Doc let me start weight training again a couple weeks ago. But no, it's fine. We're here about her ankle."

"I see," she answers bored, assessing me.

Sitting on the end of the table, I grab one of Robby's hand and pull it into my lap. He angles himself behind me and strokes my hair with his free hand. Anastasia takes in the motion, and I see her stiffen as she surveys my ankle. Yeah, that's right, this man is mine. She turns my ankle a little too hard, and I let out a whimper.

"Careful!" Robby barks.

"Sorry, I had to test the mobility," she apologizes, giving me a faker smile than a pageant queen. I grumble in response.

"You twisted it. Nothing too serious, but you'll need to stay off it completely until Saturday and take it easy for about a week afterward," she states flatly.

"Tweaked my ass," I hear Robby snort. I glare up at him.

"Are you sure it's only twisted? It hurts," I admit.

"Yep. I'm sure. If your pain tolerance is that low, I can give you some meds to take tonight to ease the pain. It should be considerably better pain-wise tomorrow as long as you don't put any pressure on it," Anastasia states dryly. "Do you have someone you can stay with for a few days, a husband or roommate, maybe?"

I give her a quizzical expression because it seems obvious that Robby and I are more than friendly, and I'm not wearing a ring.

"I can stay with my mom."

She gives a nod and wraps my ankle.

"Your mom and Steve leave for their cruise tomorrow, remember?" Robby reminds me. Uh, no. Obviously, I did not remember that. Crap. Mom and Steve are celebrating their belated anniversary with a cruise. I could ask Lola to come down if she has the PTO, but she's been acting weird lately. Haley would stay with me if I asked, but I hate to burden anyone.

"I'll be fine on my own."

"Hell no, you won't," Robby declares. "Not with the steps up to your porch."

"I have to agree with your coach here," Ana says. "You shouldn't be taking any stairs until this weekend, and I can't in good conscience give you these pain meds if you're going to be alone."

"She'll stay with me," Robby replies as he grabs the meds.

Before I object, he levels me with his no-nonsense face and grabs my face between his hands. "No arguing, Kitten. No girl of mine is staying on her own when I could take care of her. It's my job. Let me do it. I'll take you by your place to get your shit. Your

boss will understand that you need to work from home the rest of
the week."

I want to push back. I do. But the shock and jealousy on Anastasia's face is too good. I shouldn't take such pride in his show of owner-
ship, but I do. I bite back a smug grin as he takes the pills from her
hand, picks me back up in his arms, and carries me out of the room.
I'm ashamed to admit I give her a finger wave behind his head as we
leave.

Chapter Thirty-Six

Robby

I pop into the concession stand as we leave the ballpark and grab a bottle of water so Carina can take her pain meds. She isn't usually one to complain. It must be hurting for her to mention it. When we make it back to her apartment, I can tell the meds kicked in. She giggles and mock salutes when I place her on the couch and tell her not to move.

My first stop is her bathroom. I grab a bag and fill it with her shower stuff. I toss in her toothbrush and other basic hygiene supplies. I know she takes her skincare seriously, but I don't for the life of me know what she would need. I grab everything off her counter and medicine cabinet and dump it in the bag with a shrug. Good enough, I can always come back.

In her room, I grab enough comfy clothes to last her a few days. When I get her pajamas, I can't help but smirk when I notice what shirt is on top of the pile. It's the one she left my house in after that first night we were together again. Smiling to myself, I opt for no PJs. She can wear my shirts while she stays with me. I'm certainly not going to complain about that.

While grabbing her things, I decide to place a grocery delivery order. I doubt she's going to want to eat the healthy shit the nutritionist meal prepped for me. I add some of her favorites to the cart and maybe a few indulgences for me. Once that is done, I grab the bags and haul them to my car. I go back inside to get her but stop in my tracks when I spot her crying into a pillow.

"What's wrong, pretty girl? Are you in pain?" I ask as I examine her.

"No," she cries. "I missed you. You were gone for *so* long."

"Baby, I was only outside for two minutes."

"Not now. I've missed you always—when you didn't want me anymore." Ah, I got it. Painkillers are bringing up some old shit, it seems.

"Hey," I say as I cup her face and wipe away the tears with my thumbs. "I always wanted you. I was young and stupid."

She shakes her head violently. "No, I was too much. Too needy. It's going to happen again now. I need you again, and you're gonna go away and not want me anymore. I'll be sad when you do because I love you, and Sean isn't here to make me eat pizza, and Tiffany's voodoo curse obviously didn't work last time."

"Tiffany put voodoo curses on me?" She nods. Rude.

"Yes, but she knows a real witch now, so it would probably be a different kind of curse. Maybe it would make your hair fall out."

That's only slightly concerning. Not the part to focus on Becker. "Baby, you aren't going to need to curse my hair. I'm not going to leave you again. I never even wanted to leave you the first time. I'll have to go back to Nashville, but that doesn't mean I'll let you go. You're mine for good. 5ever and always."

"5ever?" that makes her giggle, my second favorite sound in the world. "You promise?"

"I promise, Kitten," I respond, stroking her face.

"I love when you call me Kitten," she whispers, nuzzling into my hand.

Grinning, I respond, "I know, Kitten. I love calling you it. It describes you perfectly. Sometimes you're my cuddly little kitty, sometimes my sassy tigress, and sometimes my sexy little hellcat."

That gets me another giggle, and she places her hands over mine. "I enjoy being your hellcat. I missed that part, too."

"Oh, yeah?" I tease. "What part exactly?"

"Hmmm, your kisses, your cuddles, your hands," she replies.

"My hands?"

"Yes, they're so strong and sexy, and you're so good with them. You're good at everything. You're the best at everything."

"Is that right? Come on, baby, let's get you home." We're getting off the rails here. I need to get her home before my cock and ego inflate too much to get out of here. She is in no position to deal with either right now.

Picking her up, I put her in the car. I buckle her and take a moment to calm myself before getting in. Her hand drifts to my thigh the second I put the car in reverse. "Whatcha doing, baby?"

"Nothing," she sings, inching up. You'd never know she was sobbing on a couch five minutes ago based on her mischievous smile right now. "I want to play with MY hands."

Fuck, this girl. Hellcat indeed. "Not right now, Care. We gotta get you home to nap. Besides, you're going to be hella embarrassed when I tell you what you said once these drugs wear off."

"Why would I do that? I only spoke the truth."

"Hmm, you might be embarrassed you mentioned something about me being good with my hands and the best at everything."

"Psssh," she scoffs. "Why would I be embarrassed by that? I should be proud I bagged the best sex I ever had again. The fact that he's got the best fingers in the MLB is a bonus."

I choke on a laugh. "God, I can't wait to remind you of this conversation."

Pulling into my complex, I take Carina upstairs and bundle her up on the couch.

While she sleeps, I bring in her stuff and unpack it, trying to make as little noise as possible. Once I'm done, I sit in the chair where I can watch her rest and reflect on everything she said. She may be high as a fucking kite, but she was always one to CUI—confess under the influence. In college, it seemed like all she needed was some liquid courage to bare her soul. The second Patron hits those lips, her filter practically evaporates.

As much as I want to focus on her saying I was the best sex she ever had or that she loves me, the other things concern me most. She's still afraid that I'm going to give her up again when I leave. I'm not ready to reveal my big plan yet. I've gotta somehow get her to realize I am in this for good. I won't leave her behind even if I can't physically take her with me yet. How do I do that without showing my cards? She has to know how much she means to me. If she doesn't know, she will by the time I'm called back if it's the last thing I do.

An hour later, a disheveled Carina shoots up from her spot on the couch. She whips her head around the room before she spots me in the kitchen putting up the groceries. Making my way over to the couch, I lean over her and adjust her blanket. "How ya feeling, baby?"

"Confused," she answers. "When did we get here?"

"What's the last thing you remember?" I ask, pushing the mess of hair out of her face.

"Um, we were in the car heading to my apartment."

"So, you don't remember telling me I was the best you ever had, and you were glad you bagged the 'best fingers in the MLB'?"

"WHAT?" She squeaks. "I did not say that."

"You most certainly did, Kitten. As much as I hate to think any other man has ever touched you, I'm ecstatic to know no one else could ever please your body like I do."

She covers her blushing face with her hands and lets out a groan.

"Don't worry. I took it as a compliment," I coo. "C'mon, let me see my girl's pretty face."

She peeks out from behind her hands. "Why did you let me babble?"

"And stop the stream of praises? No way. You're not the only one who likes hearing how good they are," I tease with a wink. I don't know how it's possible, but she turns an even deeper shade of red. I can't help myself and lean forward and kiss her on the lips. I run my hands up and down her arms.

"Don't be embarrassed, pretty girl. My bosses pay millions to get access to these hands. You get 'em for free," I say against her lips. My fingers move down her body and start to toy with the ends of the shirt I changed her into. "How's your ankle?'

"It feels okay. Why?"

"Well," I say as I kiss her neck. "You used to love my curveball, but it's changed over the years now that I'm up against better batters. Maybe we should see if it still makes my Kitten purr sweetly for me."

"Robby..." she warns.

"Yeah, baby?"

She doesn't respond but pushes her hips so that my hand brushes up against the already-wet fabric of her panties.

"Seems someone is into that idea."

"Yes," she pants.

I pull her into my lap and carefully position her ankle on the coffee table with a pillow underneath it. "Stay still. No moving your leg, or I stop. Got it?"

"Yes, Robby, please," she mewls.

"So fucking sweet when you beg me like that," I mutter. I run my hand back up her thighs and shift her panties out of my way. I swipe my fingers up and down her slit. "You're so wet for me. Is this pussy needy? Does it need the best fingers in the MLB to make it cum?"

She glares and asks, "You're never going to let me live that down, are you?"

"Doubtful," I respond as I thrust two fingers inside her, causing her to bow. "Keep still, baby."

I twist my fingers in and out. She is writhing in my lap. Every little movement causes my dick to grow harder underneath her. Sorry buddy, this isn't about us. As her walls clamp around me, my middle and index fingers stoke that spot inside her that makes her moan, and my thumb dutifully flicks her clit. She's fighting hard to keep her leg from moving and her knees from slamming shut, but I am not sure how much longer she'll win that battle. Time to finish this. "That's it, Care. You're so close, almost there. Come for me. Come all over my hand. Show me how much you love these fingers."

With a strangled cry, she does just that. I tenderly circle her clit as she comes down. I kiss her temple, easing her off my lap and back to the couch. "That should hold you over until you can take painkillers again. Chinese sound good for dinner? Not many places open this late."

She gazes at me, dazed with glassy eyes, and nods. With a contented sigh, she throws herself back down on the couch. I go into the kitchen to place our order and finish putting away the groceries with a smug grin.

Chapter Thirty-Seven

Carina

I take Wednesday off work and spend it lazing around Robby's apartment. Thanks to his baseball schedule, he is in and out all day, meaning I'm never alone for too long. Which is good for me because if he even suspects I'm about to get myself up, he's on me. For being such a laid-back guy, he's a strict nurse.

There is no game today, but he has morning batting practice followed by a team workout. He comes back for lunch, bringing me a salad, and then heads in for a meeting with the pitching staff in the afternoon. While he's gone, Justin comes by to entertain me. He brings a set of cards, and we both brush up on our poker skills. He says he wants to prepare for our next game night, where Kim plans to wipe the floor with the boys.

"You seem to be extremely concerned with impressing Kim," I remark nonchalantly.

He glances down and clears his throat, "I just don't want to lose. I'm a competitive guy."

"Hmm, if you say so."

As I'm about to interrogate him more, Leo strolls in. "If it isn't my favorite softball captain and my fourth favorite teammate."

"Hi, Leo. How was the meeting?"

I beam as Justin yells, outraged, "Fourth?! I figured Robby was over me, but who are the other two? Ryan? I know it sure as hell isn't Trevor or Romero."

Ignoring Justin, Leo plops down on the couch behind him. "It was good. Pitchers had to stay back for a few, so I thought I'd keep you company, but my boy Justin here beat me to it."

"I'm teaching him how to play poker," I respond.

"Yep, except the student has become the master. I'm whipping her ass," Justin retorts.

Leo glances down at our piles of chips, a.k.a. Oreos. "Looks about even to me," he says.

I roll my eyes. "That's because *someone* keeps eating their chips, and someone else isn't about to waste all her precious cookies on him."

Justin shrugs innocently. When I peek up from my cards, I see Leo mouthing that Justin has two queens. Smirking, I up the ante by two Oreos because I've got two pairs with Kings high. Sighing, Justin folds. We play a few rounds, with Leo feeding me Justin's cards before he decides to give up. Patting him on the knee, I say, "Don't worry, buddy. Maybe Kim will go easy on you."

"You think?" he asks hopefully.

"Yeah, easy as putting bacon back on a pig," Leo snorts. "Good luck with that one, bro."

I laugh as Justin's face pales a little. As I'm about to respond, the door opens again, and Robby comes in. "Well, isn't this cozy? You fuckers decide to have a party in my apartment and forget to invite me?" Walking over to me, he kisses me and says sweetly, "Hi, pretty girl."

God, this man has a way of making me melt. He can be flippant with other people but so sweet with me.

"You're not tiring my girl out, are you?"

"Nah," Leo says. "I just got here. Been watching her own Justin in poker."

"Really?" Robby questions with a cute scrunch in his brow. "Carina is terrible at poker."

"I am not!" I shout, outraged.

"Baby, the only way you're beating anyone in poker is if Justin is the worst player in the world or you're cheating."

"How dare you, Robert Anthony Becker. I would never cheat."

"Hmm, a likely story. If you aren't cheating, why is Leo about to burst from holding in a laugh?"

"So, you're not only accusing your girlfriend of cheating but also the golden boy of the Midwest? He was a Boy Scout, for goodness' sake! Maybe I got good at gambling in the last few years. Have you ever thought of that?" I ask sassily.

"I'm sorry, baby. You're right. You could have gotten better, and Leo is too nice to help you cheat," he replies, properly chastised. Leo and I share a conspiratorial glance.

"I saw that," Robby whispers into my hair with a grin. "Alright, you two, say goodbye to the pretty lady. It's time for her pain meds and snuggling on the couch."

"We like to snuggle, too," Justin pouts.

"Then go snuggle Leo in your own apartment. There is only enough room on the couch for two, and you are not my first-choice cuddle buddy," Robby replies.

Mocking offense, Justin grabs Leo's hand and hauls him out of the room, laughing. "Let's go! We don't have to take this abuse."

"Now that dumb and dumber are gone, how's my girl?" Robby drawls. Puddle. Right here on the couch. I hope the team has a good cleaner because I'm going to leave a stain.

"She's good, except Justin ate half my cookies while we played."

"Well, we can't have that, can we. I'm sure I've got something in the cabinets that will feed your chocolate addiction. But first, you need dinner. I've got some fancy bullshit from the trainer to eat. How do Spaghettios sound to you?"

"You got me Spaghettios?" I ask, shocked as he heads into the kitchen area.

"Of course, baby. You always loved them when you were sick. Original, right?"

"Yeah..."

"What?" he asks, noting the quizzical expression on my face while he pulls the can out of the cabinet and pours it into a bowl.

"You really did remember everything about me, didn't you?"

Smiling at me softly, "The important things I did."

"The fact that I like Spaghettios is important?"

"Knowing the things that make you happy is important, yeah. How could I ever forget what makes my girl smile? The only thing I love more than putting a smile on your face is you," he responds.

Air catches in my lungs. "You love me?"

Putting my dinner in the microwave, he comes back over to the couch and crouches in front of me. "I thought that was obvious. I never stopped loving you, Carina. I may have lost my way a bit, but you never left my heart. I've told you, baby, you're it for me. 5ever and always." With those words, he kisses me deeply. I feel his whole soul mingling with mine in this kiss. He doesn't let up until the microwave beeps. He kisses me on the forehead as he stands to get the food.

It isn't until later that night when we're cuddled up on the couch watching baseball highlights, that I realize I never said it back. I just ate my Spaghettios silently like an asshole while he recounted his meeting. Rolling my head over his shoulder, I take him in. He notices me staring.

"What is it, Kitten?" he asks.

"I-I love you, too."

He smiles softly at me. "I know, baby."

"What do you mean 'you know'?"

"You might have told me already when you were flying high on those pain meds. But it's nice to hear them when you're sober."

"Why do I get the feeling you didn't tell me everything I CUI'd?" I mutter.

He smirks and kisses me. I snuggle deeper into his arms, content in the knowledge that we both love each other, and we know it. This still may end in an absolute disaster, but that can be future Carina's problem. For now, I'm going to enjoy this sweet, sexy man who buys me Spaghettios while he eats grilled chicken, rice, and Brussel sprouts.

Thursday passes without incident, with Robby pitching a shutout against Savannah. We spent some time together before the game today, but he wouldn't let me go because I am still supposed to be resting my ankle. It's much better. I haven't had to take any painkillers for the last twenty-four hours. I'm tired of resting, and I'm bored now that the workday is well over.

He should be home any minute from his game, and his time treating me as if I'm made of glass is coming to an end. He's being too freaking sweet and touchy without being overtly sexual. It is killing me. I've never been edged before, but if this is what it's like, do not sign me up. Since I'm not allowed to put any weight on my ankle, getting myself ready is tricky. Luckily, I showered with Robby this morning—where he painstakingly washed my entire body with zero inappropriate touching. My hair has a beachy wavy thing going on. All I have to do is find something to wear. Normally, this wouldn't be a problem, but seeing as I'm at Robby's and he only brought me a few options, I need to improvise.

I peek into his closet with the idea of throwing on a dress shirt when something purple and teal catches my eye. It's Robby's jersey from college. I have no idea why he brought this to Memphis—probably some weird baseball superstition—but I'm glad he did. Kim stopped by earlier after grabbing a Target pickup for me. It's not lingerie, but the cute lace bralette and panty set I ordered will suit what I have in mind. I don't plan to wear them for long anyway.

I finish lighting the candles I bought when I hear a key enter the lock. I scurry over to the couch and take my place while sipping a glass of wine. It's been a minute since I've seduced anyone, but it's like riding a bike, right? He hasn't been getting any, either. Hopefully, it won't take much to push him over the edge.

As he walks into the apartment, he stops in his tracks as he surveys the scene. Candlelight bathes the studio, and I sit on the couch, turned to face him. He can't see what I'm wearing over the back of the sofa, but it won't take long for him to notice. "Hello, there," he says.

"Hi, baby," I return with what I hope is a seductive smile.

"What's going on here?"

"Relaxing and having some wine. Care to join me?"

"Sure..." he replies suspiciously.

"How was the game?" I ask as he rounds the couch.

"It was... uh, what are you wearing, Kitten?"

"This old thing?" I say, pulling the jersey open. "It's something I found lying around. I used to look pretty good in these colors, so I thought I'd see if that was still the case."

"No one pulls off teal and purple like you, Care. I can't help but notice you're not wearing much underneath."

"That's not true. I've got on a bra and panties."

"Calling those scraps of fabric a bra or panties is a stretch," he states. "How is your ankle?"

Ugh, this again. I'm about to sass him that my ankle is fine, it's other parts of me that ache, but I get a better idea. "It hurts," I pout.

"You need me to get you something to make it better?" he questions with genuine concern. Reaching for me, he comfortingly runs his hand up and down my shin.

"The wine will help soon. Distract me," I say breathily.

"Hmm, do you want to watch a movie? Or we could play a game?

I could read you something? How does my baby want to be distracted?"

"Oh my God!" I whine, frustrated. "I want you to fuck me, Robert. Distract me with your dick! Is that not obvious?" He grins at me with a twinkle in his eye. "Ar-were you messing with me?"

"Is that not obvious?" he mimics.

I throw the pillow at him. "How dare you, Robert!"

He easily catches it. Damn, baseball players. "Okay, okay. Enough with the Robert bullshit, baby. I was just fighting fire with fire. You were clearly messing with me. Where did these candles even come from? And I know I didn't pack this." He runs his finger underneath the strap of my bra.

"I wasn't messing with you. I was seducing you," I retort.

"Ah, my mistake. Continue you on then."

"This was kind of all I had in mind," I grumble. "I thought you'd be as hard up for it as I am. I mean, I've practically soaked the couch since you've gotten back."

His eyes darken dangerously. There's that spark. "I've been sitting here imagining your hands running over my body as you make me come on your cock over and over again."

Robby groans and wedges his knee in between my legs, and he looms over me. "Don't toy with me, baby. You're still healing."

"In case you need an anatomy lesson, my pussy isn't anywhere near my ankle."

"I know all too well where your pussy is. Trust me. I'm feeling the heat from it against my knee right now."

"Babyyyyy," I whine, trying a new tactic. "I need you, please. I need you inside me." My plea finally does him in, and his mouth crashes into mine. He brushes his fingers down to my panties and curses.

"Fuck, Kitten. You are soaked for me. You need me to fuck that pretty pussy, baby? Is that what you want?"

"Yes," I hiss.

He rips the lace thong from my body, leaving me bare from the waist down. "Fine," he says. "But we're doing this my way, and I'm not risking your ankle." I nod my head vigorously.

He gets an evil glint across his face. "Mmm, I wouldn't be so quick to agree, baby. Because I'm going to take my time and go nice and slow. Build you up until you're going to explode before I push you over again and again. You sure you can handle that?"

"Yes, please," I moan.

He spreads the jersey open further and sucks my nipples through the lace bralette causing them to pebble. I arch into him. He seats his pelvis against my core as I reach for his waistband. "Not yet," he barks. "My way."

I slam myself back down in a huff. He pulls the cups of my bra down and continues his attention on my nipples, licking and sucking them. They have always been super sensitive, and he is driving me up the freaking wall as he hums against them. I reach the back of his head to try to pull him off, but he uses his free hand to grab my wrists and hold them above my head.

Without a word, he kisses up my chest and to my neck to the spot right below my ear that gives me tingles all over. "Impatient," he tsks. "Don't worry, baby, I'll give you what you want. When I'm ready. Right now, I'm enjoying the sight of you wrapped up in my old jersey."

He starts nibbling on my neck as I buck against him, trying to find purchase, but there is nothing there as he pulls back his hips. "Tell me what you want, Care."

"You, I want you!"

"Tell me who you belong to. Tell me you're mine."

"Yes, yours," I cry. He lifts up off me and releases my wrists enough to pull off his shirt. I claw at his abs. He lifts up further until he's standing over me and shucking off his pants and boxers. Stroking his cock, he taunts me. "This what you want, Kitten? Is this what has you making a wet spot all over my couch?" Fuck, I probably am, but I'm too turned on and needy to care.

"Yes, fuck me, please."

He grabs my calves and places the leg with the injured ankle on his shoulder. "Leave this leg here. I don't want you to hurt yourself." God, I cannot handle his hotness. I didn't know anything could turn me on more than his teasing me, but how he can tease AND be careful with me at the same time... it's almost too much to handle. Realizing he is waiting for me to acknowledge what he said, I nod.

"Good girl," he coos as he rubs the head of his cock against my clit. "Ready, baby? This is gonna be fast and deep."

"Yes, please!" I mewl.

As the words leave my mouth, he slams into me. He wasn't kidding. The way he has me spread open for him is getting him so freaking deep. He's hitting every spot. It only takes a few strokes, and I shatter.

"Shit, that's it, baby. Grip my cock. God damn. You really were ready, huh, baby?"

He gives me a few moments to come down while he slowly pumps in and out of me. Opening my eyes, I see him staring down at me as if I'm a goddess or treasure. I smile up at him. "I hope you didn't think that was it, Kitten. You're gonna come for me again."

"I don't know if I can," I heave. And I honestly don't.

"You can do it. I know you can. Hang on, I'll get you there."

He moves in and out of me faster again. His grip on my thigh tightens until his fingers turn white. His rhythm is punishing but perfect. I can see the strain on his face, and I know he's getting close. I am, too, but I need more. Robby senses that and reaches his free hand down to my clit and rubs it in circles.

"Robby," I say, writhing.

"I know, baby. I know. It feels incredible. Let it take over, baby. Let it crash over you." With a few more thrusts and circles, it does. His cock expands inside me as he finds his release, which triggers mine. My legs are shaking as I come around him again with a scream.

He falls on top of me, and my leg drifts down to his hip. He supports his weight with his arms. As he catches his breath, he kisses me deeply on the lips and then on the forehead. After another minute, he pulls out, and I wince at the loss. "Be right back," he says.

He returns a few minutes later with a washcloth and cleans up the mess on my thighs.

"Sorry about your couch," I mumble quietly. Apparently, that is hilarious because he busts out laughing.

"Christ, I love you," he proclaims before kissing me again. Scooping me up, he gathers me in his arms and carries us over to the bed, where he climbs in beside me. Wrapped up in his arms, I drift off to sleep with Robby telling me how much he loves me and how glad he is to have me again. As sweet as it is, I can't help but wonder if something is lurking right around the corner, something that will burst the bubble of happiness we've found ourselves in.

Chapter Thirty-Eight

That bubble bursts the next morning. I stir in the bed and reach for Robby, only to find his spot empty. Since it's still warm, I know he hasn't been gone long. I sit up and search the living space and see him pacing while on the phone.

"Yes sir, absolutely. I'm fully healed. I'm up for it and ready to be back with my boys. The Blues Birds know? I understand, sir. You can count on me," he says to the person on the other line. My stomach sinks. I know what this call is. What it means. Robby is going back up. Back to Nashville and away from me.

When the call ends, he stares at his phone for a second and, I assume, shoots off some texts. Taking a deep breath, I put on my happy face, get out of bed, and slink toward him.

"Good news?" I ask.

"Kitten, you're up. You shouldn't be standing on your ankle." He rushes over to me, but I shoo him off.

"Robby, I'm fine. Anastasia said I could put weight on it again Saturday, and that's today. The call, good news?"

"Uh huh," he replies sheepishly. "That was Mr. Norris, the GM of the Songbirds. They're ready for me to come back up. It's the beginning of August, and they believe I've rehabbed my arm as much as possible in the minors. They want me back in Nashville Monday afternoon for a meeting and Tuesday practice."

"That's great," I exclaim a little too loudly. I hope it doesn't appear as fake as it was. I'm happy for him. I am. But I can't help but fear that this is the end of what we've been building. I know he said he loved me, but that was true last time, too.

"It's good to know they need me back. I knew they would, but it's nice to get the confirmation."

"Everyone loves to hear that they're wanted," I reply.

I grab my bag and pull on some clothes, gathering up my things. I glance over and see him scrutinizing me.

"You realize this doesn't change anything, right? I want you. I'm in this, whatever we have to do to make it work. We'll figure it out. I'm working on a plan for us. Do you trust me?"

"Yes, I trust you. I know you're in this."

"Are you?"

"What?" I ask.

"You're not having second thoughts, are you?"

"No, I love you. You know that."

"I do..." he replies skeptically. "But that doesn't explain why you're packing your bags, getting ready to make a break for it."

"That's a touch dramatic, don't you think?" I scoff. "I'm not making a break for it, but I am going home to my place."

"What? Why? You're still healing."

"Robby," I sigh. "I'm fine. It's been four days. I'm not even taking ibuprofen anymore. If you're leaving Monday, you have a ton to get done, right?"

"Uh, yeah, kinda. I've got to check in with the team here and pack up all my shit so I can get on the road Monday afternoon."

"Exactly," I agree. "And you don't need me in your way for that, and I need to stop ignoring my other responsibilities and get back to my place. I bet Camila is going to be on a tear about me working from home the last several days, and I have plants to water and laundry to do. Plus, you didn't grab any manicure supplies. These babies need a refresh."

"That makes sense," he says skeptically. I nod.

"I'll finish gathering my stuff, and you can take me home? Or if you're too busy, I can get a rideshare."

"I'm not too busy to take my girlfriend home," he says, almost offended. "Are you sure you're okay?"

"Yes, I'm happy for you," I repeat. I give him a quick peck on the lips before heading to the bathroom to get my toiletries and hopefully come out more convincing than I went in. While there, I send an S-O-S text to Lola and Tiffany asking for a group call this afternoon.

Before he leaves my apartment after dropping me off, Robby promises to see me again before he heads out. He seems put off that I didn't want him to stay, but he had stuff to get done, and it wouldn't make sense. I spend some time unpacking and picking up as I wait for my call with Tiffany and Lola. When 6 p.m. rolls around, I call them both and put it on speaker.

"Hi, Tiffany. Hey, Carina," Lola says.

"Hey, Meatball! Hi, Lo," Tiffany responds cheerily. "What's this emergency you need to talk about? Are you pregnant?"

Lola chokes, and I sputter. "God, no."

"Just checking," she singsongs. "I figured it'd be best to get it out of the way in case you were going to bitch around it for twenty minutes."

"No, it's nothing like that. It's not that serious. I hope."

"What is it, Care Bear? Don't leave us hanging here," Lola asks.

"Robby got called back up," I state.

"And he broke up with you? That rat bastard. I know my voodoo curse didn't work last time, but I know some real fucking witches now. We can do some serious damage."

"Down, girl," Lo urges. "She'd be way less chill if he dumped her again."

"Hey! He didn't dump me the first time. I broke up with him," I exclaim.

"Semantics," Tiffany scoffs.

"Anyway. No, he didn't dump me, but I'm scared. I'm afraid this changes everything, and he will hurt me again."

"What did he say about it?" Lola asks.

"He said he wants me, and we'll figure this out, whatever it looks like. And... that he loves me."

"Whoa, he dropped the L-bomb already? It's only been a few weeks," Tiffany panics.

"Calm down, Babs. He didn't say it to you. Your track record of running from commitment is safe," Lola chastises.

"He said he never stopped loving me but lost his way for a while," I recall.

"Aww," Tiffany fawns. "That's the JTT, I know. I knew..."

"What exactly is the issue here?" Lola interrupts. "The man loves you, he's apparently been pining for you for years, and he wants to remain faithful to you even from hundreds of miles away. Sounds hunky dory to me."

"I mean—I guess. But what if it doesn't work out? I'm afraid it's going to end up like last time."

"Carina," Lola sighs. "You need to spend less time worrying about what could happen and appreciate what you have. A lot of women would kill for a man as devoted as Robby, and the fact that he is hot and rich to boot? Come on. You're being a spoiled brat in this scenario."

"Lola..." Tiffany warns.

"No, some people have actual problems. Relationships are hard and require work. You can't only exist in a happy little bubble. The real world comes calling, and you have to put up or shut up. Spend your time building what you have and not worrying about what *may* happen. Otherwise, you're going to gaslight yourself into seeing your fears everywhere." With that declaration, Lola hangs up.

"Uh... what the hell was that about?" Tiffany asks.

"I have no idea," I respond, equally confused. "That was weird, right? Was she overreacting, or am I out of line?"

Tiffany sighs. "Both? I mean, listen. I get it. Losing Robby wrecked you; it would be hard to go through that again. But on the other hand, what is your other option? Leave him now before he can leave you?"

"What?" I gasp. "I can't do that."

"Exactly," she responds. "You're going to have to push your worries aside and do what you have to do to make this work. Don't overanalyze every move he makes and everything he says, searching for proof that he's going to hurt you again, but don't ignore the red flags, either. You get to build the relationship you want. If he says he has a plan, I trust him. He's done nothing but prove himself trust-worthy since you got back together, right?"

"Yes."

"Then you're going to have to put some faith in him," she states.

"You're right," I sigh. "Okay, enough about me. We need to talk about whatever the hell that was with Lola and what we're going to do about it."

We spend the next hour scouring social media and past convos to see if we can figure out what is up with Lo and plan to check in with her more regularly. Tiffany is going to invite her to go to a job in Miami Labor Day Weekend for a mini girls' trip. Satisfied we've got a good plan in place, I say goodnight and curl up in my bed while trying to keep my anxiety over Robby at bay.

Chapter Thirty-Nine

Robby

It's Sunday night, and Carina yet again told me she didn't need me to spend the night. Some bullshit about wanting to get ready for work the next morning. It's my last night here for God knows how long. Frustrated, I march up to Leo's apartment. I'm no longer playing for the Blues Birds, but I know they had an afternoon game. He should be back by now, though.

Not knocking because that fucker never does, I barge into his place. I find the man in question sitting on his couch eating a bowl of cereal shirtless, watching SportsCenter highlights. "Um, come on in?" he says.

I grab a beer from his fridge and sink beside him on the couch. "Everything okay, man? You're subdued for a guy about to return to his dream job."

I sigh, "Everything is fine on that front. Carina is acting weird, though."

"How so?"

"I don't know how to explain it exactly. She's been distant over text and hasn't wanted to see me since I got the call from Norris, but she hasn't outright said that."

"She told you she didn't want to see you?" he asks with an eyebrow raised.

"Not in those words, no. But when I offer, she claims to be too busy getting resettled after spending all week with me."

"Maybe she is busy getting resettled after spending all week with you."

"Maybe, but I don't think so. I'm about to fucking move out of the city. Who knows how long it will be until I see her again. We have several details we need to iron out, and she's acting astonishingly chill about it."

"So, you're suspicious she's being chill?"

"I know it sounds dumb, but I honestly expected her to be glued to me and kind of needy. At least pretend she's going to miss me."

"Ah, that's it. She seems like she doesn't care that you're leaving."

"I guess," I grumble.

"Isn't the whole reason you broke up that first time because you said she was too needy?"

"I guess..."

"That's your answer."

"I'm not following," I admit.

"She's afraid of the same thing happening. She's trying to be the opposite of how she was last time. It's one thing to be afraid something will happen, but it's another thing to be afraid something will happen knowing it has before."

"But that's dumb," I reply. "She knows I'm committed to making this work. Hell, I'm working on a plan to convince her to move with me. I'd take her with me tomorrow if I thought she'd come."

"Does she know that?"

"Know what?"

"Jesus, you're dense, dude. How are you the one with the smoke show girlfriend?" he complains. "Does she know you'd take her with you? Have you even mentioned that option to her? I bet she's afraid you're excited to return to your life the way it was and have her here as hometown honey that can't distract you."

"Hometown honey? Bro?" I ridicule.

"Whatever, you know what I mean," he challenges. "You've got to spell it out for her so she knows that you want her and that you've got future goals in this. Right now, y'all are planning to be in limbo with no end date."

"I'm not ready to tell her my plan," I complain.

"Then don't," he states. "Ensure she knows this setup isn't forever and that things are happening behind the scenes to get you back to where you've been the last few weeks."

"That's smart," I remark. "How are you single?"

"My mom asks me that every week. When I figure out an answer to tell her, you'll be the first to know. For now, I'm sticking with 'I haven't found the right girl yet.'"

"Well, here's to her. I hope she isn't a vegan," I say and cheers my beer to his cereal bowl.

"From your mouth to God's ear," he comments.

The next day, I meet Carina for an early lunch on a patio in Midtown by her work. She's already sitting when I get there. I walk up and kiss her on the head. "Hi, pretty girl."

"Hi, babe," she greets.

"What's good here?" I ask as I sit down and grab a menu.

"Um, I enjoy several of them. Usually, I'll mix and match a few different sliders like the fried chicken, West Coast, and the original."

"I'll do that, too." I put my menu down and grab her hand.

"How are you doing, ankle okay?"

She rolls her eyes at me. "Yes, worry wart. My ankle is fine. I'll be back dancing the night away at Paula's in no time."

I don't love that. The idea of her out dancing without me, no thank you. But it's my fault I won't be here. I can't exactly say anything about it.

I give her a playful glare, and she giggles. She seems to be in a better mood today. Maybe Leo was right; I have been reading too much into her texts. But the levity is short-lived as the light dims in her eyes again. I rub my thumb across her knuckles.

"You know I love you, right?"

"I know. I love you, too."

"This limbo with me in Nashville and you here will only be for a few months, until the offseason. I can come back after the playoffs, and we can figure out a plan that works for us long-term. If I thought you'd go for it, I'd throw you over my shoulder and kidnap you right now."

"You can't kidnap an adult," she snarks. Sassiness is a good sign. "It's called an abduction."

"Does that mean you're down to be abducted?" I tease.

"Nooo, I've got stuff here, Mom, my job, a life."

"I know, Kitten. Just give me a little time. I'm gonna make it all work for us. I promise. Okay?"

"Okay," she responds.

She doesn't appear fully convinced, but I'll take what I can get. I hate seeing the doubt in her eyes. I want to spill all my secrets. Reassure her that I have this handled and I will take care of everything; take care of her. Before I can, though, food arrives.

By the time we're done, she has to head back to the office. I walk her to her car, which is next to mine, and take out macarons I got from her favorite bakery on the way over. "Sweets for my sweet," I croon.

"You're cheesy," she laughs.

"It's a good thing that cheese is one of your favorite things, then. You want to know what my favorite thing is?" I ask.

"What?"

"You," I answer honestly. "My favorite girl, my favorite snack, my favorite everything."

I grab her by the waist and pull her to me for a searing kiss. It goes on longer than is decent for noon on a Monday, but fuck all these people. I need a taste of my girl before I say goodbye to her for, at minimum, a few weeks.

"God, I'm going to miss your taste. Last chance, you're positive I can't adultnap you?"

"Yes, I'm sure. I love you, baby. Call me tonight?" she questions.

"I'll be calling you every single night until I have you back in my arms," I promise. "I love you, too. Don't forget about me."

She scoffs, "That would never happen."

I nuzzle into her hair as I squeeze her to me. "Be a good girl for me while I'm gone, okay?"

"Okay," she sighs.

With one last kiss and a pat on the ass, I shut her in her car and watch my girl drive off.

I keep telling myself it's only for a couple of months. I have a plan in the works, but as much as my head is convinced, my heart hurts knowing I'm leaving a piece of it here.

Chapter Forty

Robby

I woke up this morning wiped after a solemn drive back to Nashville, meeting with the team trainers and coaches, plus a late-night call to Carina. Trying to shake off my mood being away from her, I head into practice, where I will finally reunite with my teammates.

"Looky what the cat dragged in, boys," Kent exclaims as I enter the locker room.

"Hey man, how are you?" I say, giving him the customary manshake and back pat.

"Good, glad to have my favorite pitcher back, that's for damn sure. It's not as fun being the only one hitting bombs. Heavy wears the crown," he jokes.

"Yeah, 'cause you killed it last game with two pop flies and one on-base hit," Miller says as he enters the room. "Hey Robby, good to have you back."

"Thanks, Papa Bear. I missed you, too," I croon.

"God, I forgot how insufferable the two of you are together in person," he says with no heat.

"What's up, Becker? Finally got invited back from the kids' table?" someone jeers. Turning, I see Derrick fucking Jones.

"Jones," I sneer. "I heard management lost a bet and had to let you on the team. I'd say it's nice to see you, but that would be a lie."

"Aww, don't be that way. It's not my fault you couldn't handle the competition and got sent to time out."

"I got sent down to rehab, not—you know what? Nevermind, you aren't worth the breath," I say.

"Whatever, man. Don't worry. I kept the city warm for you while you were gone."

Our second baseman, Clapp, scoffs, "By sleeping with every chaser and Broadway Barbie you could get in your bed?"

"It's a tough job, but someone's gotta do it. Couldn't let them get lonely in Becker's absence," Derrick quips.

"If they were lonely, it wasn't because they were missing me, but have at them all you want. I won't be curing their loneliness anytime soon."

"Find a nice side piece to play with while you were away, did you? Be careful. Just because they aren't from here doesn't mean they don't have dollar signs in their eyes," he responds.

That riles me up. "You don't know what you're talking about. I'd advise you to shut the fuck up before you see how hard I can hit with my arm in working order."

"Touchy touchy," he tsks. "Must be some magic pussy in Memphis. Maybe I'll try to get sent down to play in the sandbox for a while."

Before I can cross the room to him, Kent has grabbed my arm, and Miller is in Derrick's face. "That's enough," he bellows. "I don't know what style of locker room Gomez was running in Seattle, but in Nashville, we respect the women around us. We sure as hell don't talk about another guy's girl that way. Got it?"

Derrick puts his hands up in surrender, searching around and realizing no one will make eye contact. Hell yeah, they won't. Miller's a well-respected player and man. No one is going to go against him on this team. "I got it, Cap," he mutters.

"Good. Now, everyone, get your asses to the field!" Miller orders, and we all go. He's a scary motherfucker when he wants to be.

Fuck, that practice was rough. I don't know if it was nerves or Jones getting under my skin, but I sucked a big one this morning. I couldn't hit for shit. After batting practice, I stuck around with our catcher, Martinez, to throw some. It went about as well as batting practice did. I was slow, out of sync, and out of practice with his signals.

As we walk in, we pass our coach. "Becker, a moment?" he says.

"You got it, bud." Martinez pats me on the shoulder and gives me a sympathetic glance as he returns to the locker room.

Not a man to mince words, Coach jumps right in. "You played like shit out there." Ouch, not pulling any punches, I see.

"Sorry, Coach. I'm doing great, I promise. Adjusting to the rigor of playing in the bigs again." This is not how I wanted to present myself after time down in the minors.

"Don't sweat it, kid. I get it. If you didn't play shitty on your first day back, I'd be worried you were pushing too hard. Just make sure you get better every practice between now and Sunday."

"Why Sunday?" I ask.

"Because that's when you're back on the mound," he says like that should've been obvious.

"You got it, Coach. I won't let you down."

"See that you don't," he says as he turns and heads back inside.

The pressure is on knowing I've only got five days to get ready to face the heavy hitters.

Sunday went decent. Better than the talking heads expected but not as good as I know it could've been. It's weird being back here. I got used to my routine in Memphis. Practice during the day, see Carina at night, rinse, repeat. Yeah, we talk on the phone at night now, but it isn't the same; something is missing.

She's in my head most of the day—not constantly, but she pops in here and there. I wouldn't say she's a distraction, but I'm not as singularly focused as before my injury. It's not fair to say it's because of her, but it's also not wrong.

I've called her too late a few times this week, and she was already in bed. She woke up to talk to me, but I felt bad waking her up and a little resentful that her life is going on easily without me. I know that's crazy, but it's true. She's working and hanging out with her coworkers, not to mention Leo and Justin. I know because they all send me selfies.

I wasn't like this when I was in Houston. Maybe it's because I was so excited to be living my dream I didn't think about the life I left behind. Plus, I knew that life. I lived it for two years. I've only been part of Carina's new life for two months, but I hate missing a second.

I'm also finding it hard to find time to connect with her. She works during the day, and we've had games or meetings late every night this week. And if we don't, I've been using that time to get in extra practice to get myself back up to snuff. It's a similar routine to what I had before, but I'm realizing it doesn't leave much time for a relationship. None of that matters, though. I've been in this position before, and I'm not going to fuck it up again.

Two months, maybe three I keep reminding myself. That is the max amount of time I'll have to maintain this schedule, and then it will be the off-season. Then Carina and I will have three-plus months to get a plan together for next year. My team is working behind the scenes to bring my vision for a nonprofit to life. I know I can get her to move here when I can present that to her. I can prove that living my dream doesn't mean she can't live hers, too.

That's all I want. To give her everything she wants. I know this is hard on her. Not that she's showing it. But I know my girl. She's more stoic when we talk, dimmer. But since she isn't talking to me about it, I have no idea how hard it is on her. My biggest fear is that she gives up on us, on me, before I can make it work for us. All I need is a little time. Two months. Time is the answer to all our problems.

The irony that time is why we broke up last time isn't lost on me. But it's different now. I can do both. I can be a good partner to her and the player my team needs. I can set records and show up for her physically as much as possible but emotionally always. All I need is time and faith from Carina.

Chapter Forty-One

Robby has been gone a week, and it already feels like forever. You'd never know the four years we were apart ever existed based on how used I became to his presence the last couple of months. His first few games back on the Songbirds have gone okay, but I know his standards are way higher than 'okay.' I can sense his stress through our brief calls and texts.

He has stayed true to his word and called me each night. It's harder to connect through the phone even compared to when he had away games, but we're doing our best. I wonder if that's because he was waiting to return home, but now he is home. Back to his life anyway. He's slipping into the routine he had before, which didn't require spending time on his phone calling and texting his long-distance girlfriend.

He hasn't said anything, but I know he's struggling with working me into his schedule. He tells me he has a plan to make this all work and that we just have to make it to the offseason. I want to believe him. But I've been down this "it'll be easier when..." road. He said things would improve when he "moves up to AA," or "the new season starts," or "we get through the playoffs." It's too familiar.

I try to remind myself that he's making an effort this time. He's keeping his commitments. He's not blowing me off to get black-out drunk with his buddies. Robby is either working out/training with the team, talking to me, or sleeping. His priorities line up with his words.

While I appreciate his efforts, I get the sense he is checked out emotionally. I try to remind myself to take his words at face value and that he does genuinely want to talk to me when I catch myself slipping into the old thought pattern of being an obligation. I don't want him to think of me as a duty. I want him to think of me as something that enriches his life.

It doesn't help that I've been crazy busy, too. A new school year kicked off this week, so I spent last week preparing to restart many of our programs after the summer hiatus. It's a great thing. It means we're back to serving kids and ensuring their nutritional needs are met—at least during the school day. But as programs director, I've had to iron out all the first-week kinks that come up with new students and administrators.

Tonight, I go back to Express Delivery Park for the first time since twisting my ankle. There is a week until the championship game for the nonprofit tournament. The team and Leo have decided to practice to ensure we aren't rusty after two weeks off.

I've seen Leo and Justin a few times after Robby left, as they've been hanging out with me, Haley, and Kim. They and the hotshot rookie, Ryan Morganson, even volunteered at a back-to-school event we hosted over the weekend. It was awesome to have their support, but it made me miss Robby. Returning to the stadium where we've spent all this time together will be a harsh reminder that he's gone.

After practice, I stick around to help Leo pick up per usual. It's hollow without Robby helping and needling us both. It must show on my face because Leo checks if I'm doing okay.

"Why wouldn't I be?" I question.

"You seem deep in thought and maybe sad? I'd be neglecting my Memphis best friend duties if I didn't check on you for my guy."

I smile at his loyalty and kindness. "I'm fine, tired. Had a busy week at work, and it's taking some time to adjust to Robby not being here all the time. It's weird how used to it I got."

"I know what you mean. He wasn't here that long, but I already miss the big guy around the complex. I can't say whether it is weird or not since I've never been in a long-distance relationship, but I imagine it's tough."

"Yeah," I sigh. "It's not only the distance, though, physically anyway. It's emotional. The pressure he's putting on himself to get back to his old standard quickly is almost tangible. All he does is train and work out. He's running himself ragged, which drains him. We haven't had a deep or non-surface level conversation since he left."

Toeing the dirt, I glance up and see Leo's face filled with sympathy. "I worry that it will end up the way it did four years ago. He keeps saying he has this master plan and needs time, but I can sense his focus shifting to his career again. I get his passion. Mine is a priority, too. I just want to make sure I'm up high on that list, too."

"Aww, sweetheart," Leo drawls, stretching his arms out to wrap around me. Leo gives the best hugs. I don't know if it's because he's built like a lineman or because he's a giant teddy bear, but there is nothing better than a hug from Leo Davis.

"I can't speak for where his head is at right at this moment, but there is no way he's going to shift you down that list. Something changed in him the second you two got back together. I can guaran-fucking-tee you are high on his list. From what I saw, you're the top priority.

"He told me on more than one occasion that you two are endgame. I don't know what his master plan is either, but I know he's been working on it for a minute. That man worships you, Carina. I've got enough faith for both of us that he'll make it work.

"There's a learning curve to get through on how to balance your lives and the distance. The offseason may feel far away, but it's closer than it seems. Then we both get our boy back."

He says the last part while batting his eyelashes which makes me giggle.

"Just know that when he does come back, he's mine for the first few days. You'll have to wait your turn," I tease.

Clutching his chest in mock outrage, "Even after that great pep talk I gave you? I thought we were one step closer to becoming sister wives!"

I am full-on cackling now. "Sorry, Leo. I don't share. Maybe you'll have better luck with Justin and Kim."

"Wait," he pauses. "What do you mean with Justin and Kim? Are they dating now? How did I not know this?"

"I have no idea what's going on with them," I say. "But those two are definitely up to something. They aren't as sneaky as they think they are."

"I'll be damned," he mutters as we grab the rest of the equipment.

Leo's talk helped even if it didn't change anything. It's nice to hear from a third party that Robby is as invested in me as I am in him.

Chapter Forty-Two

My relief is short-lived. Robby misses our nightly call the next evening. I heard from him before practice when he said he was going to work out and watch TV until it was time to climb into bed and chat. The time for bed came and went about two hours ago. Sighing, I set my alarm and try to think happy thoughts as I drift off.

After a fitful night of sleep, I am running on iced coffee and a prayer. Robby flooded my phone with texts when he got up for his 6 a.m. workout apologizing for falling asleep and missing the call. He had a busy day with practice and a film session with his pitching coach and passed out when he got home.

I honestly don't get why he's working out so hard. He didn't lose any strength or muscle while he was healing and doesn't need to bulk up. Maybe it makes him feel more in control of the situation. I can relate to that desire. I'd love some control right now.

He's calling earlier tonight to make up for some of the time we missed last night. I'm not surprised that my phone rings as soon as I finish dinner. The familiar picture of Robby goofing off in Haley's pool pops up with his contact.

"Hi, stranger," I say.

"Hey, pretty girl," he answers.

"No video call?"

He answers, voice slightly muffled, "As much as I miss your beautiful face, I'm packing for the away series we leave for tomorrow. I wasn't going to be close to my phone the entire time. I'm taking this call with my headphones."

"How very corporate of you," I deadpan.

"What's that mean?"

"Nothing," I sigh. "Where is this trip taking you guys?"

"Chicago, then Denver."

"It's your first road trip back," I remark. "How do you feel about that?"

"I'm excited. I've always done well on the road. I feed off the energy of the crowds in other cities. Ever since my days in Seattle, the boos from other crowds have fueled me. Remember that game against Boston when that batter ran up on me because he thought I was trying to peg him? I crushed it in the next game against them."

"Um, no. I don't remember..." I respond awkwardly. I didn't exactly pay attention to his career or anything related to him after we broke up.

He goes quiet. "Right, you wouldn't; that was dumb of me to say. I guess on some level, it feels like you've been a part of this entire journey with me, in spirit at least."

Well, damn. That's sweet. I melt at the fact it was momentarily unfathomable that I wasn't there for part of his come-up.

"There is something I wanted to run by you."

"Okay... that isn't worrisome," I murmur.

"It's nothing bad, I promise. We leave for Chicago tomorrow, and we're there through Sunday afternoon. After that, we are in Denver for games on Monday and Tuesday."

"I remember," I confirm. "Then you fly back to Nashville Tuesday night and drive down Wednesday for the championship game."

"That's what I wanted to talk about." My stomach drops.

"I may not make it," he states cautiously.

My heart hammers in my chest. I will myself to calm down and push away the sense of déjà vu threatening to take over. "What do you mean?"

"Since the game will run late Tuesday night, we're returning Wednesday mid-morning. Assuming that goes off without a hitch and everyone makes it on time, I'd cut it close to get back there. After landing, I'd still need to get my car from the stadium and then drive all the way to Memphis.

"The trip will be tiring as it is with five days of games back-to-back. Plus, I pitch again on Friday, meaning I'll need to be back in Nashville Thursday afternoon."

"Can't you fly from Denver to Memphis Tuesday night separately? Is there some rule you have to travel with the team on the jet?"

"It's not a rule per se, but traveling separately doesn't look great, especially because I've been away for a while. Flights are a good time to bond with the team and grow morale."

"So, team morale is more important than supporting me and the team you coached in our final game?" I am full-on bitter now.

"Kitten, please don't be mad. It's a tricky situation, and I have to weigh all the sides. I'm trying to communicate and properly set expectations. I want to be there, trust me. But I don't think it's plausible. I don't want to make waves. I haven't been back long or producing at the level I was before my injury."

"Trust you," I repeat. "That's all I've heard from you for the last few weeks every time I admit something is hard. Trust you. You have a plan. Well, I'm not seeing one, just a bunch of excuses."

"Baby-" he tries to interject, but I'm on a roll.

"No, don't 'baby' me; don't 'Kitten' me. Pet names aren't going to get you out of this one. You're using the travel schedule as a cop-out. If you *really* wanted to be here for the game, you would make it happen. It doesn't conflict with a game, practice, or even another team obligation, just bonding time. You get that the other one hundred eighty days of the season."

"Ugh." He lets out a frustrated cry. "This would be easier if you lived in Nashville."

"Why, so you could ignore me in person?" I ask sullenly. "Or that way, I'd be there sitting around at your disposal whenever you deigned to spend time with me. Obviously, it would be easier to prioritize me if I lived there. You certainly wouldn't have nearly as many excuses for blowing me off."

"I'm not blowing you off," he grits. "I'm trying to balance what the team needs from me and what you do."

"The team doesn't need you at 3 p.m. on August 17. I do. This is fucking déjà vu. I'm being left behind for something better."

"I am NOT leaving you behind. I fucked up last time, I know. I'm trying to be better. This is me communicating with you before an issue arises so we can discuss it and find a compromise."

"You say you want to compromise, but I don't see what you're sacrificing here. You don't want a compromise. You want me to tell you it's okay for you not to come. You don't want to deal with letting me down, so you're hoping my permission will ease your guilt. Not granted.

"This is important to me. And not just from an 'I want my boyfriend to watch me' way but in a 'this can have an extremely meaningful impact on my career' way. If we win, it means funding and PR for Feeding Memphis and the ability to launch the FM Mobile Market. If we lose, I will be bummed and want your emotional support. No one else understands how much this means to me."

"I told you, baby, I would help you fund the program either way."

"That isn't the point," I mutter softly.

"Then what *is* the point? I don't know what you're trying to do aside from making me feel guilty!" he shouts back.

His anger at my reaction fuels mine. "The point is, your girlfriend needs you to be there for her. And if you can't see why this would disappoint me, I don't even know what we're doing anymore."

"What does that mean?" he demands.

"It means I can't be in a relationship with someone who doesn't prioritize me. I spend my life putting everyone and everything else first. I need my partner to do that for me."

"I do put you first. It's one event, Carina. I'm missing one thing. I'll make it up to you," he argues.

"The first thing. This is the first meaningful event since we got back together, and you're missing it when you don't have to. It's only been six weeks, and you're already pushing me down the list.

"Deeper than that, it seems you haven't thought about the impact of missing this 'one thing.' Let's pretend for a second that this event isn't super important to me. Let's say you miss it, and it doesn't leave me disappointed. When will I see you again? Your season is heating up as you get closer to the playoffs, and you have road games coming up. If I don't see you Wednesday, when were you planning to see me again? When were you going to make this up to me?"

"I-I don't know, but we'll figure it out," he stammers. He has no answer because he hasn't even thought about it. He hadn't thought that the team is about to have an almost two-week road stretch after next weekend at home. Seeing me in person again hadn't even crossed his mind, only missing the game."

"I don't know if I can make it work under the circumstances, baby."

"Fine."

"Fine?" he questions. "All that arguing to say 'fine' in the end?"

"I can't make you do anything you don't want to do. I learned that lesson a long time ago."

"That isn't fair."

"Maybe not," I reply. "But neither is always having to come

behind everything else in your life. I didn't expect to be prioritized over games or contractual obligations, but bonding time? I thought I'd take precedence over sitting on a plane with a bunch of guys you spent several days with and will probably be sleeping. You do whatever you have to do this week. I've clearly communicated my needs," I say that last part mockingly. "This is the last time I'm asking you this, Robby. Put my name at the top of your list. I need to matter as much to you as you do to me. You do what you have to do. And I'll deal with it, however, I need to deal with it."

"Care," he pleads.

"Maybe, I'll see you next week. Maybe I won't. We both need to consider what we want and whether this is working for us."

"You! I want you!" he croaks.

"Prove it." I hang up before he has the chance to respond and spend the rest of the night crying into my pillow until I pass out.

Chapter Forty-Three

Robby

I hardly slept at all after the brutal call I had with Carina last night. I'm able to catch a few hours on the plane en route to Chicago, but I'm still unsettled by everything she said.

I knew she'd be mad I couldn't make the game, but I thought she'd understand. I thought it would cushion the blow if we talked about it before instead of me saying "maybe" and then not showing up. I thought it would make it different from the dick move I pulled four years ago, but apparently not.

I wish she could see the uncomfortable situation it puts me in with the team. They aren't going to be sympathetic to me going back to the Triple-A city to see a girl that, in their minds, I must have met fucking around the last few months. I could try to catch an earlier flight or fly direct to Memphis, but I've already missed out on so much team time this season. People think group chemistry isn't as important in baseball as other sports, but it is.

She wouldn't really break up with me over this, right? She said she was in this as much as I was. One missed event is not breakup worthy. She made a good point about making it up to her, though. I have no fucking idea when I would be able to do that. The team's schedule is packed for the next month.

I ponder these thoughts and more as I sit in the bullpen during tonight's game. It's 9 p.m. here in Chicago, which means tonight's Blues Birds game is over. Carina told me earlier in the week that they were having another game night with my old teammates. Justin finally gets to take Kim on in poker. I wonder if they're at Leo's now. I haven't spoken to her since hanging up yesterday. This is the longest we've gone without talking since we got back together, and I hate it.

I miss hearing her sleepy voice when we talk before bed. I miss the forty-seven million videos she sends me throughout the day. I miss seeing her 'work fit OTD' selfies that she sends every morning. It's killing me not to reach out to her, but nothing has changed. I haven't figured out how to make traveling with the team and being there for the game work, at least not without traveling on my own.

If I travel on my own, I feel like I'm letting my team down. Like I'm not giving them one hundred and ten percent. On the other hand, Carina has never shied away from telling me how important this event is to her. She's repeatedly reminded me what it means for her future—at least, what she thinks her future is. I talked to my agent and PR rep this morning, and everything is almost finalized for my nonprofit.

I'm this close to making our dreams come true. I need her to give me more time and faith, but I'm afraid I've burned all my goodwill. I'm terrified of discovering what "I'll deal with it, however, I need to deal with it" means.

Once the game is over, I return to the locker room to clean up. I check my phone on the off chance my girl texted me. She's always been one to drunk text. Instead, I find a notification from Leo. It's confirmation of my worst fears—that if I make the wrong move here, I'll lose Carina, again. That's not something I can handle.

LEO DIVINCI

You're fucking this up, man. I don't know what happened, but everything about Carina screams trouble in paradise and not the temporary kind. Fix it.

Fuck. I have no idea what I'm going to do.

I don't know how, but I was able to put all this Carina stuff out of my mind and have the best fucking game of my career. I was on fire tonight. Not only did I hit a homer, but I ended the game with 5 RBIs and pitched a shutout.

Crossing home plate that final time, with my team hooting and clapping for me, should have made me feel like a king. Instead, it was empty. Empty because the one person I want to share it with isn't talking to me right now and may not ever again. I know what people mean when they call something a 'hollow victory' now.

Chapter Forty-Four

Carina

It's been three days since I've talked to Robby. I've done everything I can to keep busy. Deep cleaning my apartment, trying on every article of clothing I own to decide what I should donate to the local women's shelter, and creating the most intricate nail art I have ever done. On the outside, the floral design says fancy, but it reeks of avoidance.

Tonight, I am heading to a family dinner where I know my mom will be able to tell something is wrong and make me spill my guts. I haven't told anyone about the fight Robby and I had or the potential implications the game this week brings. I was afraid that speaking it out loud would make it real, so I haven't. Unfortunately, that streak ends tonight. Teresa Francelli-Ballerini Shaw is not about to let me get away with keeping anything from her.

As I pull up to my parents' white brick McMansion, I take a deep breath and try to put my game face on.

"*Mia bambolina!* How I missed you!" my mother says as she rushes in for a hug and kiss on the cheek. "Are you okay, Carina? You seem tense." One foot in the door, and she is already taking notice.

"I'm good, Mama," I lie. "You are so tan! Two weeks in the Caribbean sun agrees with you."

"It certainly does," echoes Steve as he enters the foyer. "We missed you, though, kiddo. Two Sundays away was almost too much for her mama bear heart to take."

"Stop, I wasn't that bad," my mom chides.

"Honey, you convinced the young couple on their honeymoon to eat with us three nights in a row. You taught the wife how to get Bloody Mary stains out of her cover-up. I think it's safe to say you missed having someone to mother."

My mom rolls her eyes—yeah, she passed all her facial expressions on to me. I use them with pride. Looking behind me tilts her head in confusion. "No Roberto tonight?"

My mom has called Robby 'Roberto' since the first time I brought him home. She said, "Robby isn't a man's name Carina. One day he will want to sound more dignified." When I pointed out that his given name was Robert, she insisted giving it Italian flair would be more welcoming. He loved it, so I guess she was right.

"He isn't here tonight," I tell her as we walk toward the kitchen. "Actually, he won't be back for a while."

Mom stops in her tracks and turns to me with sympathy swimming in her eyes. "What happened, Carina?"

"Nothing happened, Mama. He got called back up to the majors. He's in Nashville. Well, he is in Chicago right now. You knew that would happen eventually."

She hums, "Yes, yes. Good for him. Though I will miss him. We'll have to send you with food whenever you visit him."

"Sure," I respond with a tight-lipped smile. "Anything I can help with?"

"We should have everything ready to go. You can go pick out tonight's wine." With a curt nod, I do just that. I'm going to need some liquid encouragement if I am going to get through this dinner with any sort of grace. I wanted to sink into that hug and crumble.

Sitting at the table a few minutes later, I pour everyone a glass of Chardonnay to pair with Mom's shrimp risotto and dig into the watermelon salad starter. This salad is one of my favorites. Mom used to make it every summer when Lola came to stay with us.

Being on a limited budget, we didn't often get to indulge, but Lola's dad always sent her with some money even though Mom insisted it wasn't necessary. Instead of using it to cover Lola's expenses, she'd use it to buy foods that were normally out of our price range and make us delicious meals. Whenever I attend a potluck in the summer, this easy salad is my go-to.

Once Mom joins Steve and me at the table, I ask about their trip. Mom lights up as she details the view from their balcony and the excursions they went on. The highlights were horseback riding on Antiguan beaches, visiting an ostrich farm, and snorkeling in Turks and Caicos. It seems they had a lovely time.

"Oh," she exclaims, "I even expanded my cooking abilities."

"You did?" I question hesitantly.

"Yes! We took a cooking class, and the chef said I was his top student."

"Honey, I'm not sure you can call making sushi cooking. It's more of assembling," Steve says.

"Wow, Mom. Sushi? Did you figure out how to give it an Italian flair?" I tease.

"Not yet, but I am working on it," she says. I can't tell if she's kidding or not. Italian sushi doesn't sound that bad. In a way, stuffed tortellini or ravioli is sushi-ish, right? Either way, if Teresa Shaw makes it, I'll try it. And that is a motto we should all live by.

"Enough about us. What have we missed with you?"

"Hmm, nothing too exciting. Aside from being sidelined with my ankle," I answer.

"What happened to your ankle?" Mom asks with a gasp.

"I must have forgotten to tell you. I twisted it during our last game. Don't worry; it's all better now. I had to stay off it for a few days, and now it is as good as new."

"Who took care of you when you were off your feet? I would have done that!"

"You were busy petting ostriches and mastering Japanese cuisine, Mom. I was fine. I stayed with Robby the first few days and then returned to my own routine."

"That was before he left?" Steve inquires.

"Yes, it timed itself perfectly. I was back putting pressure on my ankle Saturday, and he left Monday."

"I'm glad you had him to take care of you," my mother comments. "He grew into such a dependable man. He was fine as a boy but he hadn't seen much of the real world. I always hoped he'd find his way back to you. He used to look at you the way your father looked at me. All young, stupid, and in love. It was sweet, but love without experience isn't always enough to get through hard times. Now, he looks at you like he knows what losing something important to him feels like. It's not the sweet love of youth, but a love that can last a lifetime."

She and Steve share a secret smile, and I break. Their love is so freaking pure and real. Admiring it makes me sob into my hands.

"Oh, Carina!" my mom coos and wraps me up in her arms. "It's going to be okay."

"I don't know, Mama. I don't know."

Clearing his throat, Steve stands. "This seems like a mother-daughter conversation. If you need me, I'll be in my office. Say 'bye' before you leave."

Once my tears finally stop falling, my mom releases me from her grip and runs her hands down my hair. "Is this a wine talk or a tea talk?"

I laugh. "We're Italian, Mama. Every talk is a wine talk."

"Too true," she agrees as she pours us each another glass. "What are all the tears about?"

With a shaky breath, I respond, "I don't know if Robby and I are going to make it. Things have gotten all mixed up. It's four years ago all over again."

"I'm going to need more than that, *bambolina*."

"He may not make it back for the championship game—some crap about needing to bond with the team and not wanting to make waves. But it isn't just that. He's been getting more and more preoccupied since he moved back to Nashville."

"And what does he say about that?" she asks?

"He says he's trying to get back into the groove and to give him time. He claims to have some master plan that will make everything better once we get to the offseason."

"Do you think you can do that?"

"I did," I sniff. "But now, I don't know. His missing another important event sheds new light on things. He knows how much this matters to me. He may not be expected to be there, and everyone would understand if I said he was still traveling with the team, but I'd know he could have done more. I think part of me needs him to prove he won't only love me when it's easy, but when it is hard, too."

"And this is a deal breaker for you? He knows this? You told him?"

"Not in so many words, but yes. I think so."

She nods. "I can't tell you what to do or what matters. I taught you what to expect from a man and how you deserve to be treated. I have confidence you will make the right choice for you."

And she did. She so did. My mom was 'that mom,' the hot one that all the single—and several married —dads hit on while the other moms leered at her. She had *a lot* of offers before Steve came along. But she held out for a man who treated her the way she deserved. Not as some trophy, not as someone he was saving, but as a true treasure.

That's all I want. Someone to treat me like I'm their whole world. Maybe that's asking too much. Maybe that kind of love is rare, one in a million. The fact that I can see it in life means I won't get it. I don't know.

"Don't think too hard," Mom chides. "As I said earlier, I saw the way he looked at you when you were here last. He'll make the right choice if he truly understands what's at stake. He made this mistake once before. He's smart enough not to repeat it. No matter what happens, Steve and I will be there cheering you on from the stands. I'm even going to make a sign."

That makes me laugh. "Thanks, Mama. I love you."

"Love you, too, *bambolina*."

An hour later, I am leaving with leftovers, thanks to dinner being one guest shorter than Mom anticipated. I stop by Steve's office to say goodbye.

"Bye, kiddo," he says with a smile and a hug. "Listen, I don't know what's going on with that boy, but I know he'd be a fool to let you go. I've been privileged enough to love two Ballerini women and know how amazing... and challenging it can be."

I roll my eyes at him. "Your life would be boring without us, Steveo."

"You got that right. You've been making my life more interesting since the day those big brown eyes that matched your mother's peered up at me. Now, be safe driving home, and let us know if you need anything before Wednesday."

"You got it," I reply. With that, I hop in my car and try to focus on the week ahead.

Chapter Forty-Five

Robby

Right after the team plane lands in Denver, my phone lights up with a call. I pull it out quickly, hoping it will be Carina, even though I know it won't. She made it perfectly clear that we won't be talking again until she's good and ready, and deep down, I know that won't be until after the championship game. She's waiting to see what I do.

I want to talk to her so fucking bad, but I don't know what I'd say. I've told her repeatedly that I have a plan and to hold out a bit longer. I can see from her perspective how those could feel like empty words. Like excuses to put her off until we can be together again. I can't expect her to accept a situation she doesn't want to be in with no clear way out.

When my phone buzzes in my hand, I see it is my dad. That's weird. He never calls me. We haven't talked since my blow-up on the family FaceTime call last month, and even before that, we never spoke without Mom or Morgan as a buffer.

"Hey, Dad, everything okay? Mom, good?" I rush out.

"Yes, everything is fine. Your mother is fine. She's at your Aunt Gail's making lemon pie. I can't call my son when I want to talk to him?" he asks.

"I mean, you can. You just never have before... what is it you wanted to talk about?"

He clears his throat. "This isn't exactly easy for me. Your Grandpa Ray wasn't exactly a talker, and I am afraid I inherited that trait from him. You needed advice on how to fix something; he was your guy, though. That man could install a sink, reroute electrical, and repair an engine. Once, I saw him fix our washing machine with a couple of screws and a can of Coke. But, he certainly never apologized to me for anything."

"Is that what you're doing? You're apologizing?" I wonder.

"Trying to."

Stunned, I say, "Oh, well, continue, I guess."

"Right. Well, I've been considering what you said a few weeks ago, and I realize I've been too hard on you. More than that, I've been a jackass."

I choke on the water I was sipping.

He goes on, "You may remember that I was supposed to play football beyond high school. I wasn't ever going to make it to the NFL or anything, but I would've been the first person in my family to graduate from college. Instead, that honor went to you. Don't get it twisted, I love Morgan and your mother and you and the life we have, but it wasn't the one I had planned. I thought I'd go to college, get a nine-to-five, then settle down. For me, football was always a way to do that, a stepping stone, never more.

"I know it appears I never support you playing ball. I will admit, I've never been one for the sport, but you had a real talent for it, and I was glad to provide so you could play. When you got that scholarship to MSC, I was proud. And I'm not too much of a man to admit now that I was a little jealous. Jealous that you were going to live the life I thought I'd have. Jealous you were going to make Grandpa Ray proud in a way I never could.

"But then you kept your focus on baseball. You graduated, but you didn't use that degree. It felt like a waste to me. To get all that education and then never use it. I know you're good at what you do, and you make good money doing it, but it's not forever. I always worried about you making it last. To me, you're still the twelve-year-old boy who spent all his money on video games. It's hard to remember the man you've grown into.

"A man—a man I'm proud to call my son. I know I've been shit at showing it, but your mother and I are proud of who you grew up to be. You are hardworking, loyal, generous, and more laid-back than I'll ever be. You put up with my shit for years before you finally had enough and put me in my place, far longer than I deserved. I'm sorry I ever put you in that position."

"I get it, Dad, I do. All I ever wanted was to make you proud. For you to see, I was making smart choices even if they aren't the same ones you'd make."

"I see that now," he responds. "I am proud of you. I'm also sorry I spoke ill of your intentions with Carina. I know how much that girl means to you."

Ugh. That kills me. If only he knew how much I was fucking that up. I let out a sigh.

"Uh oh, is everything okay there?" he asks.

I'm apprehensive about sharing based on our past, but he seems genuine. "I don't think so," I respond. "We're in a stalemate right now. She thinks I don't make her enough of a priority, that I only fit her into my life when it's convenient for her."

"And is she right?" he interrupts.

"Of course not. She is everything to me," I snap.

"Okay, just checking. No need to bite my head off."

"I have this big plan to show her she is, but I need more time. I don't know if she'll give it to me, though."

"You didn't ask for my advice, but I'm gonna give it anyway," he says. "If there is anything I learned in twenty-nine years of marriage, it's that most of the time, women don't need the big gesture. They care about the small ones."

"What does that mean?" I ask.

"It means that she isn't waiting for some grand scheme, some master plan for you to unveil. She wants you to show her in all the little ways that she matters. Do you know why your mother and I watch crime shows together?"

For as long as I can remember, my parents have watched at least two or three episodes of Law & Order, Criminal Minds, and similar shows together every week. Growing up, that was their time, and we weren't allowed to bother them when they watched unless it was an emergency. It's a running joke between me and Morgan that they were both plotting how to kill the other, but they'd never do it because the other would know the same tricks.

"Because you enjoy them?" I guess.

"To be honest, I don't care for the genre all that much," he confesses.

"What? Dad, you've watched hundreds, if not thousands, of episodes by now. Why would you watch them if you didn't enjoy them?"

"I imagine I have seen quite a few. I don't watch them for enjoyment. I watch them for your mother. One day when you were about three, your mom complained that we didn't spend enough time together. Now, I'd recently gotten a raise at work. I could have whisked her away for a weekend together in a big gesture, but that would have been a Band-Aid.

"Instead, I found small ways to spend more time together throughout the week and used that money to get our first new piece of furniture—the green sectional. TV time made the most sense for us to spend together based on our schedules and responsibilities. For me, it wasn't about watching something for my entertainment. It was about showing your mom I heard her concerns and validated them by making a real effort. I invested in the couch because it was where we would spend all our time doing that. Got something similar you could do?"

I run my hand over my hair. I know exactly what I could do to prove to her she is a priority to me, show up at that damn game. "I have something. It will be tricky to make it work, but it may be the only thing that will make a difference."

"Well, son. I can't tell you what to do, but it seems if she is 'everything' like you say she is, you'll do whatever it takes."

Fuck. He's right. I can say Carina is my number one priority until I'm blue in the face, but it's only words until I prove it. Even when I unveil my big plan and get her to move to Nashville, I will still always have to show her that she is my world.

I've been focused on all the reasons it doesn't work to travel to the championship game, but the simple truth is I could make it work. I just have to make sacrifices. I'd be willing to trade anything to keep her happy and keep her mine.

"Thanks, Dad. That helps more than you know."

"You got it, son," he replies. "Your mom and I were talking about taking a trip to Tennessee to see you play before the end of the season. Let us know some dates that work."

Wow. That's never happened before. They didn't come to a single game in college, and it was less than an hour away. "I will. Morgan mentioned wanting to come, too. Maybe you guys can coordinate. Love you, Dad. Thanks again for the talk."

"Love you, too, Rob. Good luck getting back your girl."

With that, we hang up. I've got about two hours until I have to report to the stadium. That means I have two hours to figure out how the hell I'm going to make it to Memphis by 3 p.m. on Wednesday.

Chapter Forty-Six

Carina

Today has been a literal dumpster fire. Okay, no garbage cans were actually set ablaze, but I might have preferred if they were. I've been slammed at work on top of the emotional upheaval of the last couple of days, and a few things have fallen through the cracks or gotten mixed up.

Nothing big, mixing up school names on a flyer or ordering too much of one cereal and not enough of another. All minor things that were easily rectified, but Camila has caught every single one. It's as if she knows my personal life is in the toilet right now and is excited to pile on. She ripped me a new one in today's staff meeting because I forgot to follow up with a vendor for the programs' fair we're having later next month.

"Carina, a word?" Camila chirps as she passes my office.

Sighing, I get up and make my way toward hers. Her office is a weird blend of native art and modern furniture. African fertility statue here, Native American tribal print there, it's an assortment of blended cultures. She speaks as I settle into the uncomfortable round chair across from her desk.

"Thank you for joining me. I wanted to have a quick chat now that we are back in full season with all our programs. I can't help but notice you've been distracted lately and appear awfully tired. Is everything okay?"

Wow. Is she genuinely concerned about me? This is a shocking turn of events. Before I can answer, she continues. "You've made several errors this past week that could have reflected negatively on the organization and me."

There it is. That train of thought makes way more sense coming from her.

"I am fine," I say. "A lot is happening with the new school year, and many of our points of contact changed. I know a few things have slipped through the cracks, and I am working hard to ensure it doesn't happen again. On a personal level, I have also been dealing with some issues that have added some stress, hence the tiredness."

"I see," she clips. "Well, as this is a professional workplace, I hope you can leave those issues at the door. When you are here, your sole focus should be on work and supporting our clients. We can't have you obsessing over outside situations when there are children to feed."

"Yes, absolutely. None of my personal issues have been brought into the office."

"See that it stays that way. From the lack of softball equipment I've seen lately, I assume the tournament is over, and you didn't win?" The gleam in her eye is almost hopeful.

"The championship game is on Wednesday at 3 p.m. It is on the work calendar. The whole office is coming to support and speak with the media," I announce.

"I see. And if you win, you still want to do your little food truck. Based on this week, are you sure you can support that program along with your current workload? I have my reservations about its efficacy, but even more, if you are already overwhelmed."

My stomach drops. Here we go again. I don't know why she is against my program. It checks several boxes in filling the gaps we are missing. It's self-sustaining and solves major issues our clients face. I sometimes wonder if she doesn't support it because it is the first program she hasn't pioneered.

Fight a grimace, I reply. "Yes, I still plan to use part of the funds for FM Mobile Market. My hope is to get it up and running early next year. That way, we have plenty of time to plan and work out the kinks. Last week was rough, but I now have a solid handle on all the programs and am not worried about workload issues moving forward."

We chat for a few more minutes about the work-related issues I faced last week. As I leave, Camila says, "With everything going on, I want to ensure we don't lose sight of our goals. We all must be fully committed to this organization and our clients if we want to succeed."

Walking back to my desk, I wonder if she is right. Have I let my personal life and wants overshadow my commitment to our clients? Am I doing as much as I can for them, or am I too focused on making my idea work?

Deflated from my chat with Camila, I pack up when the clock strikes 5 p.m. As I am preparing to leave, Jada heads toward the door after a meeting with Kim about an upcoming project. "Hi, Carina," she greets.

"Hi Jada, I see Kim kept you here late. I hope Jalen isn't missing you."

"He's fine. He had a competition with his Electronics Club today at another school. I'm sure I haven't even crossed his mind. I'll tell you who he's missing, though, is that boyfriend of yours."

"Him and I both," I mutter.

She gives me a sympathetic glance. "I don't know how you do it, girl. It takes a strong woman to be with a man like that. Some of them are worth it, I guess. Lord knows I never found one, but I'm happy you did."

I smile at her. "Don't lose hope, Jada. You're a total catch. Any man would be lucky to have you."

"I know that, honey," she replies. "But finding one who would video call into an eleven-year-old's electronic club to say 'hi' even after he moved away? One who will meet up with said eleven-year-old in a video game world to keep their relationship going? That's a special breed of man."

"He does that?" I ask, shocked.

"You didn't know? He even got Jalen hooked up with some fancy professor at Vanderbilt. They invited him to attend their robotics camp next summer—fully paid. They said it's a scholarship, but I'm not entirely convinced."

"We aren't exactly on speaking terms right now." I am gobsmacked. I didn't know Robby and Jalen were still talking. I figured once he left, he would peace out on everyone here. That's what he did after being drafted.

"I can't say when I first saw the man, I expected him to have such a kind heart. All that swag, that pretty boy hair, but when it comes to you, he's a big softy. I don't know what bump you two are encountering, but I hope you get through it because I've never seen a love as pure as yours.

"I've dated my fair share of men, and in my experience, none has ever looked at me like Robby looks at you. Hell, none of my sisters' husbands look at them the way he looks at you. Any man who will talk to eleven-year-olds about computers over video chat for an hour deserves a little grace in my book."

"Maybe you're right," I agree.

"Speaking of," she says, "time to pick up my little tech hellion. See you Wednesday?"

"See you Wednesday."

My week doesn't get better, and I have the Monday-est Tuesday ever. I almost run out of gas, my favorite dress gets stained, and one of the schools has plumbing issues, resulting in no water for the kids or their meals.

When I arrive at my apartment, I immediately change into my comfiest clothes—leggings and one of Robby's t-shirts—and snuggle up on the couch. I want to call Tiffany, but when I called her earlier today, her phone went straight to voicemail. She must be traveling again and forgot to tell me. When I checked her location, it said LAX. She and Lo's Miami trip isn't for another few weeks, so I'm not sure where she could be going.

I decide to indulge and order sushi and fried rice from my favorite Japanese restaurant and throw on some comfort TV.

Cutting through my thoughts, I hear a knock on the door. Huh, that's weird. The delivery app says my food hasn't been picked up yet. When I peek through the peephole, I see a mess of blonde hair covering and nearly scream as I fling the door open.

"OMG, BABS!"

"Surprise, Meatball! I had to come see you. I've missed you too much." She wraps me up in a hug as we do that annoying, girly, jumping squeal. I'm so wrapped up in her being here that I don't notice another presence until I hear a throat clear.

"Sean?!" I gasp as I turn and see him standing there. "Hi, pipsqueak."

"How-Why-What are you doing here?" I sputter.

"Well, I figured you showed up for all my championship games. I had to show up for yours."

"I can't believe you're here. I can't believe you're both here. Come in, come in."

I shuffle them into my apartment and then properly hug Sean, who places Tiffany's suitcase on the ottoman.

"We wouldn't miss this for the world!" Tiffany says. God, I love my friends. I can always count on them to show up for me. Even though I haven't seen Sean in forever, he still showed up. A knot forms in my chest as I think about the man who didn't show.

"How did you know?" I ask my male bestie. "You told him?" I turn to Tiff.

"You've got too much faith in me if you think I pulled that off," she scoffs.

"No," Sean answers, "Rob planned for me to come. Technically I was supposed to come up for your birthday, but it didn't work out with my schedule. We decided this week was the perfect backup."

"He arranged for me to come, too," Tiffany chimes in. "But that was a few days ago. Said if he wasn't able to make it, he wanted you to have another one of your 'people' here. And who am I to say no when a man offers me a first-class ticket?"

"Hasn't that mantra bit you in the ass before?" Sean asks.

"You end up in Ibiza indefinitely with a sitcom star one time, and no one lets you live it down," she murmurs.

"I'm glad you guys came! I can't believe you're going to be there tomorrow. I can't wait for you to meet my new friends."

"I can't wait either, babe," Sean responds. "Now, as cute as this place is, I booked a hotel nearby. I wanted to ensure FSB got here safely before checking in. I know you girls have catching up to do. I will leave you to it."

"You don't have to go," I stop him.

"Nah, it's cool, babe. I had a long week. I'm gonna hit the hay so I can get up for my run tomorrow. But I'll meet the two of you at the game, and then we can go out for dinner to celebrate."

"Okay, bye, third wheel. Give me back my girl!" Tiff says, breaking Sean and me out of a hug. Twenty-five minutes later, Tiffany and I are snuggled up on the couch, splitting my dinner.

"I'm so glad you're here," I confess.

"Me, too. I don't know if Sean knows you and Robby are in a weird spot right now—it isn't my place to tell him, and you know how he is." Yeah, I do. When we broke up the first time, Sean almost flew to Houston to kick Robby's ass. It took me, Tiffany, and our friend Blake to talk him down.

"But I do know that Robby arranged Sean's trip months ago and mine Sunday. You can't say he isn't trying to take care of you the best way he knows how."

"I know you're right," I concede. "I wish he could be the one to show up for me for once."

"He still might," she replies. "He said he was sending me as a precaution. Something about it taking a village. I don't know. I just said yes to the free vacay and packed my bags."

"You get paid to be flown around all the time. I don't see how this is much different. Your passport has seen almost as much action as your lady bits this year."

"Hey!" She exclaims. "That was rude."

"Doesn't make it untrue," I singsong.

"Still," she mutters. When I study her, I see something in her eyes. Something different—something dimmer, vulnerable.

"Everything okay, Babs? You're living your dream, right?"

"Yeah," she answers. "It's different than I thought it'd be. Traveling all the time is fun and sexy until you realize you have no deep friendships because you aren't anywhere long enough. Living out of a suitcase gets boring. And when I am home, my mom insists I go to all these events with her and meet all these high society douche bags she says would make good husbands.

"And they might, but not for me. They reek of entitlement, and view doing makeup as a hobby I'll do until it's time to pop out their heirs. Besides, I can tell from one glimpse at them that none of them could find a G-spot to save their lives."

I bubble out a laugh. "You always have had your priorities straight."

She smirks at that. "You know it."

"If that isn't the dream anymore, what is?"

"I don't know," she admits. "Something more permanent. Not a movie or anything. I'm not into special effects makeup, but maybe a talk show or at a salon where people come to me. I don't want it within reach of Mommy Dearest, though. But moving to New York seems drastic, and everyone I know there is vapid and out for themselves."

I pull my friend in for a hug. "I wish Memphis had a market for you. Maybe you should see if Charlotte has one? Or St. Louis if Lola decides to stay put. Did we ever figure out the deal there?"

"No," she huffs. "But we travel to Miami next month, and I'll get it out of her for sure."

Chapter Forty-Seven

Robby

The last two days have been a clusterfuck. I had hoped to fly out after the game last night. Unfortunately, we went into extra innings thanks to an error by Derrick fucking Jones that helped the Mountain Lions tie it up. By the time the game was over, I'd long missed my flight and had to settle for one that left this morning.

I managed to snag one that leaves at 9 a.m. central time, which is a miracle considering how few direct flights there are. However, it's also on a budget airline which is not ideal. I am a large man. Whenever possible, I buy seats with extra legroom. This last-minute flight didn't have many options, but seeing my girl will be worth any soreness.

I could've taken a flight with a connection, but I was afraid something would go wrong, and I'd get delayed in God knows where and miss the whole game. It turns out those worries weren't unfounded.

There was a freak storm in Boston that kept planes from taking off, including mine. With the next direct flight not scheduled until after the championship game already kicked off, I was stuck waiting on this one to show up. The team jet isn't leaving until after lunch.

The plane eventually arrived, and we finally boarded around 11:25. Then we had to wait another thirty minutes for them to fit us into the takeoff schedule, and now I'm going to be cutting it hella close. Thank God I didn't fly into Nashville and try to drive. Who knows when I would've gotten there.

I haven't told Carina I'm coming because I didn't want to get her hopes up, and I want to see her reaction in person. Her eyes always give her away, and I need to see the emotion in them. Plus, we've got some other things we need to discuss along with it.

As the plane takes off, I fidget in my seat, anxious we aren't going to get there fast enough. The older woman beside me notices and asks, "Nervous flier?"

"No," I answer, "more nervous about what's waiting for me back on the ground."

"Girl trouble?" I nod.

"I don't know how that's possible with a fine-looking specimen such as yourself," she appraises me.

"I'm afraid I'm the one who messed up this time," I reply.

"In my experience, a lot can be forgiven when a man is as tall as you. And with that charming smile, you could get away with murder. I'd certainly let you."

Is... is this lady hitting on me? Because she is older than my mom. Not that I am against cougars or anything, but I am not at all interested in this one, Carina aside.

"I'll keep that in mind," I say, pulling out my earbuds.

Handing me her card, she remarks, "If it doesn't work out, give me a call. I've got a few nieces who I'm sure know how to appreciate a man like you."

"Um. Okay?" I take the card, thoroughly weirded out that this lady is practically pimping out her nieces to a stranger who is clearly hung up on someone else. I pop in my headphones and think about what I want to say to Carina. I know showing up is a big gesture, but there has to be more. She deserves to know where my head is and that she is the most important thing in my life.

Around two hours later, the plane touches down in Memphis. I've got forty-five minutes to make it to the stadium. When we hit the tarmac, I message Jerold, the driver who brought us home for karaoke, that I will give him a fat tip if he is waiting for me outside in fifteen minutes. Thankfully, Miller agreed to take all my gear back home. All I have to carry is my backpack. I believe his exact words were, "I got this; go fix your fuck up, you dumbass." But same-same.

When I make it outside, Jerold is waiting for me as he promised. "Hey man, I need to get to Express Delivery Park as fast as humanly possible." The man of few words nods, and we are on our way.

Feeling a sense of relief for the first time in days, I rest my head against the back of the seat. I am minutes away from seeing Carina's face again. I hope she'll be happy to see me and that she missed me half as much as I missed her. I know the gist of what I want to say to her. I hope I can get it out without fucking it up and that it's something she'd be willing to try.

I'll do anything she wants to make her happy. Even commute to Memphis weekly if that's what it takes. These few days without her spotlighted how unknowingly lonely the last few years have been. I know, without a doubt, she's the one for me. I just need to convince her.

At approximately 2:37 p.m., Jerold and I pull up to the stadium. Having already shot him off a Venmo, I grab my bag and run inside. Since it's for charity, the event is free today. Once I pass the gate, though, I realize I have no idea how to get to the field from here. As players, we come through the dugouts and underground tunnels. I could run down and jump the fence, but surely there is an easier way.

Walking toward the elevator that would take me to the club level and basement, I run into Ryan. "Hey, man," he exclaims, giving me a manshake. "I didn't know you were coming!"

"No, it's a surprise. Can you help me figure out how to get to my team?"

"Absolutely, it's this way. Weird being on this side of the fence, huh?"

"It's strange, for sure. Why are you up here?"

"As a spectator, I wanted the authentic experience, including a hot pretzel, obviously."

"Obviously," I repeat. What a goofy dude. But he's leading me to Carina so he can be as odd as he wants. As we get to the underground level where the locker rooms are, we run into Stacy.

"Robby Becker! I didn't know you would be here. Why didn't you let us know? We could've done press about it," she chides, somewhat annoyed.

"Sorry, I didn't know if I'd be able to make it myself until last night."

She nods. "Amber," she shouts at who I assume is her intern, "be sure the cameras get shots of Robby in the dugout with his old team."

I don't stay to hear what, if anything, Amber's response is. I've got a team and a woman to reunite with. Rounding the corner to the home team locker rooms, I stop when I hear that voice I know so well. Standing in the doorway, I have a view of Carina's back as she gives the team what I imagine is supposed to be a pregame pep talk. Leo catches my eye from the back of the room and grins a mile wide. Carina is too in the zone to notice. I stand there and listen to her gas up the team. We can chat when she's done.

Chapter Forty-Eight

Everyone is gathered in the locker room as we prepare to take the field for the championship game. I haven't heard a peep from Robby. I've accepted that he isn't coming and is once again unable to prioritize me, but I can't consider what that means for us right now. As the team captain, my teammates need me to put on a brave face and motivate them for this game.

"Bring it in, y'all," I request. All fourteen of my teammates, plus Leo and Justin, are here. Sean could've gotten a fancy pass to sit in the dugout with us, but he opted to sit with my parents and Tiffany.

As everyone gathers around me, I speak, "Alright, team, this is it. This is the thing we have been working to achieve for the past few months. We are one game, nine innings, twenty-seven outs away from victory.

"At this point, it isn't simply about winning the money. It's about pride. Marshall and his merry band of butt munches think they have this in the bag. Despite beating them once already, they think they're going to walk in here into OUR house and take away a championship that is rightfully ours. Are we gonna let that happen?"

"No!" they all shout.

"That's right. We're going to go out there and show them that just because we don't spend all our time wielding power tools or sweltering in the summer heat pouring concrete doesn't mean we can't kick their butts! Now let's get out there and show them what Feeding Memphis can do!"

After a few cheers, we grab our gear and walk out to the field. The second I turn toward the door, I'm stopped in my tracks. Standing in the doorway is all 6'4" of the man I was convinced wasn't going to make it. Everyone filters past me and high-fives him on their way out until only Haley and Leo are left. Haley shoulder bumps me and says, "We'll see you out there. Five minutes until the opening ceremony."

I nod wordlessly. Leo smirks in my direction. Did he know?

Still frozen where I stopped, Robby walks over to me with a soft smile on his face. "Hi, Kitten," he says tentatively.

"Hi," is all I can get out. After staring at each other for several long seconds, I manage more. "You're here."

"I'm here," he repeats.

"Why?"

"Why? I heard there was going to be a softball game today, and I had a craving for BBQ nachos," he chuckles. "I'm here for you, baby."

"You are?"

"I am," he confirms. "I would love to tell you everything on my mind and in my heart right now, but you've got some ass to kick. We can talk after the game, okay? I want you to go out there knowing I love you. You mean everything to me, and I have total confidence you can knock the smarmy smile off that douche canoe's face."

"Okay," I rasp out. Apparently, I am not so with the words right now. Robby chuckles in the sexy way he does and grabs my hand.

"Come on, pretty girl, let's go win us some food truck money." He then leads me into the dugout right in time for the National Anthem.

We open the first inning with two runs. We're able to hold Restore 901 off to one run for the next four innings, but we don't add any more to our total, either. Their pitcher is good. Really good. I'd say she was a professional if I didn't know better. But I am friends with Mandy on Facebook, and she is the founder's wife, not an Olympic softball player. Could've fooled me, though.

During the sixth and seventh innings, we score another run each. It took me a few innings to get my bearings back. I was totally shocked when I saw Robby's face. There was always a tiny voice inside me that said he'd show up for me, but every other voice called that one stupid until she was barely a whisper. Turns out she was right and jokes on all the other voices.

I am absolutely elated he is here. And by his reaction to me, he is genuinely excited to be here. He's been by my side the entire game when he's not out being a base coach. We haven't talked about anything, but sensing his presence and his arm brushing against mine has been comforting beyond measure. I can finally breathe again.

Even though I'm thrilled, a small part of me, not that one voice, another one, is worried this doesn't mean what I hope it does. That his showing up is only a reaction to me alluding to ending it. I can't be in a relationship where I have to scare or coerce my partner into meeting my needs. He said he wants to talk after the game, and I'm nervous to hear what he has to say.

Shaking off those thoughts, I grab my bat and step up to the plate as it's my turn. I can see Marshall's smarmy smile through his catcher's mask. Ugh. "Look who it is! It's the Produce Princess. Eating all that spinach isn't going to help you win," he taunts. He's devolved into insulting vegetables now?

"Well, we're winning right now," I quip.

"There's still plenty of game left to be played."

As he finishes, the pitcher unleashes the ball. Crap. It was a strike. I let the jerk distract me. I can't let that happen again.

"Your team is currently being carried by an old lady and a computer nerd. How long do you think that will last, Cares Too Much?"

My lack of response annoys him as he amps up his trash talk. "Nothing to say, Ballerini? You've gotten cockier since dating Mr. Baseball over there. Do you think that's going to last past this tournament? That's cute. Hopefully, the fling at least keeps you from striking out before he dumps you for some country singer."

Okay, that one hit a nerve. Spinning around, I put my empty hand on my hip and yell, "Too far!" I notice Robby making his way down the baseline, but I shake my head at him. "I got this." He lifts his hands up in surrender.

"Listen," I say, returning to Marshall. "I don't know what made you such a sad, threatened little man, but you won't be taking that out on me. I get that you have some issue with me, but you don't know anything about my relationship or my man. Why don't you stick to something you actually know: losing."

Smiling at his stunned silence, I reposition myself in the batter's box and await my next pitch. I see it coming right down the middle and manage to make contact. It sails into the outfield and gets me safely to first. When I get there, I turn to Marshall and give him a salute. I wish I could see his face right now because I bet it is priceless.

I don't make it home in the eighth, but we're still up 4-3 at the top of the ninth. All we have to do is hold them to no runs this inning, and the championship will be ours. They've got two outs already, one from a strike-out and one from a ground ball to second. They do have a player on base, though.

One of their interns is up to bat, and the guy is jacked. This ball is going places. I hear Leo yell for everyone to back up. I can see Marshall smirking from the dugout. He acts like he's got this in the bag despite never leading once this entire game. The audacity of men, I swear.

Jada winds up her pitch and lobs it right across the plate. Strike one. He tips the next one into the net, but it falls before Angela can catch it. This next pitch is it. I can sense it. Jada sends another perfect pitch, and the intern makes contact. We all turn in slow motion and watch as it flies right toward a panicked Alex.

"Glove up!" I hear Robby scream.

Right as the ball is getting to him, Alex manages to come out of his trance and throw his arm in the air. The sound of that ball hitting his glove is sweet, sweet music to my ears. We won! We did it. We won this whole freaking tournament, and now I have the money I need to fund the mobile market.

I stand there in disbelief while everyone runs to Alex. As I walk over, big arms sweep me up from behind. Robby grabs me under my thighs and lifts me over his shoulder, cheering. When we make it to the rest of the team, he lets me slide down and join in on the group hug.

When we're done, I turn and see him beaming at me with that gorgeous smile. "You did it, Kitten. I'm so proud of you."

"I didn't do it. The team did," I reply.

"They won the games," he agrees, "but you made all this happen. You wanted something, and you went for it. You are incredible. I knew you could do it."

I get teary at his praise, but before he can say more, our fans are running toward us. Tiffany almost knocks me down when she makes it to me. From the corner of my eye, I see Robby and Sean embrace in a hug, not a bro hug, but a hug hug. I'm glad those two were able to work it out. They've got decades of friendship behind them.

"You won!" Tiffany yells. "This is even more exciting than when the guys won the College World Series."

"Hey!" They both shout.

"What?" She shrugs. "It is."

"The College World Series is a huge deal," Sean quips.

"Yeah, but it's not nearly as exciting as my bestie winning her tournament and getting the money to fund her own program," she retorts.

Sean mutters something we don't hear under his breath, but Robby is smiling at us.

"Hey, FSB," he says as he pulls me from her grasp and back into his side.

"JTT, you've clearly been eating your Wheaties," she comments.

"Thank you for noticing. That means a lot coming from a beauty expert such as yourself," he teases. They always had a somewhat adversarial relationship, even if it was in a playful way. Their egos always counteracted one another's well.

Tiffany rolls her eyes. "Don't you have some groveling to do?"

"I do indeed," he says as he turns to me. Before he can say anything else, though, Mom and Steve make it to my side.

"*Bambolina*, that was incredible. *Ottimo lavoro!*"

"Great job, kiddo," they say at the same time. They chat with us for a while, but then Stacy needs the winning team to come over for the trophy ceremony. We tell my parents' goodnight' and Tiff and Sean where to meet us for the after-party, a.k.a. dinner.

What feels like ten hours later but was actually only forty-five minutes, we are done with all the post-game stuff. We took pictures with all kinds of Blues Birds and city officials and gave interviews to some local journalists. I enjoyed that part, though. They asked some great in-depth questions that allowed me to speak on Feeding Memphis' mission and tell how FM Mobile Market will fill in some gaps. Plus, Camila stood beside me, lying through her teeth in agreement. It's on written and video record. I'd love to see her take back her support now.

After all that is said and done, we have thirty minutes until we are all supposed to meet at the restaurant. That hardly gives us enough time to talk, but I can't go another minute without hearing what Robby has to say. I grab his hand as we make our way to the parking garage. "Let's talk."

"Here?" he questions. We're in the middle of the stadium plaza. I can see why it's not an ideal spot, but I need some context into what he is thinking. I lead us over to a bench and sit down.

"Better?" I ask.

"I guess," he says. He seems nervous. "Alright, I don't know exactly how to do this, so I'm just going to say what is on my mind, okay?" I nod.

Chapter Forty-Nine

Robby

Sitting on a bench outside the stadium and on a time crunch is not exactly how I envisioned this conversation. I can see how much she needs reassurance before spending the next few hours surrounded by our friends. And to be honest, I do, too. As we sit down, I say, "Alright, I don't know exactly how to do this, so I'm just going to say what is on my mind, okay?"

Carina nods.

"I love you. 5ever and always. I've loved you since the first moment I met you, and even when I tried to convince myself otherwise, I never stopped. I know I can be shit at showing you how much you mean to me. I think it's because you mean so much that there isn't a universe in which I even question your place in my life. You're my everything.

"But I know you need more. As much as your love language is words of affirmation, I've got to put my money where my mouth is, too. You deserve the acts as much as the words. I thought I needed to do this grand gesture to prove how much you mean to me. Considering how much that is, getting a gesture ready that big takes time."

"I don't need some big gestures; I just need you," she proclaims.

"I know, Care," I reply, "but you deserve the big gesture. You deserve the world, and I want to be the one who gives it to you. I was talking to my dad the other day, and he made the point that life isn't about the big things; it's often about the little things. The small things we can do every day to show people we care. That's what I envision for you, for us. I will work every day to ensure you know how special you are to me.

"I know it's hard, and we're in this weird limbo with my career in Nashville and you here. I know it may seem soon," I take a deep breath, "but I want you to move in with me. I'd move here to be with you in a second if I could, but that isn't possible unless I retire. I don't want you to doubt for a single second *anything* in this world is above you. You are my number one. My world starts and ends with you."

"You want me to move to Nashville? With you? Like into your condo, not a place of my own?"

"If you want a place of your own, I'll help you get one. Hell, I'll buy you one, but I really, *really* want you in my house, our home. I want to see you when I go to sleep and kiss you first thing every morning when I wake up. I want all those small moments we can have during the day. I want it all."

"I can't up and leave," she hesitates. "I have responsibilities and things here. People who count on me, a job."

"I know you do, baby. If I could move here, I would, but that isn't feasible—not right now. You don't have to move right away. You don't even need to move until April. When the season ends in two months, I can come back here, and we can plan our future. I'll have four months where I can focus solely on you and us. We can build an even stronger foundation, and you can tie up any loose ends."

"And then I'd move to Nashville? Find a job there? I don't even know how I would do that," she blabs, thoughts spiraling. I can't tell what she's thinking. I can't tell if this is going my way or not. She's always been a planner who needs security. I know she needs to know all these details, but damn, a small part of me was hoping she'd jump immediately at the offer.

"Uh, yes. That was the biggest part of the plan I was working on. It's not fully done yet. We still have a few Ts to cross and Is to dot, but I thought maybe you'd come to work for me."

"For you? As what? An assistant or something? You want to pay me to be your girlfriend?" Now she sounds slightly offended. I can't help but laugh at the indignation on her face.

"No, baby, not to be my assistant. I've been talking to my team about creating a nonprofit. They're already in the process of securing 501 3(c) status and getting all the licenses we'd need to get it running."

She studies me curiously. Now I know I've got her attention. She can tell it's serious because I have other people setting it up. It's no longer a pipe dream. "What type of nonprofit?"

I release one of her hands and run mine up her arm to cup her face. I stroke her jaw as I talk. "The one we always talked about in college. A nonprofit that combines sports and nutrition. One that would give kids a place to play a sport and stay active. It would give them mentors and the opportunity to gain the discipline sports can provide.

"It would also have a nutrition component where we would feed them meals AND teach them how to fuel their bodies and make healthy choices. My publicist hooked me up with a nonprofit consultant who can even help us get a similar program to FM Mobile Market. We could set the truck up in the parking lot of the games and practices. Hell, we could get a whole damn fleet of trucks and blanket the city for all I care."

"You did all that for me?" she sounds surprised like she doesn't know I'd do anything for her.

"There's nothing I wouldn't do for you," I reply quietly. "It's not entirely for you, though. This was a dream we once shared. A dream

I forgot I needed until I volunteered again and saw the difference you make here. As much as I want to leave behind a legacy of baseball greatness, I want to also leave one of generosity. Look at all the good Pujols did. He's respected for who he is on and off the field. I want to be that kind of man."

"So, you're offering me a job running the program for your nonprofit and giving me a free place to stay at your condo?"

"Kitten, I'm offering you a job to run our entire damn nonprofit, and I'm begging you to live with me in our condo. I've told you before, you're endgame. I know it's only been a few months since we've reconnected, but we've spent years getting to know each other and growing—separately and together. Why wait any longer?" I press my forehead to hers and stare into her eyes, praying she can hear my sincerity and desperation.

She takes a sharp inhale, and I can see the wheels turning. She's quiet for a minute, and then I see her eyes wet with tears. Fuck. Is she going to say no? I knew it was a possibility, but I didn't consider it a real one. Is my offer not good enough? What else can I give her? Can she not forgive me for making her doubt? Fuck. Red alert. Is it getting hotter out here?

Chapter Fifty

Carina

I can see the moment Robby starts to panic. I've been quiet too long. I didn't mean to be. It's just he said so many things, and it's a large amount of information to process. I don't want to leave him hanging for too long. I lean in and press my lips gently to his.

"I love you," I whisper with a smile. The tension releases from his body, and he smiles back at me. "I love you, too."

"That was a lot to take in at once. And I don't know what to address first. Most importantly, I don't want you to give up anything for me, especially not your career, not the thing that brings you purpose. You're not you without your passion, just like I'm not me without mine. I would never ask you to give up such a big part of yourself, but hearing you would means everything because I feel the same way about you."

"The nonprofit, was that the big plan you were working on?" I ask.

"Yes," he answers sheepishly. "I wanted to have it ready and buttoned up before I told you about it so you knew I was serious. You'd know this wasn't just an empty promise to get you to move."

"To move in with you, for like ever?"

He smiles at that. "Yeah, Kitten, for like *ever*."

I know the answer my heart wants to give. She's always been easily swayed by his ocean-blue eyes. When I tap into my gut, she's also on board. Living away from Robby has always felt wrong. Living with him, that feels right. Even my brain is warming to the idea. He thought of all the things that would cause me apprehension—where to live, where to work, and leaving my current job hanging. Six months is plenty of time to get everything ready to hand off. I know he'll be at spring training for the last six weeks of that. That would give me time to set up his home—our home—exactly how I want it before the season.

"What about Mom?" I wonder out loud.

"The condo has three bedrooms. We can set one up for her and Steve to stay in whenever they want. Or we can buy another unit in the building to use when family and friends want to visit. We'll rent it out on other weekends. I've been meaning to diversify anyway.

"To be honest, babe, I don't think it would be long after you moved that your mom would follow, anyway. None of her family is tying her there, and Steve's family has dispersed all over. Once he retires, they'd probably follow you to Timbuktu if you'd move there. Plus, Steve is only in court a few days a month, and his firm has an office in Nashville. He could relocate and go back to Memphis when he's needed."

I grin at him; that is a good amount of background knowledge to have on Steve and Mom's circumstances. "Have you talked to Steve about this?" I tease.

"He might have mentioned some of those facts when you and your mom were cleaning up dinner a few weeks ago. Said he knew I'd eventually be called back up and that your future was never there," he shares with a shrug. This man. I kiss him again. A little harder this time.

"Is that a yes? You want to do this? Move to Nashville sometime in the next six months?"

"Well," I sass, "it seems as if you've covered all the reasons I'd say 'no,' so I don't have another choice, do I? I love you. I want to be with you, and you made it as easy a transition as possible."

"You're serious? Don't fuck with me, baby. I can't take it."

I nod my head. "Yes, it's a yes."

The man fist pumps. "Hell yeah!" He grabs my face and kisses me hard. The kiss quickly turns more passionate, both of us telling the other without words how much we missed each other and how happy we are to be back on good terms again.

Pulling away suddenly, he rasps, "We gotta leave for dinner, baby. If we don't stop now, I will end up taking you back to your apartment and making you scream your answer over and over again until you can't speak at all."

Yes, please. Those words are all it takes for my body to heat and tingle all over. His eyes darken as he licks his lips. "I love where your head's at, Kitten, but we've got people waiting on us, and I don't want to explain to Steve or Jalen why we ditched them."

"Fair," I sigh.

He gives me another quick kiss and then takes my hand as we walk toward my car in the garage. "You remember Tiffany is staying at my place, right?" I comment.

"I'll get her a hotel room close to Sean's, don't worry. She's not going to want to be anywhere near the plans I've got for you," he says, taking my keys and opening the passenger door for me.

When he settles into the driver's seat and turns the ignition, my filter malfunctions, and I blurt out, "So, do you like want to get married?"

He turns to me, surprised. Crap. "Do you?" he asks hesitantly.

"Cause if you do, we can go to city hall tomorrow and take care of that." He must see my eyes widen at the suggestion.

"Or we plan a big flashy wedding for six months, a year, two years from now. It doesn't matter to me. You're already mine. Whenever you're ready, I am, too. I've been ready to marry you since I was twenty-one. We can move in for now and figure out the rest later."

"Um, moving in is good for now," I stammer.

He chuckles at my embarrassment. "Okay, pretty girl, but you will be my wife one day. I'll give you my last name, and then you can give me some little Italian surfer babies who play the banjo or whatever the fuck they want to do."

That thought makes me giggle. "Okay."

He puts his hand on my thigh and squeezes. "Let's go tell our friends the good news and get the party started so the real celebration can begin."

Yes, please.

Epilogue

Carina

December, four months later...

As I sort through our Christmas ornaments, I can't help but reflect on how much has changed in the last few months. Even though Robby offered to spend the offseason in Memphis, I decided to move to Nashville sooner rather than later.

Taking a sip of my coffee, I survey the condo. We're spending the weekend decorating for Christmas. Mom and Steve will be coming to stay with us. Mom is a little suspicious about the concept, but I assured her I had all the pots and pans she could need to make her Christmas Baked Ziti. I even offered to show her this specialty grocery where she can buy all the spices her heart desires. The kitchen in this condo is incredible. She's going to have a fit when she gets to cook in it.

My favorite part of this holiday season is that we're going into it

engaged! Whenever I catch the sparkle on my finger, I'm taken back
to when Robby and I went to California for Thanksgiving to see his
family. He told me we were meeting friends for dinner, but instead,
he led me to a private picnic in Malibu near where we went to school.

November, three months later...

"We're meeting them on the beach?" I question as we park a few
blocks from the MSC campus.

"Kitten, could you go with the flow for a second? I know what I'm
doing," Robby huffs.

"Fine."

After slipping between two beach shacks, we move closer to the
water. I'm so busy watching where I'm going that it takes me a
minute to notice the bonfire in front of me. When I peek closer, I see
a picnic set up.

"What's all this?" I ask.

"Dinner, duh."

"I see that. But what is it doing here? Where are Blake and
Kelsea?"

"They'll be here soon. Let's sit and enjoy the food while it's
warm."

"Oh my gosh," I gush. "It's guacamole from AvocaJoe's! And
pizza from *Quel Posto*. This is such a weird combination, but I'm too
excited to question it."

As I take a bite of pizza, my eyes shift to Robby staring at me
indulgently. "I'm glad you are enjoying it, baby."

"Are you going to eat, or is watching me eat a new kink?"

"Sassy," he tsks. "I'll eat in a minute. Do you want something to
drink?"

"Yes, please."

He pours me a glass of champagne and laughs when I wrinkle my nose, pulling out sparkling water.

"You get me," I coo.

"I hope so," he says. The glint in his eye holds some deeper meaning, but I can't decipher what it is. He finally grabs a slice of pizza, and we talk about everything that has happened in the last few months.

I spent the last two months training my replacement at Feeding Memphis and implementing some systems to make the processes more seamless before I left last week.

Ultimately, I didn't purchase the food truck since I wouldn't be there to run the program. But the money was used to create farmers' markets in some of the city's largest food deserts, filling the same gaps and keeping our promises to the community. It's now FM Markets—drop the mobile. Local businesses donated space to keep the markets open in the winter months so the community will have fresh food all year.

The biggest change came a few weeks after I resigned: Camila stepped down. She decided to take an administrative role with a national organization that does similar work. She is basically a glorified schmoozer in our region, but whatever. It fits her skill set and interests, AND it meant that the board could promote Haley to the director! The small changes she's made are already having a big impact on the community.

Robby stayed with me in Memphis through the move, but his reps and legal team have been working hard to get our nonprofit ready to launch next year. He used his off time to volunteer more with Jalen and spend time with Leo, Justin, and Ryan—the rookie Leo has taken under his wing.

As we finish our meal, Robby pulls out his laptop. I thought we could watch a little something. He plugs it into a portable projector, and it shines onto a sheet I never noticed set up a few yards ahead of us. The opening scene of *Bridget Jones* 2 starts, and I laugh. Five minutes into the movie, though, it starts to fritz. I peer over at Robby, but he doesn't move to fix it.

As I am about to say something, footage of us flashes on the screen with my favorite Ryder Brothers' song playing in the background. The images span our entire relationship. There are photos from our earliest days together and the video of us hugging after my epic slide. I have no idea where he got all of them. He must have scoured our friends' social media memories and anything else he could get his hands on.

While entranced watching, I don't notice Robby slip behind me and rise onto one knee. I turn around when I hear him clear his throat, and promptly stop breathing. He smiles at my reaction.

"If you pass out, you won't hear the end," he says. "Breathe, baby."

I inhale but am still frozen.

"Carina, since the first time I saw you, I was captivated. Your beauty, sass, and caring soul showed me how bright the world could be. I lost sight of that for a few years, and I didn't realize how dull my life had gotten until you brought the light back into it. In some ways, this seems fast, but in others, this moment has been building for a lifetime. I can't imagine another day without my ring on your finger. I want to spend the rest of my life protecting your light and letting you shine. Will you do me the honor of spending the rest of your life sharing it with me? Will you marry me?"

His eyes are burning into mine as I kneel, mouth agape. He waits patiently for me to shake out of my shock and give him an answer.

"Yes," I whisper.

"Yes?"

"Yes. Yes. Yes! I love you. I want to spend every day loving you and being loved by you."

"You will," he states. He pulls me into him. He crushes his lips to mine as we collapse on the picnic blanket. With sweet kisses, one hand trails my cheek as the other slips a gorgeous duchess-cut diamond on a gold band onto my finger. It's accented with a halo of baguette and round stones.

"It's beautiful," I note.

"Nothing less for you, pretty girl. Are you ready to celebrate? I don't know how much longer I can hold them off."

"Who?" As the words come out, a rush of people descends on us. Through the blur of hugs and congratulations, I realize Robby invited our friends and family to enjoy this moment. I see his parents smiling beside Mom and Steve. Lola, Tiffany, and Morgan are swooning over my ring while the men pat Robby on the back.

"Did you know it was coming? Your manicure is on point," Morgan states.

Tiffany snorts. "Like it would ever be anything less."

I laugh. Catching my eye, Robby saddles beside me and nestles me into my side. "Thank you, everyone, for coming tonight. Your support for us means everything. We've got the beach all night. Grab a drink, and let's celebrate!" he announces.

Hours later, we're sitting around the fire with Tiffany and Sean. My parents and Lola went back to the hotel. They're drained from flying in today.

"Have you thought about when you'll get married?" Sean questions. "I need time to prepare my speech."

"Me too," Tiffany agrees.

"Oh God," I say as Robby groans. "Can we just do it tomorrow and avoid that?"

"Aside from the fact that it will be Thanksgiving and the courts aren't open, I think we need a marriage license and all that first," Robby laments.

"Fine, we can plan a proper wedding then," I fake pout.

"Whatever you want, Kitten."

The ring of my phone pulls me out of the memory. It's Tiffany. She has been helping me manically plan. Robby and I decided to get married during this season's All-Star break. She mentioned she also had some exciting news to discuss. I can't wait to hear it.

Tiffany's news was a shock but in the best way possible. She's moving to Nashville! She'll arrive next week and stay with me through spring training. Having a friend here while Robby is in Florida will be nice. None of his close friends are in relationships, and I haven't had time to meet any of my own yet.

Robby made good on his idea to buy a unit in this building. Once he is back in March, Tiffany can rent it from us—at a steep discount—until she can afford a place of her own. Since it's a two-bedroom, she can even have a makeup studio there if she wants to take private clients. Though her job at a well-known music venue should keep her plenty busy.

This will be a great move for her. It will get her back around her true friends (me, obviously) and give her some much-needed space away from her mom. I can't wait to watch her flourish here, and I'm excited to have an extended sleepover while my *fiancé* is gone. God, I love saying that. I didn't think I'd be one of those girls, but I so am.

I hear the keys jingle in the door, and I turn around as Robby comes strolling in.

"Hey, babe," I greet.

"Hi, Kitten," he says with a kiss. "How's my girl today?"

"She's good, except she woke up alone," I pout.

"I'm sorry, baby. I had to pick the Casanono up from his latest booty call's house and then had a meeting with Molly from my PR team."

"How did that go?" I ask.

"Picking up Kent? It was hilarious. You'd have thought he was a freshman doing the walk of shame the way he hightailed it out of that building. He hasn't slept since yesterday, so we got breakfast, and then I brought him back here to pass out while I worked out. I kissed you each time I left, though," he coos, giving me a soft one on the lips.

"No, the meeting, not Kent. The less I know about the Filanderer's exploits, the better."

He chuckles at my nickname for Kent, but he is the biggest playboy out of Robby's friends. He is upfront with all his 'buddies,' but he has all these crazy rules I can't keep up with.

"The meeting was good. Trying to get all my ducks in a row before preseason. The consultant believes she found a perfect spot for the warehouse, and we can move in before we launch the programs in May. It used to be owned by this old Nashville family, but their grandson took over warehouse operations and moved them into a bigger space. She says it's perfect for what we'll need. It even has office space, but I'd still prefer you work in the retail space downstairs and not out there."

"You just want to keep me close."

"Hell yeah, I do," he agrees with a smirk. "I'm gonna heat up some soup and make grilled cheese for lunch. You interested?"

"Mom's Italian Wedding Soup?" I ask, and he nods.

"Tomato jam on the sandwiches?"

He scoffs, "What am I, an amateur?"

"Excuse me, I didn't realize I was dealing with a sandwich savant," I apologize.

"You're excused. Don't worry; you can make up for the insult later."

"And how will I do that?"

"Oh, I'm sure you'll come up with something," he challenges with a wink.

As Robby heads into the kitchen, my phone lights up with a text from Lola in our group chat with Tiffany.

LOLA 🐰

I'm coming to Nashville. I'll get there next Wednesday, same as Tiffany.

Yay! Double sleepover.

LOLA 🐰

More like a permanent couch resident…

BABS

Lo?

LOLA 🐰

I was right the whole time. Phil heads out for another "conference" Monday, and I'll be gone with all my stuff by the time he gets back Friday.

Wait, am I missing something?

LOLA 🐰

I married a cheating bastard who I let gaslight me for too long.

What. The. Fuck. I knew Lola was having some problems, but I never expected this. Phil was so mild-mannered I can hardly imagine him having sex with Lola, let alone with anyone who wasn't his wife. What a prick. He was batting way above his average with my cousin. They weren't even playing the same game, let alone the league.

BABS

You sure this is what you want? I can get some people to fuck him up either way; I just want to know what I'm working with here. Are you ready to uproot your life?

LOLA 🐰

I can't stay here. Aside from a job I don't enjoy, nothing ties me here. Dad moved into his lake house full-time, so he isn't even in St. Louis. I need friendly faces, and everyone here knows me through Phil or us as a couple, and if I get one more pitying look from someone who obviously knows, you're going to have to help me hide a body.

Oh, Bunny, I'm so sorry. He was always a douche canoe. I am thrilled to have you for as long as you want, but I'm a little surprised you aren't going to Chicago. You usually run to George when shit hits the fan.

BABS

More like douche yacht, and hand on the Bible, I'll be lying through my teeth, Lo.

LOLA 🐰

I need to be with my girls. Besides, if George saw me upset like this, he'd kill him.

BABS

Sounds like my kinda man.

Ha, that is a match I'd LOVE to see.

BABS

Excuse me, I am a catch.

You are Babs, but let's focus here.

Lola, we have a room for you whenever you need it. You can stay with us until you're ready for your next move. Tiffany will be here through the end of March, so it will be an estogrenfest.

LOLA 🐰

Perfect. The fewer men, the better, in my book.

I look up just as Robby is bringing in my lunch. He must notice the emotion on my face because he asks what is wrong almost immediately.

"I hope you're ready for the full girl group package."

"Sounds ominous," he says. "What does that mean?"

"It means Lola is moving to Nashville, too."

"That's awesome! She and Phil decided to relocate?"

"Nope," I say with a big emphasis on the p. "No, Phil."

He gives me a dubious look. "Tiffany has already mentioned calling in her witch friend," I add.

That somehow satisfies the rage I saw flash in his eyes, and he takes a second to process the news and sits down. Digging into his soup, he says, "Start from the beginning."

Thank you for reading Robby and Carina's story. For more of this couple, visit my website (katsummerswrites.com) for a bonus scene of their first night together in Nashville.

Want more Songbirds? Keep reading for a sneak peek into book two of this series, *Stepping Up to the Plate*.

Stepping Up to the Plate

Lola

My first days in Nashville have been amazing. Robby hasn't left for spring training yet, but it's been a total estrogen fest at *Casa de Becker*. Considering he is about to leave his girl for several weeks, Robby has been a good sport about all the rom-coms and rosé present in his swanky condo. Tiffany and I are going to stay here with Carina until he gets back and then we'll move into the two-bedroom unit they bought a couple floors below.

A few nights before Robby leaves, he wants to make Carina a fancy dinner at home. To make ourselves scarce, Tiffany and I spend the night exploring Nashville. We stumble across a cute champagne garden that is right up Tiff's alley. As we sip our bubbles, I can tell my blonde bestie is buttering me up for something.

"So..." she probes. "You left Phil over six weeks ago. Have you made any movement in the separation front?"

"I've contacted a lawyer in Missouri, but I haven't done anything yet. He hasn't been bugging me lately and I know the second he gets served papers he's going to harass me again. I'm enjoying the peace while I can. I think he finally got the message that it's over but I don't want to tempt fate yet."

"Speaking of tempting things, are you ready to get back out there? Meet some hunk to break your two-month dry spell?"

"Two months? Try eight," I say before I can stop myself. Tiffany chokes on her drink at the announcement.

"Eight?! You haven't had sex eight months?" she whisper-shouts causing people at nearby tables to turn their heads.

"Can you shut up? People are staring!"

"I'm sorry. I just... I know you hadn't gotten physical in a while, but your husband didn't have sex with you for that long, and you didn't suspect he was cheating? Oh honey, I didn't know it was that bad. You'd think the dude would throw you a bone now and then, especially when you were offering. Who turns down a free lay?"

"Excuse me," I huff, affronted.

"I wasn't calling you easy, babe. I'm simply pointing out that it is a lot more work to go and find a mistress or a rando than it is to have sex with your wife. Wow. And you're a knockout. Phil is dumber than I thought he was."

"Can we not talk about this in public?" I ask with heated cheeks.

"Oh, no ma'am. We are talking about this. I cannot let this injustice stand. We are getting you laid ASAP."

"I am not going home with some random guy we meet at a bar tonight. I can't handle that stress or potential rejection right now."

"Fine," she sighs, then perks up. "What if I knew a way you could have sex with someone who would for sure not turn you down?"

"I'm not hiring a hooker," I deadpan.

"Not a hooker, babe. There is a club here that offers a service for finding sexually compatible people and getting them together. It's all between consenting adults and no money exchanges hands – except the membership fee."

"I don't want to have sex in some shady nightclub."

"Not a nightclub, a sex club. And it's not shady, it's super classy. You fill out a profile and they find someone who matches your preferences. Everyone who is approved has been vetted. I signed up a few weeks ago but haven't been yet."

"Tiff, you have guys hanging all over you. Why do you need to go to a club for sex?"

She shrugs. "Sometimes it's nice to have a partner who already knows what you want. That way, you don't have to go through all the pesky guesswork and pretend you don't want him to spank your ass and call you his 'naughty girl.' Plus, there are a few things I enjoy that aren't exactly one-night stand or first date material like—"

I hold my hand up to stop her. "I don't need to know all that, and I don't think this is a good idea."

"Come on, Bunny. It's perfect. It's a sure-fire way to rip off the Band-Aid with someone who won't reject you and knows exactly what your boundaries are. It's ideal for a novice!"

"A novice, really?"

"Oh, I'm sorry. Did you have a lot of sexcapades you never told me during between homecoming and freshman spring semester when you met Phil?"

"No..."

"Exactly," she exclaims. "You need someone who knows how to get you off and how to keep you comfortable. I'll help you complete your profile and make sure you get the match you need."

She's staring at me with big blue puppy dog eyes. It's hard to say no when I know she's trying to help me.

"Fine," I concede. And that's how later that night I end up huddled in bed with Tiffany answering an exceedingly thorough questionnaire about my sexual preferences.

"I don't even know what some of this stuff is," I say.

"Like what?"

"Like water spots. Do they mean jet skis?"

"They mean being peed on," she replies nonchalantly.

"Seriously?"

"Seriously."

"Why do you know that?"

She smirks at me before answering, "I've been with my share of kinky former child stars."

"Oh my God."

"Hey, don't knock it till you try it. *I* didn't get peed on."

"That is way more than I needed to know. Ugh, this is going to be the most vanilla questionnaire they've ever received. They aren't going to let me in."

"Oh please. I'm sure you've got some secret kinks in there you don't even know about. Let them worry about that. All you need to do is answer honestly."

After another hour of filling it out, Tiffany convinces me to submit an application. Later, I go to bed embarrassed but also optimistic that I'm taking steps forward even if I have no intentions of stepping foot inside that club.

"I can't believe I let you convince me to do this," I yell over the blow dryer.

"Shut up. You're going to love it," Tiffany replies with an eye roll. "You're going to meet some hunk to rail you into forgetting all about that small-dicked son of a bitch who called himself a man."

"Are we sure this is a good idea?"

Tiffany puts down the blow dryer and meets my eyes in the mirror. "This is going to be great for you, Lo. I promise."

I nod my head and she returns to helping me get ready. After she's done, I slip into the navy velvet dress she forced me to buy for the occasion. The fabric is smooth against my skin and the cinched waist gives the illusion I was gifted the curves of my Italian ancestors.

"Damn, it pays to have someone who went to beauty school as

your bestie," Tiffany comments, coming into the room. I haven't had the nerve to peek yet.

"Holy shit," I breathe at my reflection.

"Yeah babe, you look hot as hell."

"You are a magician, Tiff. I can't believe you made me look this good."

"Yeah, whatever. You're a little Aphrodite and some guy is going to cream his pants at the sight of you tonight," she says as she downs the rest of her champagne. "Alright, Bunny. Let's roll out. Don't forget to grab your mask if you want to keep up the mystery."

"Here goes nothing," I mumble as we walk out the door.

Acknowledgments

I want to say a big thank you to everyone who helped me bring this book to life. From friends who heard me talk about this story and the entire Nashverse to the ones who read sections to offer feedback. An extra big shout out to Haley, my alpha reader and ride or die. Your support throughout this process is appreciated more than you'll ever know.

I owe a huge thanks to Emma from EJL Editing for helping me navigate this process, offering her colorful commentary on my story, and ultimately making it that much better.

Lastly, I want to shout out the person who inspired this couple with a few lines over Snapchat. I won't say your name but thank you for getting my wheels turning and being a supportive sounding board of the past. If you ever read this, I hope the character makes you smile.

Thank you, thank you, thank you,

– Kat

Also by Kat Summers

Want more Nashville Songbirds? Check out the other books in the series.

Need some hockey romance in your life? Read the story of Robby's sister, Morgan in Backcheck Heart.

Read bonus scenes from your favorite couples by visiting bit.ly/katsummersbonus and signing up for my newsletter!

Along with more Songbirds novels, Kat has a few surprise releases and a new series planned for this year. Country rockstars, anybody? Get updates on upcoming projects through my newsletter, by following me on social media (@katsummerswrites), or visit my website katsummerswrites.com.

About the Author

Kat Summers is a millennial spicy, contemporary romance author living in Tennessee. Her books are filled with just enough angst to hurt your feelings, witty banter to make you laugh, and steamy, swoon-worthy men to make you blush. She creates stories with strong, sassy heroines who can hold their own but love being called a "good girl."

Kat has had a love for reading and writing her entire life. After consuming what some would call way too many romance books, she decided to take the stories she told herself to fall asleep and put them on paper.

When she isn't writing, she can be found reading (duh) and spending time with her family and furbaby or gossiping over Mexican food. Fueled by Diet Dr Pepper and a dream, Kat is excited to bring the couples that live in her mind to the rest of the world. Follow her for sneak peeks of future projects.

Find her at @katsummerswrites on all the things.